THE
DARKEST
THREAD

A FLINT K-9 MYSTERY

THE DARKEST THREAD

A FLINT K-9 MYSTERY

JEN BLOOD

Adian Press
Maine

THE DARKEST THREAD
Copyright © 2016 Jen Blood
First Edition
ISBN: 978-0-9982296-0-7

Adian Press
934 River Rd. #1
Cushing, Maine 04563
www.adianpress.com

Publisher: Adian Press
Cover Design: damonza.com
Author's Photograph: Amy Wilton Photography

To Killian.

My overgrown, soulfully sweet, and ever-fretful
canine compadre for the past decade.

1

THE BRUSH WAS THICK and the air cool, and rain pelted my chilled skin. My shirt was drenched, and my ponytail had gotten snagged so many times I was debating cutting the damned thing off. Up ahead, I caught sight of a flash of dark fur and cursed under my breath.

Phantom is my lead dog, a German shepherd who was closer to death than life when I rescued her from the needle at an animal shelter in my hometown back in Georgia five years ago. She's one of the best search dogs I've ever had, but she can also be a willful old goat—particularly when she sets her mind to something. This morning, that was exactly what she'd done.

"Phan!" I shouted. The dog continued on, oblivious. Beside me, my seventeen-year-old son, Bear, glanced at me. I tried not to look as frustrated as I felt. "She's got a scent."

"Not the one you set, though," he pointed out, as though I hadn't noticed.

"I gave her the go-ahead," I said. Nothing like the present to seize a teaching moment. "Eventually, you've got to get to a point where you trust your dog. Sure, she passed by the scent trail I laid. I gave her the go-ahead when I realized she had something else in mind, though."

"Like squirrel for dinner?" he asked. At the end of the lead Bear held, his own dog—a white pit bull named Casper—strained to join Phantom in the search. Thankfully, Bear held tight. One rogue dog was more than enough for what should have been a quiet Maine morning.

"Very funny," I said with a grimace. This was supposed to be our version of a field trial, since Phantom was getting on in years and it had been a while since I'd put her skills to the test. My business, Flint K-9, is run from the mid-coast Maine island where I live with Bear, a small staff of misfits and miscreants, and a slew of dogs and other assorted wild things in need of a respite. Bear and I had decided to take a couple of days on the mainland to put our dogs through their paces—and, in the process, give Bear some time in the field himself, since he'd been on my tail for the better part of the past year to give him more responsibility.

The night before, I'd come out and set a scent trail that wound through a stretch of woods in Appleton, Maine, and then Bear and I returned first thing this morning with Phantom and Casper. It wasn't long before I realized Phantom had caught a whiff of something I'd never laid down, however. Now, an hour later, she was in hot pursuit of...something.

"Up ahead!" Bear said. I heard the distant sound of the bell Phantom wears to keep me from losing her when she's off lead, but when I followed Bear's gaze, I saw nothing. Not surprising—where wild things are concerned, Bear's got a sixth sense I've never been able to top or tap into.

Sure enough, the next thing I heard was Phantom's

telling double bark, deep-throated and clear. *I found it.*

The question was, what exactly was *it?*

I was none too pleased at the answer we got once we'd followed the reckless trail Phantom had blazed. At the end, I caught sight of a felled doe just to our left.

"Keep Casper back," I warned Bear. He obligingly ordered the dog to 'leave it,' and I noted somewhere in the back of my mind that Casper followed the command immediately. The dog was coming along, no question.

I moved closer to Phantom's find and knelt next to the body of a large white-tailed doe. Based on the rate of decomp, she'd been killed at least a day ago. Anger grew like fire in my belly at sight of the wound in her side. Not only had she been shot off-season, but the jackass who'd done it hadn't even cared enough to follow up, find her, and finish the job. I looked around. I'd expected to find Phantom with the deer, but she was nowhere to be seen.

"I guess we know what scent she was following," Bear said, forehead furrowed.

"I'll call the ranger, let him know he's got a poacher out here." I looked around. If Phantom had found what she was looking for, where was she now? I couldn't hear her bell anymore. Bear scanned the thick woods, rain dripping from his shaggy dark hair. I glanced at the doe one more time, for the first time noticing a key piece of information I'd missed before: the swollen teats of a nursing mother.

"There!" Bear said. He pointed into a stand of spruce and pine, and I caught sight of a black and tan tail whipping through the underbrush.

I moved forward, Bear and Casper beside me. The woods smelled of overripe berries and fresh earth, but the scent of blood beneath it made my heart go still. Bear's face was tense, no hope in his green eyes.

He'd been in this business long enough to know the likelihood of what we'd find.

Ahead of us, I saw Phantom move carefully into the underbrush, until her head and muzzle had disappeared.

I watched as the dog lay down, settling her aging bones on the cold, wet ground. At eight years old, she's coming up on retirement age—something I've been doing my best to avoid thinking about. Her head reappeared as she twisted to look at me, wet brown eyes meeting mine. She barked again, twice, just in case I hadn't heard her the first time. That second alert always seems a little patronizing to me, like she's suggesting I might be slow on the uptake for not getting there sooner.

She turned back to whatever was in the brush and crawled forward until she was half swallowed by the bushes herself. I lay down on my belly beside her and inched in, ignoring the thorns that tore at my cheeks and hair or the mud that drenched my front, focused instead on the animal I was sure I would find.

"Well, hello there," I said quietly when I finally caught sight of her—a young fawn speckled with white, caught in blackberry brambles and too tuckered to fight any longer.

The fawn flailed at sight of me, letting out a pitiful bleat, then stilled when Phantom whimpered and ran her tongue over the deer's tawny fur in long, leisurely strokes.

The fawn calmed, focused on Phantom now. I crept in further.

"Good girl, Phan," I said. "Good find."

•

It took just under twenty minutes to get the fawn untangled once we'd found her. In the meantime, we found her brother farther in the brush, also alive. Both were scraped up and plenty scared, but there were no broken bones. That didn't mean they were home free, of course—I've seen plenty of animals succumb to shock after something like this, when they'd seemed just fine. Still, it was a start.

I'd offered Phantom the knotted rope she usually gets after a successful search, but she turned up her nose at it. She was too concerned with her new charges to play games.

From here, our destination was Windfall Island— formerly Payson Isle, an island ten miles off the coast of Maine. The island had been very generously donated by Erin Solomon, a reporter who had inherited the place and assured me she never, ever wanted to set foot on its shores again after the drama she'd faced there several months ago. *Call it Fantasy Island and hire a couple of guys decked out in white suits and bad accents for all I care—the place is yours now,* she'd told me in our last conversation. Thus, Windfall Island was born. There, Bear and our crew run a wildlife rehab center and Flint K-9, a business devoted to training rescued shelter dogs for individuals, law enforcement, and search and rescue divisions around the world. The fawns would get medical care and some R&R out on the island before they were ideally released back into the wild as soon as they were able.

We'd just gotten back to the Jeep when Monty, my second-in-command, called. I answered my cell while Bear was getting the fawns safely situated in one of the padded crates we carry for just such emergencies, his voice low as he whispered sweet nothings to the babies.

"Funny story," I answered as I hit the 'Accept Call' button. "We hit the woods with two dogs and a few scent markers… We're coming back with both dogs, half the scent markers, and a couple of injured fawns who'll need tending to. I need to get in touch with the warden, but will you let Therese know we're coming? I think they're fine, but they'll need the usual intake and a vet should give them a good once-over. We should be back on the island by nine if she wants to meet us at the dock."

"And good morning to you too, Jamie Flint," he said, in his finest New Orleans drawl. "I'm just fine, thanks for asking. How was your night in the big city?"

Monty had been on me lately about my interpersonal skills. I'd told him more than once, though: I'm a single mother and a business owner with anywhere from two dozen to a hundred mouths to feed on any given day. I don't have time for interpersonal anything. "It was just fine, thank you. Did you hear what I said?"

"Two more babies to add to the zoo," he said. "Got it, boss. I'll meet you at the dock in Littlehope, and I can take it from there."

"No need. The boat's at the wharf, we can bring the fawns straight over."

There was a pause on the line. "Actually, I'm not sure you'll be back on the island for a few days yet."

I didn't like the sound of that, and said so. Monty wouldn't give me any details as to why I couldn't head home yet, but something in his voice got my antennae up. The rain had cleared, but there was still a lingering heaviness in the air. I've been called superstitious more than once in my time, but I've learned to listen to the chills that climb the base of my spine, the voices that ride the wind.

Right now, those voices were all I could hear.

2

TRUE TO HIS WORD, Monty met me at the town landing in Littlehope, a fishing village off Route 97 with a population of 753, including the team of seven I'd relocated with me to the island a year before. Two people stood beside him. One was a big, burly man with graying hair and a wool overcoat I was guessing cost considerably more than my car—though, granted, I got the car used from *Uncle Henry's Swap & Sell It Guide*. It seemed unlikely Mr. Overcoat had ever heard of *Uncle Henry's*.

I did know the other man, though. He stood at the dock in a worn trench coat, taller by several inches than the man beside him, a pensive expression on his face. Despite myself, I couldn't help but notice that it was a very handsome face.

"Will you get the fawns on board and ready for the trip?" I asked Monty, without greeting Special Agent Jack Juarez or the man by his side. Bear and I carried the crate between us, careful not to jostle it. Monty—five-foot-nine and 190 pounds of pure muscle—took my end.

"Will do," he agreed. "Did you get in touch with the warden?"

"I talked to him in the car," I said. "They already caught the guy. Some numb-nuts who got drunk last night and decided going out in the dark off-season and shooting things was the perfect way to pass the time. The warden didn't know the doe had fawns, though."

"So they'll string the guy up by his balls till he rots?" Monty said cheerfully.

"Fingers crossed," Bear said, with no trace of Monty's good humor.

"He'll get his day in court," I said. "We'll hope for the best from there." The incident was actually a serious one; shooting a deer out of season is already a punishable offense, but going out at night under the influence considerably ups the stakes. Depending on the judge, the offender was looking at a fine of at least a thousand dollars, jail time, and confiscation of any weapons used in commission of the crime. Personally, I hoped they threw the book at the guy. Not all judges agree with me, however.

"Did you talk to Therese?" I asked, returning to business. Therese is our veterinarian out on the island, a necessity when you deal with as many animals as we do—many of them in less-than-ideal condition when they come to us.

"I told her to expect us," Monty said. "Any idea when you'll be back?"

"I don't even know that I'm going anywhere," I said with a pointed look. "I still don't have a clue what this is about. Once I have some idea, I'll let you know."

Monty eyed Jack with a hint of distrust, but made no comment.

Monty and I have worked together for six years now, ever since he was first recommended to me—two days after being released from the Maine State Prison. There, he'd been part of a dog training program for inmates that's run by a friend of mine. Marie Finnegan's endorsement isn't one that comes easily. I hired Monty on the spot, and haven't had a moment of regret since.

He is, however, occasionally a little overprotective.

Once Monty and Bear were on the boat, I refocused on Jack Juarez. His dark hair was cut shorter and his clothes hung looser than they had when I'd seen him last, almost nine months ago. Half circles shadowed his dark eyes. Though at five-foot-ten I'm taller than most of the women and a lot of the men I work with, Jack always makes me feel smaller. Petite, almost. He has broad shoulders and an athletic frame that easily tops six feet, his darker skin tone thanks to a Mexican mother who died when Jack was young and a Cuban father he never knew.

Those parents are just a few of the ghosts who haunt Jack. Right now, it looked like they were doing a bang-up job.

"Monty tells me someone's been asking for me?" I said.

"I guess you could say that. There's a situation…of sorts."

He looked uneasily at the man beside him. Since I didn't know what he was talking about and he hadn't so much as dropped an email to let me know he was still alive in the past nine months, I folded my arms and waited. Maybe it was petty, but I wasn't going to make things any easier for him. Jack cleared his throat.

"This is Special Agent in Charge Gerard McDonough," he said, introducing me officially to Overcoat. "And this is Jamie Flint, sir."

The man stepped forward with his hand extended before

Jack had the words out of his mouth. "I've heard a lot about you, Jamie. It's a pleasure."

I shook his hand, noting that the iron grip stopped just shy of bone crushing. "What can I do for you, Agent McDonough?" I asked.

"We have a situation," he said immediately. I'm not a fan of small talk myself, so the fact that he'd jumped right in earned him a point or two in his favor. "Two sisters have gone missing."

I couldn't hide my surprise. "If you're looking to organize a search, all you needed to do was call. We've got—"

"It's not as simple as that," Jack interjected.

"Of course it is," McDonough said coolly. The tension between them could have cracked lead.

"What isn't so simple about it?" I asked, directing the question to Jack.

"The girls went missing up in Vermont, along the Long Trail on Glastenbury Mountain."

"You're not working with Vermont K-9?" I asked. "That's their turf."

"They're out there," Jack said. "Police are there, forest service is there, reporters are there. It's a three-ring circus."

McDonough didn't look happy with his assessment. The second he mentioned Glastenbury Mountain, though, I knew what Jack was talking about. Any time a search is organized around the country, it's my business to at least take notice. In this case, that wasn't hard since it was all over the news. K-9 search and rescue teams were out looking for two girls in their teens who'd been missing since the previous morning.

"VTK9 is good," I said. "They know that area well. I'm

flattered you think I'd be helpful, but I think you're better off with that crew. I've worked with them before, and I've always been impressed."

"We actually got a special request to bring you in," McDonough said. "That's why I'm here. I know you and Juarez—uh, Jack—have worked together before, so I asked if he would make introductions."

"A special request by whom?"

"The father of the girls who've gone missing," he said. There was something about the way he said it, a look in his eyes, that made me think I wasn't getting the whole story. "He doesn't trust us, and we were the ones who brought in Vermont K-9. He's gotten it into his head that the search and rescue team may be collaborating with the FBI."

"But Vermont K-9 has nothing to do with the FBI," I said.

"Trust me, we've told him that," Agent McDonough said, a bit wearily. "But we have a history with the family, which means they don't believe much that we say."

I considered things for a few seconds before I said, "Would you give Agent Juarez and me a few minutes? I'd like to ask him some questions."

"If you're talking to him, you can include me in the conversation," McDonough said shortly. "I'm the agent in charge here." I was surprised at his tone. Clearly, he was a man used to getting his own way.

I didn't really give two horse hairs what he was used to, though. He was on my turf now. "That's not how this works," I said. "You came to me. If you want me to pack my crew up and horn in on an established search that's already being led by an experienced team, I'd like to talk to Agent Juarez privately to get some details."

He stood his ground for a second, intractable, before he seemed to realize that I wouldn't change my mind. I waited until he was well out of earshot before I shifted my focus back to Jack.

"What exactly have you stepped in?" I asked. "Why is the FBI even in on this thing? You said you've already got the local and state police in the mix, not to mention the forest service. What made your guys throw their hats in the ring?"

"You don't know the story?" he asked.

"I know there's a search on Glastenbury Mountain. There's more of a story than that?"

"There's definitely more to it than that. I guess you probably don't have a lot of time for the news out on the island these days," Jack said.

"I've got seven people—two of them teenagers—helping me build a business and the buildings that will house that business, from the ground up. There's a lot I don't have time for these days."

He looked guilty at that, not without reason. Nine months before, I'd offered him a job when it seemed his career with the FBI was most likely a thing of the past. I would have been fine with him saying no—hell, I was glad he'd been able to salvage what had seemed an unsalvageable career at the time. But he could have at least called to let me know what was happening.

"Right," he agreed. "Well, Dean Redfield is the patriarch of the family—the oldest of ten siblings, though there are only five left now. About a month ago, he and his family bought up land in an unincorporated town in southwestern Vermont called Glastenbury. There was no real fuss about it, but Dean's got a history with the FBI so we were keeping an eye on him."

I thought the name—Redfield—sounded familiar, but I couldn't put my finger on exactly where I'd heard it before. "Agent McDonough mentioned that. What kind of history are we talking about, exactly?"

"Tax evasion, for the most part. And..." He hesitated. "Do you remember a case in Western Mass about seven years ago? Two sisters..."

That was all it took for the memory to click into place. "I knew the name rang a bell. His sisters were murdered, weren't they? By..." I paused, realizing the implication for the first time. "By an FBI agent, wasn't it?"

"Exactly," Jack agreed, grim now. "Gordon Redfield was—is—Dean's brother. He was also a seasoned federal agent. He was convicted of killing their sisters, twins a decade younger than him. Gordon, incidentally, has maintained his innocence since that time."

"But you guys don't buy that."

"No. Most of us don't," Jack said. There was something steely in his eyes when he said it, and I realized this case had some deep roots for him. "Back in 2009, the government had taken over the Redfields' land after Dean refused to pay taxes for...well, ever. We'd just moved in on the place when the bodies were found. Two women, twenty-nine years old."

"Yeah, I remember. A pretty grisly case, as I recall. Or am I remembering wrong?"

"No, you got it right." His dark eyes held mine for a second. I felt that inexplicable warming I always feel in Jack's presence, and resisted the urge to take a step back. "Their names were June and Katie Redfield, two of only three sisters in the Redfield clan. When they were found, both had been drugged, raped, and tortured. Both of them tied together through the whole experience."

The violence of the act stopped me for a moment, the cry of two dead sisters bound for eternity echoing in my head. "Both found with purity rings, weren't they?" I finally managed.

"They were," he said with a nod. "Genital mutilation of both bodies—while the women were alive and conscious. All the victims were killed in pairs, strangled with gold chains. Each found with an antique purity ring on the right ring finger."

"All the victims?" I echoed. "I only remember hearing about the sisters."

"There was never enough evidence to bring the other murders to trial. But eight other women had been killed in crimes that were almost identical, all killed in pairs. All prostitutes."

"This is why I prefer dogs," I said with a shiver.

"I'm not arguing with you." He paused. "There were some…extenuating circumstances with the case, made it kind of a nightmare around the office for a while."

"In what way?" I asked.

I caught something in his eyes, a hint of whatever story I wasn't being told, before he glanced back toward Agent McDonough and the look vanished. "It's not relevant here," he said. "The bottom line is that Gordon had all of us fooled, but ultimately the evidence put him away. Dean is a hard man, but he isn't heartless. You can imagine what the whole thing did to him."

I'm from a family of eight myself—six of them sisters. When I was seven, one of those sisters—Clara, four years old, the youngest among us—went missing. Half of Georgia rallied to try and find her. Search dogs were called in. I watched how hard the dogs worked; how much the handlers cared. For two weeks, we searched high and low. My folks put up bulletins. Offered a reward of three thousand dollars cash money raised by strangers who'd seen the whole thing play out on the local news, for any information that helped bring Clara home.

At the end of the day, though, none of it mattered. Clara remains lost in the Georgia woods to this day, a piece of my family with her.

"Sure," I said quietly. "I can imagine." I waited for him to continue. When he didn't, I added, "There's no question that this family has suffered. I'm not sure I understand what it has to do with me, though."

He frowned. "Honestly, it doesn't have anything to do with you—at least, not as far as I'm concerned. But, as McDonough said, Dean doesn't trust us. None of his family does. And now that his daughters are missing, they're convinced it's happening again."

"What's happening again? The murders? You said Gordon Redfield is behind bars, though."

"The Redfields always thought the FBI had more to do with it than we did," Jack said. "Dean was convinced there was a conspiracy. And now he's sure that we're somehow responsible for the other girls going missing."

"Well, whatever he might think, he should know that Vermont K-9 doesn't have anything to do with it. And they're the ones who should be running the search."

"No one's disputing that," Jack said. "But the FBI feels that it wouldn't hurt to have another pair of hands on deck."

"The FBI feels," I said, catching the implication. I can't

deny, it stung a little. I studied him. "What about you?"

His jaw hardened. He glanced back at McDonough, and I caught the glare that passed between them. "I'm here in an official capacity, Jamie," he said, quieter now. "They're trying to get me to use the relationship between you and me to their advantage, but I won't do that."

He paused on 'relationship.' I felt my cheeks warm, even though there's never been a relationship between Jack and me—not really. We've worked together a few times. Shared a hotel room one night, but separate beds. I cut his hair one cold winter morning out on the island. And once, when I was feeling particularly brave, I kissed him on the cheek.

That's the extent of our 'relationship.'

"If you don't want to come, I won't try to persuade you," he said.

"Does McDonough know that?" I asked. One look in his eyes at the question, and I could tell McDonough had no idea.

Before we could continue talking, McDonough got tired of waiting and rejoined us. I noticed that his shoes were leather and freshly polished, though to his credit he didn't seem concerned at the rain and mud now spattering his wingtips.

"I'm sorry, Ms. Flint, but we don't have a lot of time here," he said. "We're not saying you need to bring your whole team out with you. Just you and your dog. You can coordinate with VTK9, explain the situation, tell them you're not there to step on anyone's toes. We're looking at a search area that could be as much as twenty thousand acres, all of it rough terrain, mountainous, with twelve peaks topping three thousand feet in elevation. You're seriously telling me they couldn't use the help?"

He was right. I had a good relationship with the organization, had trained with a lot of the handlers there, so they wouldn't get territorial if I showed up and offered to lend a hand. With a search area this big, other K-9 organizations had most likely already been called in. If I were a gambling woman, I'd bet the house that nobody would blink if I joined their ranks.

"They still haven't found any sign of either of the girls?" I asked.

Jack shook his head. "Not a trace. Dean Redfield has been through this with June and Katie—his sisters. Those two had taken off a couple of days before and dropped out of sight from there. You can imagine what he's going through now that the girls missing are his own daughters."

I glanced back at the boat, where Bear was standing with Monty. I was barely sixteen when my son was born, and I've lost more than my share of sleep since that time worrying over everything from chicken pox to first crushes and a thousand things in between since that time. What Dean Redfield was going through, though, was incomprehensible. Torture was the only word for it.

I asked for a minute from Jack and McDonough, and nodded Bear and Monty over. They came as if they'd been waiting for the signal for a while.

"You need us to gear up?" Monty asked.

"No," I said. "Just me—I'll take Phantom, probably be gone no more than a couple of days. You think you can handle things without me?"

"You're going on a search?" Bear asked. "You sure you don't need a hand?"

"Positive—" I began.

"Because we could get geared up fast," he pressed. "You saw how good Casper's been the last couple of days—he listens better than Phantom half the time. And this would be good experience. I could come, maybe bring Minion. Three teams are better than one."

"Minion and Ren, you mean?" I asked.

Bear's never been much for subterfuge. He blushed, while Monty snickered beside him. Urenna—Ren—is the seventeen-year-old daughter of another of the Flint K-9 staff, Carl Mensah, a former Nigerian soldier who fled his homeland after his wife and sons were murdered. He and Ren have been with me since first immigrating to the U.S. a few years before. The growing bond between Ren and Bear—completely platonic, Bear insists—has been one he's denied for years. I know his feelings for the girl run a lot deeper than simple friendship, though.

"We don't really need more teams, Bear," I said. "This is just a quick operation for me. To be honest, I'm not even clear why I'm going, much less why I'd bring anyone else."

"It'd be a good road trip," Monty said, always helpful. "Get the kids out there, show 'em how the Feebs do it."

I shot him a glare, but all he did was grin in return. "We'd do whatever you need," Bear added.

"You really think Ren can handle things out there?"

Bear looked at me pityingly. "Seriously?"

"Yes, seriously," I said. "If we actually end up pitching in, we're talking cold temps, rough terrain, and two girls your age who may well not even be found alive. Conditions don't get much tougher than that."

"Ren can handle it," he said, with the unshakeable confidence of youth.

I glanced at Monty, who shrugged.

"Trial by fire, right?" he said. "I say give her the call, see what happens."

I weighed the argument for a few seconds before I finally nodded. "Okay, fine. Gear up Casper, and call in Ren and Minion. I'll give VTK9 a call, clear it with them."

"Yes!" Bear said, half under his breath. I shot him a look, which he ignored. "You won't regret it, I promise."

Famous last words. McDonough and Jack returned then, McDonough just ending a call. "I've got a plane on standby. You think you can be ready by ten hundred?"

I nodded without a second thought. "We'll be there."

Special Agent in Charge McDonough said he had business to take care of and would meet us at the airport, but Jack joined us on the boat. Monty got behind the wheel, piloting us across the harbor with the engine at full throttle. The seas were calm and the sky had cleared, but there was a heaviness to the air that suggested we weren't through with the rain yet. We'd need to check the weather for Glastenbury, as well as the maps. Jack and I stood portside with the wind in our hair and watched as the island got closer.

"One question," I said. "Agent McDonough said Dean Redfield has heard of me. That's flattering, but I'm not exactly a household name."

"Apparently, Dean was friends with someone you used to work for," Jack said. "A Brock Campbell? I know Campbell died a few years ago, but I guess he spoke highly enough of you when he was alive that Dean had heard of you, too."

Jack watched me as he fed me the details, reading my expression. I kept it as clear as I could. He already knew the truth—he would have to. Or at least as much as the rest of the world did: that Brock Campbell had been my mentor, yes, but that he had also left his entire estate—including a thriving business and a barren mansion that I sold the second Brock was in the ground—to Bear and me.

"I've never met any of the Redfields," I said. "Apart from the stories I remember from the news, I've never even heard of them."

"I know," Jack said. "I wouldn't have let McDonough talk me into coming here if I didn't think you could help, though. I expect the girls just wandered off somewhere. Hopefully, they'll be found by the time we get there. But I remember how good you were during the search up in Black Falls a couple of years ago—the way you handled me when I was going crazy, how hard you worked. You have a way of setting people's minds at ease."

Two years before, I'd led the search when Jack's girlfriend at the time, Erin Solomon, was run off the road by a madman up in the Northern Maine woods. Thankfully, that search had ended well. Not all of them do, though, and I didn't have a great feeling about this one. I shrugged at his praise, never easy with compliments. "I was just doing my job."

"Which is all I want you to do here," he said. "Dean's not a bad man, and he's had a hard time over the years. I think it would do him good to know someone he feels like he's hand selected is out there looking."

"Well… I'm happy to help if I can," I said. "It sounds like it'll be interesting out there, anyway—I haven't done a search in that area before. I'm glad you called." I hesitated. The elephant in the room yawned, stretched out, and made himself comfortable between us.

Silence fell. A shimmer of light caught the sun over Jack's

right shoulder. I stared at it for a few seconds. A familiar tremor slid beneath my skin. I'd seen that light before. It followed Jack, shining brighter the worse things got for him. Right now, it was blinding.

"Are you all right?" I asked him.

He looked surprised. I noted again how thin his face was. His complexion was a shade lighter than usual, like he hadn't been in the sun much in recent months. Though he's only a few years older than my thirty-three years, just then Jack looked a decade beyond that.

"I'm fine," he said. He sounded tired, though. His professional Man-in-Black persona wavered. "I mean… I guess I'm fine. I get up every day. Put one foot in front of the other. Try to find answers."

"And?" I asked.

"And…none yet. But I'm still looking."

Jack's wife—that brilliant light shining forever in the distance for him—was raped and murdered in Nicaragua a few years ago. He'd learned last year who had actually done the killing, but I knew he'd been working hard to bring the killers to justice since then. Apparently, with no success. Based on what I was seeing now, it was eating him up.

"I'm sorry," I said, and meant it. I resisted the urge to ask him why he hadn't called over the past several months. How he'd managed to get his job back. So many questions. I wasn't sure that any of them were really my business, though, so I kept quiet.

I thought again of the uneasy feeling I'd gotten that morning; the loaded glances Jack had been trading with Agent McDonough.

"I noticed some energy between you and McDonough,"

I said. "Is there anything I should know?"

A pulse ticked in his jaw, though he shook his head. "I don't like the man, and he knows it. We have a history, but that doesn't have anything to do with the search for the Redfield girls. This should be fairly straightforward. Dean's family lives up in the cabins they bought at the top of the mountain, and I think his younger brother has a couple of friends he brought up there. I'll go with you and we'll talk to them, see if there's anything they can tell us that wasn't mentioned before. Other than that, you'll be out with the rest of the searchers."

Which meant it really would be good experience for Bear and Ren, both of whom were chomping at the bit for another chance to get out in the field. A search like this, as horrible as it was for those directly involved, was a once-in-a-lifetime opportunity for us.

I still wasn't able to completely dismiss the unease crawling beneath my skin, but I put it out of my mind. Ahead, I nodded toward a darkened land mass that loomed above the water. "All right, we're here. If you can keep yourself out of trouble for twenty minutes, I'll get everything pulled together and we'll get out of here. We're used to gearing up fast."

He nodded. For a moment, our eyes caught. He managed a naked smile. "I really am glad to see you, Jamie. I should have called sooner, but it will be good to work together again."

I shrugged, trying to ignore the blush that climbed my cheeks. "It's my job, Jack. This is what I do."

3

JUST UNDER TWO HOURS LATER, we left the Owls Head Airport in a private charter with Jack, McDonough, Bear, Ren, and me, along with our three dogs: Casper, Minion, and Phantom. We landed in Bennington at noon that day. William H. Morse State Airport consisted of a single airstrip, a complex of modular buildings, and a virtually empty parking lot. A trim, athletic-looking woman with coal-black hair met us in a cargo van. McDonough gave her some orders I didn't hear, then excused himself and drove away in a black SUV the size of a tanker.

"Jamie, this is Agent Rita Paulsen," Jack said once McDonough was gone. "She's assisting me on the case."

"Good to meet you, Agent Paulsen," I said. Her handshake was firm and her gaze keen as she greeted me, and I got the sense she didn't miss a lot. Not surprising, I supposed, given her line of work.

"Rita, please," she said. "Agent Paulsen was my mother. I went ahead and booked a couple of rooms at the inn where we're all staying—they take dogs, so it shouldn't be a problem. It's not fancy, but it should be a good enough place to lay your head."

"Thanks. I'm sure it will be fine," I said.

"Thank you for coming out. Jack's said great things about your work. Anything we can do to bring Melanie and Ariel home safely, I'm in favor of."

Melanie and Ariel. It was the first time I'd heard the names of the missing girls. It had the impact I suspected Agent Paulsen had intended: for some reason, nameless faces are so much easier to forget. The simple act of giving these young women identities apart from victim instantly drew me in deeper.

"We'll do whatever we can," I said. It was hardly a promise, but Agent Paulsen still looked pleased. She helped us with our gear, and a few minutes later we were on the road.

Since Glastenbury is set among thick woods and a whole lot of mountains, there's no easy way to reach the town from the airport. We followed Route 9 to 71, traveling winding highways where mountains rose in all directions, and ultimately ended up on a pitted dirt road all but washed out thanks to the heavy rains over the fall. The trees closed in around us on that dirt road, and a pall seemed to hang over the vibrant colors that surrounded us.

The vehicle was a simple cargo van, with no actual seats apart from the ones up front. I sat on a cast-iron bump over the wheel well. Jack stood beside me, his hand fisted around the Jesus handle in the roof of the van as we drove. Bear and Ren sat across from us. The dogs were already wired at the prospect of a search, Casper and Minion both pacing in their crates as we rolled on. Phantom alone seemed peaceful, alert but apparently at ease.

"They call it the Bennington Triangle," Ren announced

a few minutes after we'd hit the road, reading from her phone. "Glastenbury is supposed to be at the apex." Bear looked over her shoulder, and I resisted the urge to push the hair from his eyes. There had been talk at one point of him joining the Marines after graduation. I couldn't deny that I was grateful that talk had lapsed in the past year. A haircut wouldn't have killed him, though.

"Okay, I'll bite," I said. "Why is it called the Bennington Triangle?"

"Five disappearances, between 1945 to 1950," Ren said, in the musical Nigerian accent that's become a familiar— and welcome—part of my world over the past few years.

Unlike Jack and me, Bear and Ren shared the wheel bump on their side of the van, the two of them so comfortable sharing space that they looked literally joined at the hip.

"They never found the people who disappeared?" Bear asked.

"This is a heavily forested area," I said. "And my guess is that those searches weren't done the way we conduct searches today. Things have changed a lot in the past sixty-five years."

"The FBI was brought in to look for the second girl who went missing—Mary Wieland," Agent Paulsen said, glancing over her shoulder with the words. "The Vermont State Police were actually formed as a result of her disappearance.

"She was last seen wearing a red sweater," Agent Paulsen continued. "And a young boy in a red jacket disappeared in 1950. After that, it was said that it's bad luck to wear red within the Bennington Triangle."

Ren looked down at the deep red jacket she wore and frowned. "Now you tell me."

We lost our cell and internet signals shortly after that,

but Agent Paulsen went on to tell us about Bigfoot and UFO sightings in the area; ancient structures built into the mountainside; mysterious lights and ghostly apparitions and voices whispering in the darkness. I watched Bear as she told the stories and couldn't help but wonder what he thought about all this. Of all of us, he was the only one who truly had something to fear. If there were ghosts to be seen, Bear was the one they would find.

He always is.

From the time he was a baby, it's been clear that Bear doesn't live entirely *in* this world. I first started hearing voices that no one else heard shortly after we lost my sister. At first, I thought I was going crazy… Later, I realized those voices meant me no harm, and had no hidden desire for me to do harm to anyone else. They are part of both my inner landscape and the world around me, and I've learned to deal with them as best I can.

Bear, on the other hand, doesn't just hear voices. He sees faces. Meets people. Makes friends with ghosts who've been walking the earth for decades, sometimes longer. It's a burden he's handled well over the years, but I know it's taken its toll.

Nearing our destination, Rita drove toward what looked like an abandoned nineteenth-century church at the end of a long dirt road. As I always do before a search, I found myself thinking of my little sister, and the men, women, and K-9s who pitched in trying to find her more than twenty-five years ago. And, just as always, I sent up a silent prayer that this search would end better; that we would provide a resolution, good or bad, for the family left waiting for their girls to come home.

Then, I got down to business. "You guys go ahead and get unloaded," I instructed Bear and Ren as Rita stopped the engine. "Let the dogs stretch their legs a little, but don't leave this area. We'll solidify the game plan once I talk to the muckety mucks running the show."

Jack, Paulsen, and I left the van and stepped into what must have passed for sunlight around these parts, and I took a moment to take in the scene.

Upon closer inspection, the building Paulsen had driven us to was indeed an old church, with peeling white paint, a bell tower, and rotting wooden steps that sagged dangerously in the middle. Forest grew thick around it, and the parking lot—if it could really be called that—was run through with pits and boulders never extracted from the cold, hard ground.

It may have been rundown, but right now it was hardly abandoned.

Three black SUVs with government plates lined the pitted parking lot, while pickups and SUVs with the VTK9 logo lined the road alongside Blazers from the Vermont Forest Service and cruisers from the state and local police. Two white news vans had been relegated to a far corner, practically swallowed by the forest itself.

"You weren't kidding," I said to Jack. "Definitely a three-ring circus."

Rita overheard and nodded. "That's a nicer word than most people use."

Jack said nothing, just remained beside me in staunch silence. He'd relaxed a little over the course of the trip, but now he looked strung as tight as a drug dog in a poppy field.

"This will be headquarters," he said. "It was the closest

we could come to a central command post out here."

A trim, overly made-up blond woman with a microphone in hand beckoned to Jack, her cameraman in tow as she sped up to reach him.

"Jack," the woman began. There was an odd tightening in my chest at her familiarity.

"No comment, Angie," he said, before she could get any further.

The woman was shorter than me, but with a fuller chest, bigger hair, and a mouth full of gleaming white teeth that shone when she smiled. "Have a heart, Jack," she purred. "I just want to know what you're doing to find the girls who've gone missing."

"Everything we can," he said briefly. I could tell even those few words weren't appreciated by Rita, however, who glared at them both.

"Is there any truth to the rumor that this is someone copying the murders that took place in 2009?" the reporter pressed.

"The girls are missing," Rita said. "That's all." The reporter had gotten in front of us by now, blocking our way into the church. She was either very brave or very, very stupid. "If you'll excuse us—"

"Dean Redfield has suggested that the FBI is to blame for these disappearances—"

"I thought I told you to stay out of the way, Angie," Paulsen said. There was a dangerous glint in her eye.

"This is public property, I'm well within my rights—"

"Not if you get in the way of my investigation, you're not," Rita cut her off. "You obstruct this search or write a story intimating the disappearance of these girls is tied to the 2009 killings, and I'm sending your tight little spin-aerobicized ass to jail."

"Jack—" the reporter began, appealing to him one last time. He shook his head.

"You're not getting anything from any of us," he said. "Sorry, Angie. Maybe some other time."

The reporter scowled, nodded to her cameraman, and retreated. Once she was gone, Rita glanced at Jack.

"That's not going to be a problem right?"

"No," he said briefly. "It won't."

I'd seen the way the reporter looked at him, though—the familiarity there. Combine that with Jack's tension now, and I knew Rita wasn't imagining things. Clearly, there was something between him and the reporter. Even though she was gone now, the tightening in my chest didn't loosen.

"Like this search isn't hard enough," Rita continued, "we've already got them spinning rumors that'll get the Redfield camp completely up in arms."

"The Redfields were already thinking the same thing, though, weren't they? That the FBI is involved?" I asked. "I thought that was the reason Dean Redfield wanted me in on this in the first place."

Rita considered the question for a beat, fatigue clear in her eyes, but she didn't comment. Instead, she switched gears abruptly. "We should get to work. The other search teams already have topo maps and GPS inside. Just let us know what else you'll need and I'll make sure you have it."

"We carry our gear in with us, so we'll be fine," I said. I looked around our thickly forested surroundings. "I'm assuming cell phones are a lost cause out here."

"Yeah, everything's run on satellite," she agreed with a

nod. I noted a large generator at the side of the building, its hum as alien as the roar of a waterfall in the Sahara. "You won't have much luck with anything else."

"And the other handlers are out with the dogs right now?" I asked.

"They are," she confirmed. She glanced at her watch. "Have you connected with Cheryl?"

"Madden?" I asked. Cheryl Madden was the director of Vermont K-9, and had been for the past decade. "Yeah, I talked to her this morning. She told me to bring a slicker, boots up to my ass, and a dog with gills."

Rita laughed. "Sounds about right. As long as she's on board, I don't think anyone will have a problem with you being out there with them. Come on in and I'll make introductions."

I followed her up the worn wooden steps, and she held open one side of the oversized double doors. They led to a surprisingly spacious inner sanctum with wooden pews still in place. Dirty stained glass windows allowed a few beams of filtered sunlight through in shades of blue and gold. A digital whiteboard was set up at the front of the worship space, and a dozen men and women from various law enforcement agencies were seated in the first few pews.

They looked up as Rita, Jack, and I walked down the center aisle toward them. McDonough stood beside the whiteboard at the head of the room. In the front pew were half a dozen men in khakis and LL Bean gear, all of them looking ill at ease—Jack's peers with the FBI, I assumed. Jack made introductions, but the names and faces quickly ran together. I have a hard time remembering anyone who doesn't have four legs and a wagging tail, so quickly gave up trying. Farther back in the room were a few hearty-looking, frowning men and women in weathered outdoor gear. The forest service. I already knew Wade Wright, the head of the Vermont Forest Service, so I went to him as soon as the others in the room began fighting amongst themselves over who should be doing what.

"Welcome to the CF," he said with a scowl. Wade was in his sixties, well past retirement age and resisting with everything he had. He had a ruddy complexion and angular features, his hair a sandy color fading to white, his teeth yellow. His body was both too tall and too lean to look natural inside.

"CF?" I asked.

"Clusterfuck," he said in a more hushed tone. "How the hell'd they pull you in?"

"Father of the missing girls," I said without elaborating. "What's your take?"

"Runaways more than likely," he told me. "That's my best guess, anyway. The family won't talk to any of us—there's an old guy in charge of the lot of 'em, seems to think the FBI went in and took the girls. Not that I can blame him, considering what they went through before—you heard about that?"

"The murders back in '09?" I asked. He nodded. "Yeah, I heard."

"Right. Well, according to him we're all in cahoots, of course. If they asked for you, maybe you'll have better luck."

"What's Cheryl say about all of it?" I asked, knowing he and the head of Vermont K-9 had worked together frequently over the years.

"She doesn't give a rat's ass so long as she gets to stay

out in the field. Leaves me to deal with the assholes and the imbeciles."

I heard the church door open behind me.

"Speak of the devil," Wade said. He nodded toward the door. I turned to find Cheryl Madden standing there in waders to her thighs and a slicker dripping rain, a cattle dog beside her with a notched ear and a bright yellow raincoat.

McDonough started to approach her, but Cheryl ignored the man in favor of Wade and me. Festus—the cattle dog, whom I'd met on searches before—trailed alongside her, paying no more mind to McDonough or the other law enforcement than his handler had.

"You sure you want in on this thing?" she asked me. "I saw your dogs out there—they all look so damn dry. Not too late to back out."

McDonough had followed Cheryl over. He didn't look happy at the suggestion.

"I think it is, actually," I said. "It's all right, we'll be fine. The dogs won't melt with a little rain; neither will we."

"All right then, let's get you up to speed," Cheryl said. She was a sight you didn't see every day: six feet tall, with thick gray curls she usually wrangled into a braid. Her front tooth was cracked, and her personal style seemed pulled directly from the field manual she'd used for the better part of her twenty years of service in the United States Marines.

"You want to show her, or you want me to?" she asked McDonough. There was an underlying hostility there that wasn't surprising—Cheryl's never been known for her deference to authority figures, particularly when they're men. And men like McDonough... Forget it.

"Why don't you," McDonough said. "You know the area

better than most people here."

Cheryl glanced at Wade, who shrugged at her. It was the truth.

She led me to a long folding table loaded with topo maps along the back wall. I'd already gotten a good feel for what we were in for, but the maps confirmed it: This promised to be a hell of a search, testing the dogs' skill and both their and my handlers' endurance.

At a word from Cheryl, McDonough brought up a digital map on the whiteboard, enlarging it with a sweep of his hand. Cheryl took the lead from there.

"Melanie and Ariel were last seen here." She highlighted an area at the center of the screen. "That's where Dean has set up camp."

The elevation on the peak was roughly 3500 feet. Photos came up to the left of the map, showing an old log cabin atop what looked like a sheer wall of granite.

Jack had given me the basics of what he already knew, which I reviewed internally in light of the new information: The missing girls were Ariel and Melanie Redfield, sixteen and eighteen, respectively. Both were daughters of Dean Redfield, patriarch of the Redfield clan. According to Dean, they'd last been seen at 6:30 Saturday morning, when they told one of the men in their camp that they were going for a walk. They'd been wearing light clothing, nothing fit for an actual hike in rough terrain, and according to reports, they'd had no gear or food with them.

None of these things boded well.

"Are you sure they didn't fall?" I asked Cheryl. "It looks like it would be easy enough, especially if they aren't familiar with the area. Where have you looked?"

"We're not sure of anything right now, but my gut says no. Not that we could actually get close enough to do a damn thing," she said with a frown. "Nobody's out there with welcome mats. What we have checked so far has gotten us nowhere. Right now, all we've got to show for the trouble is swamp foot and a hell of a lot of tick bites."

"What else has the family said?" I asked. "Do you have any information on where the girls were going? Why they were headed out in the early morning in light clothing in the middle of a rainstorm?"

"The Redfields aren't exactly the talkative sort," Wade said. He stooped to pet Festus, who leaned against the man and continued to drip rainwater on the wood floor.

"Which is why we're glad you're here," McDonough added. "Dean's said he'll talk to you, and so far he's shown no interest in anyone else. To be honest, I think this whole exercise will prove to be a waste of time at the end of the day. The girls probably got tired of swimming in their own gene pool and decided to head for open water for a change. Eventually, they'll show up on the other side of the country and we'll be done with it."

"I don't think so," Cheryl said. "I've got a feeling they're out there somewhere." The words surprised me, given Wade's counterargument moments before that they had most likely run away. "Of course, I don't have much to back that up just yet. Just doesn't seem like given their history and what they saw their old man go through a few years ago, they'd up and take off without saying something to someone."

I hadn't met Dean Redfield yet, so I had no way of knowing whether it was likely that his daughters had simply run off. There was only one way to find out. "All right, so let's go talk to Mr. Redfield and see what he has to say about all of this." I looked at Cheryl. "You mind getting my handlers up to speed? I don't want them stepping on your toes, and they could use some guidance. Just send them wherever you think they'll be most helpful."

"Sounds good," she said with a nod. Her gaze drifted to Jack and Rita, then the other law enforcement. Wade straightened, though Festus remained leaning against his calf. Cheryl's jaw hardened as she returned her attention to me. "You be careful out there, all right? Tweedle Dee over there"—she nodded in the direction of McDonough—"doesn't know shit, as far as I'm concerned. There's something not right about this. And I'm not so sure the Redfields are the only ones at the heart of it."

•

It was pouring again when I went back outside. The two news vans were still parked where they'd been before, a couple of reporters—one of them Jack's blonde—and a cameraman huddled beneath umbrellas talking. They glanced toward me when I left the church, and I looked away in the hopes of discouraging any interest. It worked, since they went back to their huddle without incident. Apparently, I wasn't worth their time. One thing to be grateful about today.

Meanwhile, Bear and Ren waited just outside the cargo van, beneath a canopy they'd set out to keep out the rain. The dogs all have their own rain gear: slickers that cover their bodies and keep out the chill, though I've never gone as far as the doggy rain boots I know some handlers like. In my experience, they just hinder progress in rough terrain—

not to mention the time it takes for the dogs to get used to them. That means extra attention is paid to paw care, but ultimately I'd rather do that than try to keep track of a dozen K-9 Air Jordans every time we hit the trail.

"What's the verdict?" Bear asked when I approached. I got under the canopy with him and Ren. Raindrops poured off the canvas roof in rivers.

"I'm going up to meet with the Redfield clan," I said. "Cheryl will get you two started. She's in charge while I'm gone—which means whatever she says goes." Bear made a face. "Problem?"

"She doesn't like me. She thinks I'm just a kid."

"She likes you just fine. And you are just a kid."

"Thanks," he said with a frown. "That's reassuring."

"I'll radio you as soon as I'm done with this Dean Redfield," I said. "In the meantime, you can get out in the field as soon as Cheryl okays it. Tell her I said I'd like you to work the outer grid."

"The outer grid always goes to the least experienced," Bear said immediately. "I bet I've been doing this longer than half the people with VTK9. There's no chance we'll find anything if you put us out there."

Ren shot him a look, clearly not pleased that he'd spoken up. I wasn't all that pleased myself.

"There are twenty thousand square miles of forest we're trying to search here," I said, in the most reasonable, I-don't-want-to-strangle-my-teenage-son voice I could muster. "These girls have been gone twenty-four hours already. They could be anywhere out here, and Vermont K-9 is already stretched thin. Which means I need you focused on what you're doing, and I need to know you don't have some damn-fool idea that you're less important to this search than anyone else. Let's try and keep in mind that there are two girls' lives on the line here—this isn't just an exercise so you can earn your next Boy Scout field badge."

Bear considered the words in the stubborn way of seventeen-year-old boys the world over. "Yes, ma'am," he finally agreed.

"Thank you," I said.

"Don't worry," Ren said, far more upbeat than my son. "You can count on us."

"I know I can," I said. "Just remember why you're here, and you'll be fine." From the corner of my eye, I saw Jack emerge from the church with Wade and Cheryl. "Okay, I need to get going. I'll radio as soon as I'm ready to join the search."

"You sure you don't need backup going up there?" Bear asked. Casper stood beside him, tail whipping back and forth and body quivering. The dog's attention was fixed on the forest.

"I'm sure," I said. "I've got Jack, and I'll take Phantom with me. I'm covered, bud."

Bear didn't look completely at peace with the arrangement, and looked even less so at Cheryl's rapid approach. Regardless, he nodded. "Stay in touch, okay?"

"Will do," I agreed. "You too. Be safe."

"Always," he said. Ren nodded her agreement. I clapped him on the back since I knew a hug would be unwelcome—*Mom, we're working*—and ignored a swell of fear that I knew could be premonition, but was more likely just the curse of every parent in the universe when leaving their kid to the world's mercy.

I left the two teens behind and joined Jack and the others. One low whistle was all it took and Phantom was at my left side. Festus perked up at sight of her, but at Phantom's glare the smaller dog gave her a wide berth.

"My team's briefed," I said to Cheryl. "I've just got the two handlers, but Bear and Ren know what they're doing. Nobody needs babysitting."

"I'm sure. You forget, I've worked with you all before—though not since your boy was not much bigger than Festus here. Give me a holler once you get done and you and Phantom can join up with me. One of my guys washed out earlier—literally. Mudslide," she explained. "I could use a partner."

"Sounds good," I agreed. "What about you?" I asked Wade.

"There are still a few local families out here in these hills," he said. "I'll go talk to them, see if they've seen anything. Then I'll check in with some folks in Shaftsbury, see what they have to say."

With the logistics settled, Jack, Wade, Phantom, and I left in Wade's Chevy Blazer, Jack and Phantom relegated to the back at Wade's insistence, while he and I manned the front. The dirt road was slick with mud, four-wheel drive required for most of the trek. The higher we climbed, the darker it got, as though the trees were converging on us. It felt sinister and chilling, and I couldn't deny my growing sense of dread the closer we got to the top of the mountain.

4

BEAR WATCHED HIS MOTHER and the others ride off, then focused his attention on his own dog. Casper had been pacing and pulling at his leash all morning, eager to get on the trail. Bear's mother's dog, Phantom, was the kind of Zen dog who'd just let things unfold the way they were going to, but Casper would push it every step of the way. That bully nose of his was always going, his body perpetually on the move.

"Chill, Caz," he said when the dog tugged on the lead yet again as they were trying to get their gear laid out and ready to go. The rain hindered progress and the cold chilled his bones, but Bear paid little attention to the weather. Not with a search like this on the horizon—especially not one with Ren.

"Someday he's just going to charge off and drag you down with him," Ren said. Her own dog, Minion, was also a pit bull mix—but a hell of a lot mellower than Casper. She was also two years older than Casper, though, so there was an excuse there. Regardless of Casper's impulsivity, the dogs were two of the best Bear had ever worked with.

"He's better once he's working," Bear said. "Put on his

harness and give him a longer lead to run with, and he's golden. He's just got a little more energy than the rest of the dogs you usually see on the trail. Nothing wrong with that."

Ren smiled. She had teeth that shone that much whiter against her dark skin, and eyes that Bear knew had seen too much in her short life. He understood about that kind of thing, though… It was probably why they got along so well.

They were interrupted at the approach of Cheryl Madden—a handler he'd worked with once or twice in the past, though it had been a few years. She stood even with Bear's six feet, with gray hair mostly hidden under the hood of her yellow raincoat. She looked hearty and strong-willed, which in his experience was a trademark of lady handlers. She nodded to them as she approached the van.

"Jamie'll be back shortly, but in the meantime she wanted me to brief you. We've got two girls missing over twenty-four hours now, both of them last seen leaving their house up on the ridge." She nodded to a peak in the distance. "I've got eight teams already in the field. The woods here are dense, and conditions are shit—pardon my language," she added, looking directly at Bear.

"We've heard worse, don't worry," Bear said. "How long have you been searching?"

"We didn't get the call till last night, and conditions were too bad to come out before first light. We've been out here since five."

"Any alerts?" Bear asked.

"A few false alerts, but nothing that yielded a damn thing. I'm not sure whether it's the weather that's screwing them up or just this particular stretch of forest, but the dogs are having a hard time sorting things."

Cheryl's own dog—a cattle dog, purebred by the look— sat at the woman's feet, head up, taking in the proceedings. His mouth was open in a relaxed pant; a friendly enough dog, but Bear could already see the focus that marked a keen working dog. At the end of his own lead, Casper canted to the right, straining to get loose. Bear followed the pit bull's gaze into the deep woods. Something had caught the dog's attention, though Bear couldn't say what.

"Chill," Bear said, keeping his voice level. Casper glanced back at him, seemed to consider the command for a second, and reluctantly sat.

Cheryl watched the exchange and actually smiled. She took a step toward them, giving her own dog a visual 'stay' command, hand extended behind her as she walked away, palm out. That was all it took for the cattle dog to settle back on his haunches and wait for her to return.

"Handsome dog," she said to Bear. She crouched in front of Casper, who was up on his feet again in an instant, body wagging. "What's his story?"

"His name's Casper," Bear said. "He's young, but he's good at what he does—has a lot of heart, too. He can handle it out here."

"Where's he from?" she pressed. Bear knew what she was asking. Casper's body was scarred, his ears docked so close to his head that Bear had to monitor constantly for ear infections. He wasn't the kind of dog you usually saw in the field.

"There was a dog-fighting bust down in South Carolina about two and a half years ago," he said. "Casper here was only about six months old, but he'd been used as a bait dog." At the look of uncertainty on Cheryl's face, he explained.

"They'd use him to work up the fighting dogs—tied him and let the others go at him."

Cheryl's jaw tightened, compassion for the dog and rage for his past at war in her eyes. Bear knew the feeling.

"They were going to put him down—he was in pretty bad shape, and they figured nobody would want a pup with that kind of history."

"They didn't count on you coming along, though," she said with a smile.

Bear blushed. Shrugged. "Yeah, I guess not." He patted the dog's head, and Casper's tail whipped back and forth.

"With a history like that, I'd be worried about dog aggression," she said. He saw her gaze flicker to her own dog before returning to Casper. "You keep him on lead?"

"When we're searching, of course—but just so I can keep track of him, not because I'm worried how he'll get along with others. I've been socializing him with just about everyone and everything I could from the day I brought him home. He's been around pups, grown dogs, aggressive dogs, passive dogs… He's good with all of them. Loves cats, goats, and babies. I've got no qualms about him starting anything, or even taking up the charge if somebody else does."

Rather than taking his word for it, Cheryl put both Casper and Minion through a quick test to make sure they were as reliable as Bear and Ren claimed. Both dogs breezed through, and Bear tried not to look too smug when Cheryl acknowledged that maybe a pit bull could be a good search dog after all. He knew she wouldn't really believe it until the search was over and done, though. That was fine—he was used to people questioning his dogs.

"So, are we ready to go?" Cheryl asked a few minutes

later, once the games were over.

"Ready," Bear and Ren said at the same time. He looked sideways and smiled at Ren, then got a little dizzy at the smile she returned.

"Then let's get on with it," Cheryl said. She surveyed the two of them. Bear's stomach twisted, and he tried not to look at Ren.

"My mom said we'd be going out together," Bear said, trying to sound casual. Cheryl eyed him knowingly, and Bear felt the color climb his cheeks.

She considered it. "You sure she's okay with it?"

"Yes, ma'am," Ren and Bear said at the same time. Ren caught Bear's eye, and he tried to contain a grin.

"We know what we're doing," Bear said. "We've trained long enough, and we've gone solo before."

"But you haven't worked together," Cheryl pointed out. "Especially not in conditions like these."

"We can handle it," Bear said, trying to keep the tension from his voice. Cheryl studied him, then Ren. Then the dogs. It felt like an eternity passed before she spoke again.

"You've got your radios?"

"Uh—yeah," Bear said, almost struck dumb at the thought that she might actually go for it. "Radios are fine, dogs are set, gear is packed."

"Check in every half hour," Cheryl ordered. "And be careful. The forest service has gone through these woods and tried to get rid of them, but there are still a few animal traps set in the brush. Make sure you mind your dogs."

"Anywhere in particular we should be watching for them?" Bear asked, unnerved.

"Like I said, they've been going through the woods to

get rid of them. But there were a couple of active trappers out here years ago. They did their damnedest to cover these woods."

"We will be careful," Ren said. Bear nodded his agreement.

"Good," Cheryl said. "Now, you're covering the southeast corner of the grid. If the dogs alert, radio and one of us will meet you."

"Got it," Bear said.

He looked toward the woods. He'd had a bad feeling about this place from the time they had arrived. That wasn't going away now that he knew they were going in, but he'd had bad feelings before. There was something different about this place—that much was clear. Every forest he'd ever been in had its secrets, though. It never kept him from stepping inside. And this time, with a shot at being alone in the field with Ren... Well, he didn't care what kind of vibe he was getting right now. Nothing could stop him from hitting the woods today.

5

ABOUT THREE QUARTERS OF THE WAY up the mountain, Wade stopped the SUV and pulled into a dirt turnaround surrounded by trees. A red pickup was already waiting there, and I watched as Dean Redfield slid down from the driver's seat and made his slow way toward me. He looked sixty but could have been a decade younger, which made me wonder about the Redfield clan as a whole. According to Jack, there had been ten siblings—two of whom had died at twenty-nine, nearly ten years ago. Had they been the youngest? Or had Mom simply started early and kept on having pups until biology put her out of business? In my own family, my mom had her first at seventeen, and didn't have Clara until she was almost forty. As a species, it's remarkable just how long humans are viable breeders. It's not always good, but it's certainly remarkable.

It was clear based on his appearance that Dean had once been a vigorous man. He looked like he'd seen better days, though, and I wondered if he'd been ill. His head was shaved, the flesh there deeply tanned and liver spotted. He was smaller than I'd expected, reaching barely to my shoulder, with arms and chest that I expected had once been thick and powerful. His arms were ropy and his chest sunken now, his face gaunt. His eyes were pale blue, his lips thin, and his nose slightly too large for his face. Despite the appearance of some physical weakness, he held a rifle easily in one hand, as though it were an extension of his arm.

As we approached, he nodded toward Phantom. "Put the dog back in the car."

I didn't argue. Whenever I can minimize the time my dogs are exposed to cagey men with guns, I'm happy to do so.

Phantom hesitated when I called to her, her gaze locked on Dean. There was an implicit message there that others might not be able to read, but it was as clear to me as if she'd whispered it in my ear.

Something was wrong here.

"Get her out," Dean repeated, a trace of menace in the words now.

"Come, Phan," I said again, more firmly this time.

She took one last look at Dean, then turned her back and trotted to me. I returned her to Wade's SUV, half listening to the conversation between Jack and Dean behind me. Half listening to the forest around me.

I didn't like it here. Dean had met us at the site of what Jack told me had been a casino in the former town of Glastenbury, long before the place was unincorporated in 1937. The casino was built after settlers had deforested the entire area; the higher-ups in town figured they'd try to cash in on the tourist trade since they'd killed the only other industry available to them. Thanks to the deforestation, though, flooding was inevitable. The casino operated for one season in 1897 before the fall rains came and washed out the railway tracks up to the mountain. They were never rebuilt, and the place fell to ruin.

The forest had reclaimed everything now. I doubted sunlight could get through, the trees were so thick. The only thing remaining of the original structure was a granite wall built into the hillside, a remnant of the casino's foundation. The leaves had turned, the forest floor carpeted in rust and red. Something beyond that had me on edge, though—a feeling that eyes watched us just outside my line of sight, secreted in the trees.

Phantom appeared to agree. As I shut her in the back seat, her gaze remained locked on the tree line behind me. I turned, but saw nothing.

"Stay," I said to the dog, returning my attention to her. She whined, but didn't move.

"She'll be fine," Wade said from the driver's seat. "A lot safer than you are. I don't like this guy."

"We'll be all right," I said, though I wasn't convinced myself. I closed the door and returned to Jack's side.

"...they've been gone too long as it is," Dean was saying when I returned. "They know our history—know better than to scare me like this."

"We're doing what we can, Dean," Jack said.

"So you say, but so far that hasn't done us a whole hell of a lot of good, has it?" Dean snapped. I thought of how fondly Jack had spoken of the man before, and was a little taken aback at the old coot's behavior. Oblivious, Dean shifted his attention to me and extended his hand, effectively dismissing Jack. "Dean Redfield, ma'am."

"Jamie Flint," I said. We shook hands, his grip stronger than I'd expected—stronger than it needed to be, really, demonstrating a powerful need to dominate in that simple interaction. I let him have the win; I had better things to do than arm wrestle old men.

"I saw Mr. Campbell speak a few times," Dean told me. "First on TV, and I liked what he had to say enough to make the trip to a couple of his training seminars."

I suppressed a grimace. My former mentor, Brock Campbell, had been a poster boy for the testosterone-driven, good-old-boy network of dog handlers who had ruled the scene up until a couple of decades ago. And still do, in some cases. If cooler heads hadn't prevailed, a prong collar and a bull whip would have been his company logo. I thought of the way Dean had reacted to Phantom, confused.

"Are you a handler?" I asked.

"Me?" He shook his head. "No, no. Don't care for dogs. But what Mr. Campbell talked about was deeper than just training dumb beasts. He had a way about him, an understanding of the order of things. What he had to say about dogs could just as easily be applied to the rest of a man's life, as God intended him to live."

Ah. If that was the way Dean felt about things, it gave me some insight into the way he probably lived his life. I was surprised he wanted anything to do with having a woman run the search for his family.

"You wanted to talk to me about your daughters?" I said, rather than stand there making small talk any longer.

He frowned, and I caught what looked like anger in his pale eyes. He was supposed to be leading this conversation.

"How long's Brock been gone now?" he asked, rather than answering my question.

"Six years. Almost seven."

"Mmm," he nodded. "No offense to you, but I was surprised to hear he'd signed over his business to a woman. A lot of us were."

"We worked together a long time. If you'd actually known him, I don't think it would have been that surprising at all."

The spark ignited in his eyes at the implied rebuke, and his face tightened. For the first time, I saw beyond the smallness of a man who was simply living in a bygone era, to something deeper. Something dangerous.

"The girls who are missing…" I prompted once more.

"Ariel and Melanie," he said. "My daughters."

He still held the rifle in one hand. I noticed that Jack's gaze had shifted to it as the tension ramped up in our conversation.

"I'm not sure what you think I can do that the other searchers already out there can't," I said. "They all know this area well—much better than I do."

"I want you here," he said. "Mr. Campbell trusted you, so I trust you. I got down on my knees last night and I prayed to God. Your name is what He came up with."

I looked at Jack, but he appeared as surprised as I was. "I'll do the best I can, but I can't make any promises."

He grunted at that. "Did he tell you what happened before?" he asked, nodding toward Jack.

"He did," I said.

"I'll bet," Dean scoffed. He turned hard eyes on Jack, then returned his gaze to me. "My brother killed his own flesh and blood. They found my sisters buried in land that had been mine, before the government stole it out from under me. Those girls were slandered. Made a mockery of in death."

His voice hardened even as his eyes grew distant, as though lost in the memory. "I told Gordon to stay the hell away from us before any of this even happened. He was supposed to be this bigshot FBI man that everybody looked up to. My family was whole before he came... Two days after the government took our home, my baby sisters were dead."

"Dean—" Jack began.

Dean held up his hand. "Be quiet," he growled. "You're the only one of any of these sons of bitches that's worth a good goddamn, but how do I know you're still on my side? They could've gotten to you too, for all I know. I'm only dealing with you now because I haven't got a choice. The fact of the matter is, everything was fine, we were safe, until your people started nosing around again. And then, suddenly, more of my family is gone."

Silence fell. Jack looked uncomfortable, but he didn't bother arguing. The focus shifted back to me. There was absolute stillness around us—eerily so, and I got the strange sense that something out there was holding its breath, waiting for me to speak. I took a few seconds before I found my voice again.

"All right... Well, I think I have a good sense of what's happening now. It seems like the best thing anyone can do is what's already being done: get out there and search."

"So you'll join them, then," Dean pressed.

"Yes," I said, though I'd thought that much was obvious. "I don't really see why I shouldn't."

"Thank you," Dean said. "Truly, ma'am. Thank you."

"Don't thank me yet," I said. "We haven't found them. Jack said you have someone you want me to talk to?"

Dean placed a call on his handheld radio. Jack followed

me back to the SUV, where I let Phantom out once more. The dog hopped to the ground with her tail held low and her eyes on the tree line again. I followed her gaze, but still saw nothing.

Jack watched both of us, clearly wanting to say something. I stroked the top of Phantom's silky head, the action more reassuring for me than her, and waited for him to speak. All the while, my focus remained on the trees.

"What he said about Gordon…" Jack finally began.

I turned to look at him. "Had you worked with Gordon Redfield before?"

"He was my mentor at the Bureau for two years."

The information made me pause. "And you never suspected anything?"

"Not for a second." It cost him something to admit that, his eyes more distant with the words.

According to the articles I'd read while traveling that morning, Gordon Redfield had insisted throughout the trial that he was being framed; that his record spoke for itself, and he would never touch his family. Or anyone else, for that matter.

Ultimately, the jury found him guilty of the murders of his sisters, but the conviction had been a surprise. There was wide speculation that he would eventually be released on appeal. Here we were seven years later, though, and clearly that hadn't happened. Massachusetts didn't have the death penalty so he'd been sentenced to life without parole instead, but so far that was the only break he'd caught in this case.

"Do you think he did it, then?" I pressed. "Dean seems pretty clear on it, but are you?"

His eyes found mine. For a moment, I was caught by the hardness there—the betrayal that was almost blinding.

Somewhere beneath that, though, I sensed something else: doubt.

"I'm sure," he said. I wondered whether he was lying to me about that, or himself.

Jack looked around again, checking on Dean's position. Since Dean had gotten off the radio, another man had joined him—this one taller and broader, with a thick beard and red hair threaded with silver. Phantom had wandered a few feet. I snapped my fingers, and she trotted back to me. Dean and the red-haired man approached, both looking as though they expected something to emerge from the forest and eat them alive if they weren't careful. Frankly, I found it a little unnerving.

"This is my younger brother, Claude," Dean said. "He was the one who saw the girls last."

Both Jack and I perked up at the words.

"And what time was that?" I asked.

Claude's forehead furrowed. His right hand sounded out a spasmodic rhythm against his thigh, his mouth slightly agape. "I…"

"It was six-thirty," Dean interrupted. "Claude's not great with time, but I'd just come off my shift."

"Your shift?" I asked.

"Guarding the place," Dean said shortly, glaring at Jack. "To make sure nobody came for us."

Claude nodded. It was hard to gauge his age, though I guessed somewhere in his forties. He swallowed hard, then wet his lips. "Dean just come off his shift," he repeated.

"And what did you see?" Jack asked. This was clearly the first time he was getting a chance to interview the man. Claude looked at Dean, as though seeking permission to continue. Dean nodded.

"I saw Ariel and Melanie—they were whispering. I asked what they were doing, and they told me to mind my own business."

The words came slowly, his voice thick and uncertain.

"Were they dressed when you saw them?" Jack asked.

"Yeah," Claude said with another nod. "They were both in their raincoats. I told them it was too cold to go out. Too early. That this place doesn't like us. I told them not to go out alone."

Dean looked away. Jack, however, remained focused on his subject. I listened intently, caught by Claude's phrasing. *This place doesn't like us.*

"Can you tell us exactly what they were wearing?" I asked. Claude closed his eyes, his brow furrowed in deep thought.

"Pants—not jeans. Tight pants, like you say they shouldn't wear out." He opened his eyes and looked at Dean, clearly expecting a reprisal of some kind. Dean stayed quiet, but I could tell he didn't like Claude's answer. "They had their boots on. Well, Ariel had her boots on. Mel had on more girly shoes, and Ari told her she'd get blisters walking around like that and Mel said, 'I don't plan on staying on my feet that long.'"

I exchanged a glance with Jack. Dean's eyes fell.

"Okay. That's good, Claude," I said. "Good memory. Now, can you tell me a little bit about Melanie and Ariel? Do they like the outdoors?"

"No," Claude said. He laughed, then sobered at the look on Dean's face. "Especially Mel. They like to be in cities. They like to go shopping."

"Do either of them play sports?" I asked, trying to gauge

just exactly how out of their element these girls were.

"Ariel does," Dean volunteered. "She's the younger of the two. Claude's right: Melanie likes cities. Boys with fast cars. This was the last place either of them wanted to be."

"But Ariel is physically active," I pressed.

"She's strong," Claude confirmed. "Really strong. Captain of the basketball team. She goes to the school and works out in the gym every morning, no matter what. Even when she's sick. After we moved, she started going running outside. And she brought weights here with her."

"So she's in good condition," I said, looking to Dean.

"Excellent," he agreed. "She's deep into that whole CrossFit thing, wants to be a trainer someday. Has all these dreams about going out to Hollywood and training the stars. She's always trying to get Melanie to do more."

"What did they say when you told them they shouldn't go out alone?" Jack asked Claude.

"They said they wouldn't be alone, and I shouldn't worry."

"They told you they wouldn't be alone?" Dean asked, his voice sharp.

"That's what they said," Claude said. "I forgot. Mel said, 'Don't worry, Claudey. We're just going for a little walk. We've got an escort.'" He paused. "Then Ariel's lips got skinny, like they do when she's mad, but she didn't say anything else."

"And they didn't tell you who this escort was?" I asked.

"They didn't say. They just told me it was a secret, and not to tell anybody they went. They'd be back before breakfast, that's what Mel said. 'We'll be back before Daddy even knows we're gone.' But then they didn't come back."

His gaze shifted to Phantom, who sat at attention at my left side. "That's your dog?" he asked me.

"Phantom," I said.

He knelt where he was, tipped his body away from Phantom, lowered his eyes, and extended his hand just slightly. It was a good greeting—sophisticated even, demonstrating empathy and an understanding of other beings that I appreciated. Phantom glanced at me.

"Go ahead," I said.

At the magic words, Phantom got up from her spot and walked sedately to the large man now kneeling before us. He looked nervous, an unsteady anticipation in the way he held out his hand. Phantom sniffed, lapped at his hand once, and then moved in so Claude could pet her.

"Nice dog," he said, only partly speaking to me now. "Nice dog. Why's she got a scary name, if she's such a nice dog?"

"When I found her, she looked like a ghost," I explained. I faded, aware that the explanation was over his head and unsure how to make it any simpler. It was true, though.

I wasn't supposed to save Phantom, when she came to me. I was at the DeKalb County Shelter in Georgia looking at a dozen mutts they'd pulled from their three-page-long list of dogs about to be euthanized. According to the DeKalb staff, those dozen dogs had all the qualities I was looking for to become professional working dogs; all I had to do was take them. As I was putting them through their paces, literally deciding then and there who would live and who would die, a worker went past dragging a German shepherd who clearly did not want to go wherever he was taking her. The dog was so thin I could count every rib through her mangy coat. Her eyes were dull, her gait halting. But she turned and looked at me, the hot Georgia sun blazing down on us both, and I knew. If anyone was going home with me that day, it would be her.

I didn't know how to explain that now, though. "When she walked," I continued, "she reminded me of something that wasn't really…" I trailed off, not sure what else to say.

"Not from here," he finished, to my surprise. "Like she wasn't from here. That's how I feel sometimes, too. Like maybe I was supposed to be some other place, but I ended up here instead, like this."

Dean set his hand on Claude's shoulder more firmly than was necessary. I couldn't tell if there was an implicit threat in the gesture or I was just reading it that way. Phantom looked up warily at him, but she didn't leave Claude's side.

"Come on," Dean said. "We'll go get everybody rounded up so Jamie and her dog can start looking for the girls."

Claude stood with some effort, every movement careful. When he was on his feet again, he looked down at Phantom, then back toward the woods. "I hope you find them," he said. "The voices get hungry at night." He paused. A chill swept up my spine.

"The voices?" Jack asked.

He looked at Jack and frowned. His gaze shifted back to the forest. Phantom likewise stared into the trees. The hackles rose along her spine.

"What voices are you talking about, Claude?" I asked.

"It's time to go," Dean said.

"Claude?" Jack prompted.

Claude shook his head. "No voices," he said, the words barely audible. "I wasn't talking about anything."

He turned and strode away—toward Dean's truck, away from the trees—without another word.

•

Two others emerged from the woods shortly after Claude had gone, delaying my ability to join the search yet again. One was a slender middle-aged woman with the same distinctive Redfield features—strong chin, prominent nose, pale blue eyes—that I'd seen in Dean. The other was taller, male, again most likely in his forties.

Dean frowned at sight of them, but grudgingly nodded them over.

"This is my sister, Wendy," he said, gesturing toward the woman. The slender woman extended her hand. Her grip was stronger than I'd expected, her palms calloused. Despite the print dress that covered her from chin to ankle or the demure bun in her hair, she was clearly a woman used to hard work.

"I'm sorry about your nieces," I said. "I know everyone's doing what they can to bring them home again."

Wendy nodded, terse, her lips thinning at my words. Otherwise, she offered no response.

"And another of my younger brothers," Dean continued. "Barrett."

I didn't care for the way the man's eyes never quite found my face, lingering instead on my body. An oily smile touched his lips as he extended his hand.

"A pleasure, ma'am. Thanks for coming out to lend a hand."

I ignored the proffered hand and focused instead on Dean. "I want to join up with the others as soon as possible,"

I said. "Is there anything else you need from me before I get to work?"

"I think we're good for now," Dean said. "You've got your radio. I'll get in touch if anything comes to mind."

At my snub, Barrett pulled his hand back and stuck it in his pocket. I got the sense he wasn't used to such treatment. Indeed, he was a good-looking man, with thick dark hair, straight white teeth, and well-placed dimples. Too pretty and far too slick for my taste, but I doubted he had any trouble finding other women more amenable to his charms. I thought of what Claude had said earlier about what Ariel and Melanie had told him before they'd left.

We've got an escort.

Who could possibly be escorting them out here in the middle of nowhere, if not family?

"Is your whole family sharing a house here?" I asked suddenly, before anyone could disperse.

"Mostly," Dean said. "There are a few cabins that came with the land, up on the ridge up there, but we stick close to each other." He nodded toward a peak southwest of us.

"Who else lives in the house with you?" Jack asked, following my line of questioning.

"Wendy, Claude, the girls, and me live together. My wife passed about four years ago."

"I'm sorry. And what about you?" I asked Barrett. "Are you bunking with someone else, or are you on your own?"

"I'm on my own for now," he said. "Make me an offer, though. We'll see what we can work out."

"Knock it off," Dean said sharply. Barrett's jaw ticked and his eyes hardened, but he didn't argue. Instead, he took a step back, head lowered. Interesting.

We went over the last of the logistics and Jack asked a few more questions that yielded very little in the way of answers before the Redfields seemed to be in agreement that they'd told us everything they could. Dean and Wendy took their leave, but Barrett lingered. Jack went to touch base with Wade, still waiting in the SUV.

Phantom was still at my side, but she hadn't been nearly as warm with the others as she'd been with Claude. Barrett seemed determined to wear out the tenuous welcome I'd extended. His attention inevitably turned toward the dog, and he took a step forward.

"Sweet dog," he said. He stretched out a hand. Phantom growled, her hackles up. Barrett withdrew with a frown. "Or maybe not so sweet. No dog of mine would get away with greeting somebody that way."

"Would you prefer she not growl and just get straight to biting you, without the warning?" I asked. "I'm not fans of everyone I meet, either—I'm not going to insist my dogs be more gregarious than I am. Besides which, she's not a pet. She's a working dog. She doesn't need to win Miss Congeniality to get the job done."

He returned his hands to his pockets. When he looked at me, the chill in his gaze was more than embarrassment—I sensed hostility there with some seriously deep roots. Barrett might make a pretense of being a playboy who loved women, but what I saw in his eyes just then was anything but love. This was a man who loathed the opposite sex, and got off on showing the world just how much control he had over them. I'd made an enemy, but I didn't have the time or the energy to try and make nice.

"We should get going," Jack said, coming to my rescue. "Wade's getting restless, and everyone's got a lot to do. Thanks for coming out to meet us, Barrett."

"No problem," Barrett said. "Just bring the girls home, all right?" For the first time, he appeared genuine. "That's all any of us cares about right now. Just bring Mel and Ariel home."

"We'll do everything we can," Jack said. Barrett nodded. He walked away without saying goodbye to me, his head down, but I couldn't shake the feeling that this wasn't the last I'd heard from him.

"Sorry about that," Jack said when he was gone. "Barrett's a jackass, but it won't hurt to have him on our side over the next few days."

"I don't know that I did anything to help that," I said. "I've never been any good at politics." I shrugged, shaking it off. "I'm not here for politics, though. Let's get on with this, shall we?"

I took a breath and looked around. The temperature hovered right around fifty-five degrees. The rains had cleared for the moment, but based on the weather report and the clouds overhead, that wouldn't last long. I was guessing these were the best conditions we'd get in this search, and I was wasting them.

"I still don't know what anyone thinks I'm going to do that Cheryl and her team aren't already doing," I continued, "but I'd just as soon get to work and give it a shot. Whatever hope we have of finding these girls alive is running out fast."

Jack nodded, and the look in his eyes said all I needed to know on the subject. He knew all too well the odds we were facing at this stage of the game.

6

BEAR AND REN WALKED together for a solid mile without speaking, content to watch the dogs work their magic. It smelled of wet earth, pine, and decaying leaves. Bear listened to the high-pitched shriek of a woodpecker nearby, then separated out the warbling whistle of what sounded like two red-eyed vireos high up in the trees. He searched the forest for a sign of the distinctive birds, but couldn't find them.

He glanced at Ren, whose attention was still focused on Minion as the dog worked the scent, pulling hard at the lead Ren held. Phantom was the only search dog Bear knew of who was allowed to work off-leash. Casper and Minion were both great dogs, but there was no way he'd want to risk just letting them run during a search in woods like these—especially if there were traps laying around. The downside to that was that both he and Ren spent a lot of time being yanked around the countryside by their dogs. It was something they both accepted willingly, knowing that the average pet golden retriever was trained to heel, but a good working K-9 had to have that fire in their belly that meant they'd do anything to get the job done. Including just about pull you off your feet once they caught a scent.

Bear kept his attention fixed on the dogs. A couple of times, Casper froze with his head in the air. He sniffed at the breeze, tail wagging, then turned back and worked in ever-tightening circles for a minute or more. Every time, it seemed he lost the scent before he got far. Bear made note of the places where the dog had paused, though, logging them on his handheld GPS before he sent Casper back through again. Nothing. He made a mental note to recheck one more time on the way back through, just in case.

As though sensing his thoughts, Casper turned his muscled, wiggling body toward Bear, pink nose quivering.

"Keep looking, Caz," Bear said. "Find them."

Casper wagged his whip-like tail in Minion's face. He looked toward Minion, then back at Bear. Woofed twice. There was a bully grin on the fool's wide face that suggested Casper had better things in mind.

"Focus," Bear said, more stern now.

The pit bull ran toward Minion, almost knocking her over as he overtook her on the trail. Minion woofed after him, indignant, and Bear shook his head. Hopeless.

"He's getting better, you know," Ren said.

"Yeah, he is," Bear agreed. "It'll still take some time, but I've never seen a dog want the find more than he does. That has to count for something."

Just then, Casper came back toward him in a burst of speed, braking a second *after* colliding with Bear's legs. Bear struggled to stay upright under the force of the impact. Any other dog and there would have been a reason for the drama, but this was just Casper's way of checking back in. Minion followed at a more sedate pace and stopped in front of Ren.

Bear stooped to ruff Casper's head, while Ren doled out

a quick treat for Minion. "Fool dog," he said. "You know, sometimes I think someone a little less rowdy could be a nice change of pace."

Casper butted the top of his head against Bear's thigh, body still wagging. Ren laughed at the antics. "You would be bored with another dog."

He sat on a felled yellow birch and Casper angled closer, slurping a kiss across his chin.

"Probably," Bear admitted.

They settled in for a break, the dogs eager for water and a chance to let off steam before they got back to business. A minute or two passed in silence while Bear and Ren watched the dogs, before Ren cleared her throat. Bear tensed at the look on her face—a calculated attempt at appearing casual, when he could tell she was anything but.

"I've been thinking about all the disappearances they've had out here—about the curse they talk about." She paused and looked at him expectantly.

"Yeah?" he prompted. "What about it?"

She took a long drink of water, wiped her mouth, and avoided his eye when she spoke again. "What do you think of it?"

"I don't know," Bear said with a shrug. "It's a lot of woods. Frankly, five people in terrain this tough, woods this thick, over the course of a few years doesn't seem like much of a curse to me."

Ren watched him for a second. He felt himself tense at the look in her eyes. "So…?" she prompted him.

"So…what?" he asked, though he knew full well what she was asking.

"So, do you sense anything? Or see anyone?"

He felt himself blush, and looked down at the ground. He'd known Ren for almost four years before he finally told her about the whole sensing thing, when he felt like he couldn't really hold back in good conscience any longer. Ever since, though, things had been strained between them. Different.

"It doesn't work that way," he lied. Though in truth, that was exactly the way it worked: he went to a place where someone had died, or their spirit was somehow tied. If there was something there to see or hear or sense in some way, most of the time he was able to do exactly that.

Ren looked at him doubtfully. "They disappeared a long time ago," she said. "So maybe you just can't sense spirits that long dead. The ones out on Windfall Island have only been dead since 1990."

"Or maybe there are no spirits to sense out here. Just because they're dead doesn't mean there's some part of them still hanging around."

"So sometimes there's no trace?" she asked. "They just… die? Then where do they go?"

"I don't know," he said. Irritation crept into his voice. "It's not like I'm some expert on ghosts or something. I don't understand how I see what I see, and I don't know when it's going to happen. I have no control over it."

She was disappointed, he knew. Ren's family—all except her father—had been murdered in Africa. She'd been trapped under her older brother's body, pretending she was dead. She was only three at the time; her father was a soldier with the Nigerian army, and had been away during the raid. When he came back to his home six months later, the village had been burned and everyone he knew was dead. It took another year before he was able to track down Ren.

All of this Bear knew thanks to Monty, who made it his business to know everyone else's. With that kind of history, Bear could understand wanting to know what happened when someone died; maybe even finding a way to contact them. He softened his tone.

"I wish I could tell you more. I just don't really understand it myself."

"I know." She nodded, then rose before he could say more. "That's ten minutes—we should be going. According to everything I've read, there's a stretch up ahead where a couple of the disappearances took place. There may be something to the terrain that makes it harder to navigate."

"Right," he agreed. He wondered if he should say more. He wasn't good with girls. With people, really. Animals were easier—they didn't require talking. You just communicated with a touch or a gesture, and it was all they needed to be on the same page. Awkward and less at ease now, Bear got to his feet and gave Casper the command to hit the trail once more.

•

"Before I give Cheryl a call and join up with them, I just want to take a look around the ravine by the house," I told Jack and Wade when we got back to the SUV. "Everything else aside, it's just as likely that Melanie and Ariel went out for an early-morning stroll, maybe to meet someone, and they slipped and fell. With the rains this bad out here, Cheryl's already said mudslides were an issue. If one of them went down, she might have pulled the other with her."

Neither of the men looked convinced, and I could understand why. If that had happened, why hadn't one of the girls been heard calling for help by now? One might have been knocked unconscious, but both of them?

"I guess it couldn't hurt," Wade said doubtfully as he put the SUV in gear.

"I also wouldn't mind getting the lay of the land out here," I admitted.

"Now that I can understand," he said.

We set out through the muck of the forgotten dirt road, tires spinning every few feet before Wade was able to get things moving again. For a while it seemed we were traveling straight up, the forest so dense a view of the world beyond was impossible. After about fifteen minutes of this, the ground leveled off again and we reached a cluster of log cabins set back from the road. To my surprise, about a dozen people—a couple of kids, but most of them men my age or older—stood in their front yards, watching warily.

"I thought you said only the Redfields lived up here," I said.

"I think this is Barrett's doing," Jack said, clearly not impressed. "He's kind of a…"

"Hustler's the word you're looking for," Wade interjected.

"Entrepreneur," Jack said instead. "He's doing what he can to start a town, provide housing for people who can pay a little rent and help out building things up out here."

Wade pulled off to the side and stopped the truck. "Good luck with that," he said, shaking his head. "I don't know what in hell he thinks he's going to build."

"These houses were all just left here?" I asked. "The previous owners just abandoned them?"

"About thirty years ago now," Wade said, "a bunch of hippie wannabes got the idea they wanted to leave civilization and get back to nature. They built the cabins, figured they'd live off the land."

"I'm guessing that didn't work out well for them," Jack said.

"They weren't too well versed in what makes for decent farmland," Wade agreed. "The leader took sick the first winter they were here, and he died shortly after the first snow fell. Once that happened, things fell apart fast. They took off early one morning, and I never saw any of them again."

"And the cabins have stayed empty since then?" I asked.

"More or less." Wade shrugged. "Somebody will come out every so often, see if they can make it work. I heard a rumor some developers were thinking about trying to make it a resort destination again." He got out of the truck and looked around, his collar turned up against a biting chill. "If I had the money, I'm not thinking this is a destination I'd choose. But rich folks are a strange breed. What do I know, maybe Barrett's right and he's got a gold mine on his hands."

Maybe indeed. Apart from the rundown cabins and the suspicious glares from the Redfields and their clan, it was actually very pretty here. The leaves were just beginning to turn, but I could only imagine the riot of colors in October. There were no power lines, no sound of engines or car horns, no exhaust fumes. It was one of the most pristine places I'd ever been. Frankly, I hoped the developers stayed away. That *everyone* stayed away. This felt like a place better left to itself.

"So, where do you want to get started?" Jack asked.

I noticed a lone figure in a smallish cabin on the left side of the road watching us. Barrett. To the right, farther back than the others, was a two-story cabin that looked slightly more well-built but no better maintained than the others. On the porch stood the other siblings I'd met thus far: Wendy, Claude, and Dean. I nodded toward that house.

"That's where Melanie and Ariel live?" I asked Wade.

"Yeah—that's the old Smithfield place. It was already here when the hippies moved in. They built the other cabins around it."

I kept Phantom on leash as we approached the cabin, Jack and Wade behind me. A couple of boys, maybe eight years old, kicked a ball across a scrubby clearing in front of one of the cabins. What looked like a Rottweiler started toward us from the same cabin and I froze. Off-leash dogs are the bane of my existence, though I could understand no one worrying too much about leash laws out here.

Before the dog could reach us, one of the boys grabbed its collar and wheeled it around and back toward the house.

"Sorry," he yelled toward us. "I'll keep him out of the way."

I wondered if the boy—or the dog—had already had a run-in with Cheryl.

"Thanks," I called back.

We stopped at Dean's cabin. The porch was in dire need of repairs. Wendy, Claude, and Dean all remained at the railing watching us, and I wondered how the structure could possibly support their combined weight.

"You got the things I gave you from the girls?" Dean asked, looking down at us.

"I've got them, thanks," I said. "I just wanted to start the dogs off here, since you said this was the last place they were seen. That's right, Claude?"

The man nodded, his eyes fixed on Phantom. "Yep. They was on the porch, sneaking out. I was at the door."

Wendy watched all of this with her hands knotted in front of her, her lips pressed into a thin line. She was likely in her fifties, and she had effectively erased any trace of femininity from her bearing. Now, she seemed ageless, sexless, as silent as a specter. I wondered at her history, and made a mental note to get more details about the family from Jack once we hit the trail.

I let Phantom get a good whiff of the items Dean had given me: a pair of Melanie's underwear—small, black lacy things that were completely at odds with our surroundings—and Ariel's T-shirt, the words "TRAIN OR DIE" written in block letters across the front.

"Find it, Phan," I said. While she was used to searching off-leash, Wade had warned me about bear traps in the area. That, combined with the density of the woods and the number of other searchers out here, convinced me she'd be better on lead this time out. She looked put out for a second when I didn't unclip her leash, though—she's a much happier dog when she doesn't have to drag me behind her.

She remained rooted to the spot for a moment, her head raised as she scented the air.

Seconds passed. I thought briefly that she might never pick up the trail—that we would be left standing there, the whole of the Redfields' extended family looking on while I was forced to tell them that apparently Ariel and Melanie had vanished into thin air.

Thankfully, that didn't happen.

About thirty seconds in, Phantom's body stilled. Her gaze sharpened, nose up, and she looked to the north, toward the steep incline on which the house had been built. She glanced at me to make sure we were on the same page.

"Find them, girl," I repeated.

That was all she needed. The next moment, she was headed straight for the hills with her nose in the air.

The sight of a bloodhound with its nose glued to the ground is the one people most commonly associate with tracking dogs, but it's just as likely that the dogs will be following air scents instead. Ground scents are less reliable; they're the reason the bloodhounds in movies were always losing the escaped prisoner when he crossed a creek bed back in the day. Air scenting means the dogs are able to follow a scent as it rides the currents of air above ground, and it's been proven to be considerably more effective for searches in the deep woods.

Wade stayed behind to check in with the others, saying he'd catch up to us shortly, while Jack and I followed Phantom along a barely discernible trail through the trees. We continued on until the house was no longer in sight, descending deeper into a ravine cut into the granite mountain by centuries of rushing water. The rainfall meant loose rocks were that much looser, the hillside leading down toward the ravine slick and tough to navigate. I grabbed hold of a piece of scrub brush as Phantom kept going, the ten-foot lead taut between us and the dog seemingly oblivious to her surroundings—focused on the scent.

"Now that we're on our own again," I said to Jack, glancing back over my shoulder, "can I ask a question?"

Despite the terrain, he looked more relaxed now, as though movement set him at ease. "Of course," he said. I kept my focus honed on Phantom's retreating backside as we walked on through wet leaves, slick granite, and cold rain. "Ask away."

Relieved, I asked for a brief history of the Redfield family. The trail widened enough for Jack to walk alongside me for a stretch and, with my gaze still fixed on Phantom, I lost myself in the Redfields' past.

"Dean was the first of the kids," Jack told me. "Born sometime in the 1960s. His parents lived in Adams, Mass, in the same farmhouse the government repossessed in 2009."

I nodded, listening as he continued. Dean's father was in the military, killed in Vietnam in 1973. At that point, there were already a slew of siblings, and rumors flying about abuse and mental illness on the parts of both Mom and Dad.

Jack hesitated. "Go on," I said. "There's clearly more to the story…"

"Oh, the story hasn't even started yet. To keep the house, Mom started taking in…boarders."

"I'm guessing these weren't kindly old spinsters looking to help out a neighbor in need."

"Not exactly," he agreed. "They weren't even boarders, really. Or they were, but they mostly rented by the hour."

"Ah. So, Mom decides to keep the family afloat by going into the oldest profession."

He smiled faintly, though his eyes remained grim. "It explained a lot, eventually, about the way everything fell apart for Gordon and the rest of the family later on. Mom continued selling herself—and Wendy, I suspect—until she was stabbed by a drunk customer one night in '87. By then, Dean had joined the military himself. He got the call after her death, got an honorable discharge, and returned to chaos. All the kids were a mess by then, and the house was in ruins."

"A lot for a kid in his twenties to deal with," I noted. We'd reached another narrow stretch, so Jack and I separated. The trees closed in yet again, the sky dark enough that I thought I'd need to haul out my flashlight. Up ahead, Phantom paused and glanced behind her.

"Hold that thought," I told Jack.

I jogged on ahead to check in with Phantom. "How's it going, girl?" I said. "Have you got a scent, or are we just taking in the sights?"

As though in answer, she lifted her nose to the air. I flashed back to the mangy, bone-thin, but strangely self-possessed dog I'd rescued from the shelter in DeKalb County.

"So you've got this—is that what you're telling me?"

She hip-checked me in Phantom's signature show of solidarity, and continued on. Jack met me on the path.

"Any luck?" he asked.

"Nothing yet," I said. He frowned, and I realized this wasn't really his area. Experienced SAR—search and rescue—are prepared to meander through the woods for long, often fruitless stretches of time. I suspected Jack was more of a man of action than that.

"You could go back to the car if you want," I offered. "Check in with the others."

He shook his head without a second thought. "And leave you alone out here? Forget it."

"You know, I can actually take care of myself. I've been doing it for a long time now."

"We all need someone to watch our backs sometimes," he said. "Today, that's my job." For a second, it seemed like he was about to say more. Tension simmered in the air between us. He wet his lips, cleared his throat, and looked away. "Anyway… Where was I?"

"Dean Redfield, now in charge of all his siblings."

"Right," he agreed. "Dean rose to the occasion, even though it had to be tough. Or he tried, anyway. Got the kids to help out and get the house back in shape. He was a hell of a carpenter, and he started getting work around the area. Took on two of his brothers as apprentices. He did everything right…except pay taxes."

I frowned at that. "So, you're saying a veteran—himself the son of a soldier who died in combat—who returns and takes on the care of his siblings after the death of his mother… You're telling me that you then went in and booted him out of his home? *Their* home?"

Jack bristled. "We did everything we could to get them set up in a new place, or else tried to help get him the resources to take care of the back taxes. I'm not in love with every aspect of this job, you know." I didn't say anything, letting him calm down first. After a couple of seconds, he continued. "Besides, more than twenty years had passed since that time. June and Katie were adults. No one had paid taxes for decades, and there were complaints from neighbors that other things were happening, as well."

"Other things like…?"

He frowned. "The girls had gotten into some trouble. It's not clear what they were exposed to in those early years with their mother, but they were troubled as teens and never quite pulled it together after that. Dean came down hard on them; the police were called in multiple times over the years, charges filed for domestic violence."

I said nothing for a few seconds, considering the story.

"So, the women who were murdered in other states were prostitutes," I finally said. Jack nodded. "And Gordon's mother was a prostitute of sorts. As were June and Katie, possibly, at the time of their deaths."

"Exactly."

Interesting. Very interesting—and dark, and damned depressing. But it cast Gordon and the murders in a new light, at the very least. I got the sense there was something Jack was holding back, but I wasn't sure how to get the information—and wasn't completely sure I needed it. The whole story might give me a better sense of things, but it didn't really get me any closer to finding the girls who were missing now.

"Okay," I said. "Thanks for the background, I appreciate it."

"Of course," Jack said with a nod. "Whatever I can tell you, I will." I caught the implication: there were things about this case that he *couldn't* tell me. He looked up ahead, and I followed his gaze. Phantom wasn't in sight, though I could hear the bell on her collar clearly.

In the time that we'd been talking, we'd slowly been descending the mountain, the terrain varying from a bitty hill to a steep ledge carved from the granite. The sound of rushing water was louder now, and I expected we must be getting close to the ravine by this time. It was hard to tell at the moment, however, since we were tucked into a narrow thread of woods so thickly forested you could barely see daylight.

Once we'd cleared the trees and I got a better look at what we were facing, I stopped dead.

"How much longer do you think we should be looking

around out here without the others?" Jack asked behind me.

I held my hand up, signaling him to stop. My heart was lodged somewhere in my stomach, twisted in there with the warm cereal I'd had for breakfast hours ago.

I wet my lips, and tried to find my voice.

"Stop, Phan," I called. She was at the end of her lead and straining forward, at the very edge of the ravine. The drop below was dizzying. The sound of rushing water was a roar now, water churning white below. A light, cold rain fell, making the already-slick granite potentially treacherous.

To my relief, Phantom braked at my command and glanced back over her shoulder at me. Her body practically vibrated with impatience. When she's on a mission, Phantom has always been oblivious to her surroundings. Right now, that could prove deadly.

"Come, Phantom," I said. She was still pointed in the opposite direction, her gaze fixed on something I couldn't see on the other side of the ledges. And then, as though watching her thoughts unfold, I saw her focus shift below. My stomach dropped.

The incline was practically a right angle that plunged thirty feet to icy, rushing waters and deadly rocks below.

And my dog was about to try climbing down.

"Come," I repeated firmly. I thought of her tracking the deer early this morning. The fact that she's an independent spirit is partly what makes Phantom an incredible search and rescue dog…but I've worked with her for a long time to instill a sense of when independence is okay, and when she needs to cut the crap and listen to me.

She paused, still looking below. I followed her gaze, but saw nothing. I heard her whine, then glance back at me one more time. She woofed, unmistakably unhappy with me. *I can do it—just let me try.*

I thought of the mangy cur she'd been when I'd pulled her from the Georgia shelter. The way she'd looked at me then, like she would do whatever she had to do to prove she was worth saving. She'd done that a thousand times over by now.

"Phantom," I said, pulling myself back to the present. "I don't care what you think you smell—we're done. Get your butt back here, or I'm retiring you tonight."

I could practically see her frown. And while I understand that dogs don't speak English, and she most likely doesn't think things through in quite the same way we do, I could have sworn she was weighing the pros and cons while I stood there. Somewhere in the back of my head, I heard Wade's voice and realized that he'd rejoined us. Jack started to speak behind me, but I held up my hand again. He fell silent.

Finally, after what felt like a lifetime, Phantom turned to face me. "Come on, Phan," I said.

She trotted along the ledge, never once glancing down, and returned to me without incident.

"So, what do you want to do?" Wade asked when we were together once more a few minutes later, Phantom safely beside me once more.

"Call in the cavalry," I said. "I'm not losing my dog because these idiots were too stubborn to get people down here the right way as soon as they knew the girls were missing."

"I'll radio Cheryl," Wade said.

"You think you can talk to Dean?" I asked Jack.

"Convince him I can't do this alone—we need people down here."

"I'll either convince him or I'll haul him in," Jack said, his face tense. I'd seen him reach for me more than once over the past hour when it seemed I was losing my footing. I'd recovered each time before his help was needed, but it was clear he wasn't comfortable here. "You want to come back up with us?"

"No, I'll wait here with Phan," I said. "We need better gear than this, though—climbing harnesses, ropes. I didn't realize what we were in for when I said we should check it out. I should have asked first."

"I'd forgotten what it was like myself," Wade admitted. "Haven't been out here in some time. The rain hasn't done anybody any favors."

Least of all the girls, if they were out here.

Phantom had returned to me and we settled on a narrow overhang that jutted out over the rock. Her nose was still up, her gaze focused on the path she'd been following before—a path that had ended abruptly where turf met granite.

I watched as Wade and Jack made their way back up and into the trees. My hand was wrapped around Phantom's collar, just in case she decided she couldn't bear sitting still any longer. Seated there, I took the time to soak in the surroundings, looking for any trace of Melanie and Ariel.

The water continued in a rush below. If it ever got dry up here, I expected things quieted to a trickle. Right now, we had a churning river of white foam, a narrow strip of rocky ground running alongside it before it steepened to ledges and inclines.

I cupped my hands around my mouth and shouted, "Melaaaaanie! Ariiiiiel!"

My voice echoed back to me. Otherwise, there was no response.

I took two protein bars from my bag—one for me, and a specially made bar for Phantom. Glanced at my watch. Ten minutes had passed.

And then, just in my periphery, I saw a flash of color in the canyon below.

I turned, fast. Phantom came to attention.

Someone in a red sweater limped along the riverbank, moving with painstaking care. The figure was fuzzy, hard to follow—as though I might not be seeing it at all. Phantom whined.

"Melanie!" I shouted again. The figure turned. A girl. She stared up at me for a moment, her face too far for me to make out any details beyond gender and race. "Wait there," I called.

She froze. I could sense the tension despite the distance between us. She looked over her shoulder, then back at me. And then, still limping, she scrambled in the opposite direction. Away from me and around a corner—out of sight.

7

"YOU'RE SURE SHE WENT that way?" Cheryl asked me for the third time since she'd arrived on the scene.

"I'm sure—I'm not blind. A girl in a red sweater. I couldn't see anything beyond that. She was too far for me to figure out how old she was, or whether it was Melanie or Ariel."

Cheryl looked below doubtfully. The water was still churning, and the rain was falling in earnest now. Other than that, the scene was still. No sign of a soul, living or dead.

"Claude didn't remember her wearing red," Dean said behind us. Much to my dismay, Cheryl and Wade had returned with a crowd: Bear, Ren, Jack, and Dean. Bear and Ren I could handle, but it's never a good thing having the family of the missing in on a search like this one.

"If there's a woman running around the countryside out here, chances are pretty damn good she's got some connection to Ariel and Melanie," Cheryl said. "There's a trail that cuts down to the river. Jamie and I will follow that." She glanced at Bear and Ren, and I wondered what had happened in my absence that morning. Clearly, Cheryl had had some opportunity to work with them both.

"You two track along the edge of the ravine—carefully," she said. "We're looking for any sign of the girls: clothing, jewelry." She paused, and I knew what she was thinking. Blood. Hair. Fibers. The residual pieces of two lives that may or may not have been lost out here. She could hardly say that in front of Dean, though.

I hesitated before giving the okay. It was clear we should be maintaining teams of two, but I wasn't so sure about keeping the two most experienced handlers together while we sent Bear and Ren—both juniors without the skill or maturity necessary to handle the situation if things went south—out on their own.

"How about Bear and Casper work with me," I said. "And you take Ren topside with you, Cheryl."

Technically, this wasn't my call—I knew that. Cheryl considered it for a moment before she nodded, and I saw Bear's face fall.

"You all right with that, Bear?" she asked him.

"Yes, ma'am," he said. No argument. No eye roll. Maybe I should have Cheryl along on more of our searches from now on.

She glanced at Dean and the others, then at Jack and Wade. Weighing who would be of value, and who would be dead weight.

"Jack, you bring Dean and help us with the search up here," she said. "Wade, I want you down below with Jamie— you know this area better than anyone."

Jack didn't look happy with the arrangement. Frankly, I wasn't either—Dean was still carrying his rifle with him, and I didn't care for the thought of him roaming the woods up here with Cheryl, Ren, and their dogs left vulnerable. I hesitated.

"Maybe it would be smarter if you went back to the house, Dean," I said. "I'd like you to take a look around the girls' rooms, see if you can come up with anything else."

"That's good," Cheryl said. She sounded relieved. "Good idea. Do that."

"The hell I will," Dean said. He stepped forward. "You think you found my daughters, I'm damned well going to be here. And I'm not traipsing around the goddamn woods like a fool. You saw her down below. Let's stop wasting time talking about it and get down there."

He was right about one thing: time was definitely an issue. Nearly twenty minutes had passed since I'd seen the figure in red. I didn't want to lose her now.

"Fine," I said. "But leave your gun behind. We won't need it down there."

Dean's jaw tensed. His fingers tightened reflexively around the barrel of his rifle. I waited for him to launch into a diatribe on the second amendment. Instead, he nodded. "Fine. We leave the gun behind. Let's just get on with this."

Moments later, the gun was safely stashed inside the hollow of an old maple tree, the bullets in Dean's rucksack. Wade led the way with Bear and me and our dogs behind him, Dean bringing up the rear. For a moment, I watched Ren's dog, Minion, pulling her eagerly along the side of the ravine behind Cheryl and Festus. My stomach turned. I reassured myself with the knowledge that Cheryl knew what she was doing – probably better than I did. Ren was in good hands.

"The trail's this way," Wade said, interrupting my thoughts. "And that's using the word 'trail' loosely."

Dean merely grunted.

Bear and I both kept our dogs at a close heel this time, much to Casper and Phantom's chagrin. Rain was pouring down hard enough that it felt at times the mountain was about to come down with it, and there was no way I wanted the dogs to lose their footing when there was a thirty-foot drop just to one side of us.

We moved forward slowly, carefully. Wade was right—his idea of a trail could use some refining. We pushed through thick brush and dense trees until we came to a rough path carved from stone, every step treacherous. Phantom stayed in a reluctant heel at my left side as we moved, glancing at me occasionally when I lost my footing and inadvertently jerked her leash.

"How was the search this morning?" I asked Bear, after we'd been walking for nearly twenty minutes and things seemed to be evening out. Wade was far enough up ahead that I didn't have to worry about him overhearing, and it seemed like Dean had enough to worry about just surviving the descent.

"There were a couple of places where Caz started to alert, then it seemed like he changed his mind," Bear said as we made our careful way down.

"Did you bring him back through to let him work the scent a little more?" I asked.

"What do I look like, an amateur?" he said, with just a little more attitude than I like. "Of course. I let them spend a good amount of time in each spot, waited for the winds to shift, worked it from different angles. Nothing."

"And you didn't see anything yourself?"

He looked uncomfortable at the question. We always

used to speak openly about his 'sensitivities,' but since moving out to Windfall Island, he'd changed. For the first time since he learned to talk, I knew he was keeping something from me.

"Bear?" I prompted when he didn't say anything.

"I don't know," he finally replied. "I mean… It's hard to say. I don't think so."

"But you're not sure?" I asked. I turned to look at him in profile. He's taller than me now, topping out at over six feet, with a chest and shoulders that have just started to develop after years of being a gangly, gawky kid. I suddenly have a knockout on my hands, one that girls—and women, for that matter—look at twice wherever we go. Thank God, he hasn't caught on to that yet.

"I don't know," he repeated. "Out on the island, I've gotten so used to it I hardly think about it anymore. Hell, half the time I can't tell who's alive and who's dead."

It might have passed for a joke if not for the bitter edge to the words. I didn't say anything, letting him work through that on his own.

"Anyway, I haven't seen anything like that here. I think I've heard something, but I'm having a hard time telling for sure." He hesitated. "I know it's weird, but it almost feels like something's whispering from the ground. I just can't make out the words. It's just sort of this…voice, that I feel beneath my feet."

"Okay," I said when he didn't go on. "You know I won't push you one way or the other. But if you do hear or see something…"

"I'll let you know," he said with a curt nod. "Don't worry. I'll let everyone know."

It took half an hour to get to the bottom of the ravine.

By that time, my rain gear was soaked through and sweat had left my underclothes damp and my skin clammy. We all stopped once we hit bottom, out of breath and shaking with adrenaline. Dean's color was bad, and he didn't look all that steady on his feet once we were on even ground. I wished someone would step up and make him go home, but I knew that wasn't up to me.

"You go upriver, I'll head down," I told Bear, shouting over the sound of rushing water. "The riverbank isn't wide enough for both of us to search the same direction."

Bear agreed. We were on a bank of loose gravel no more than four feet across, the water so close I was doused with cold spray every time I looked toward it. I told Dean to stick with me, and sent Wade with Bear and Casper. I watched for only a second or two as Bear and Wade strode off together before I returned my attention to Phantom.

I still didn't want her off lead given our surroundings, but I loosened my hold on the leash and gave her the command one more time. "Find them."

I waited. Unless I'd gotten completely turned around, this was roughly the spot where the girl in red had stood. I'd seen her run in the same direction we were headed.

Phantom didn't move, her nose in the air, searching for a scent.

Dean shifted impatiently beside me. "What's wrong?"

"Just give her a second," I said.

I took out Melanie and Ariel's clothing and gave the dog another good whiff. She snuffled both items top to bottom, intent, before I took them away again and replaced them in the plastic bags that would ideally retain their scents. "Find them, Phan," I said. "Go on, girl."

Once again, she lifted her nose into the air. Apparently

finding nothing, she snuffled at the ground for a few seconds. Just under the roar of the water, I heard her whine. She looked at me, puzzled.

There's nothing here. There's nothing to find.

Then who the hell had I seen down here?

"What the hell's going on?" Dean demanded. "You said you saw her—saw one of the girls."

"I said I saw someone," I corrected him. "Let's just move. Phantom may pick something up along the way."

She didn't.

We walked for fifteen minutes, until the riverbank had narrowed to a two-foot strip of gravel and going any farther would put everyone at risk. We'd gone around the same bend I'd seen the figure in red follow, but there was nowhere she could have gone but straight up—another five yards ahead of us, the riverbank vanished completely. On either side, rain-soaked granite rose at an impossible angle.

"You sure whoever you saw went this way?" Dean asked. He mopped his brow, his color still gray. His rain gear wasn't nearly as effective as mine, and it was cold out here—if he stayed out much longer, he risked hypothermia.

"I could have been wrong," I said, certain that I wasn't. "Let's go back, meet up with Bear and Wade. They may have had more success."

I expected an argument, but apparently Dean was too tired for it. He went on ahead, and I thought suddenly of my own father on the days and weeks that followed Clara's disappearance. I knew firsthand how deep the pain ran for Dean Redfield right now, and I wanted more than anything to offer some reassurance; to tell him that we would find his daughters. That we would find both girls, and they would be all right.

I kept my mouth shut, all too aware that that was most likely a lie.

We met back up with Wade and Bear a few minutes later. They, too, had found nothing.

"I still don't see how anybody could make it down here," Wade said. "What the hell they'd be doing all this way down. They'd have to do some serious hiking before they even got to the edge of the ravine."

"Hikers come through here sometimes," I said. "This isn't far off the Long Trail and the AT. Maybe the woman I saw was someone else."

"A hiker who vanished into thin air?" Wade said doubtfully. "Seems like a stretch to me."

More likely that my eyes had been deceiving me—that was the implication. That I'd led them all on a wild goose chase.

"We should get back up topside and catch up with the others," Dean said. "Maybe they've had better luck."

We started back up, the climb even steeper than I remembered it coming down. We'd almost reached the trees again when Bear stopped short ahead of me, his gaze fixed on a stretch of dense forest about fifty yards from us.

Dean was struggling to keep up behind us, while Wade had gone on ahead.

"What is it?" I asked Bear.

His body was tensed, his focus riveted on that single stretch of forest. I followed his gaze, but saw nothing.

He didn't look at me when he answered. "A...woman, I think. I don't know. A shape. Something running. You don't see it? She's wearing red—maybe the same woman you saw in the ravine."

I searched the woods once more, Phantom still beside me. Behind us, I could hear Dean closing the distance. I shook my head.

"I don't see anything."

He looked frustrated at that, and shifted his focus to Casper. The dog's usually vibrating body was still while he waited for Bear's command.

"Find them, Caz."

He gave the dog enough lead to run, and Casper tore through the woods with Bear behind him. Meanwhile, Dean caught up to me, gasping for breath.

"What is it?" he asked. "You found something?"

"I don't know yet," I said.

"What did he see?" Dean pressed. There was a combination of fear and hope in his eyes that was unmistakable. Visceral.

"I'll go check, but I want you to go back to your house. I'll report back as soon as I know anything."

"The hell I will," Dean said. In the distance, I heard two sharp barks break through the stillness—Casper's alert. Dean paused for just a moment to look at me, his strength magically restored at the prospect of news. "If it were your boy, could anyone make you stay behind waiting for news?"

Just the thought sent a bolt of dread through me: the scenario no parent ever wants to face. I shook my head.

"Come on," I said. "Wade should already be there. I'll get in touch with Jack, and have them meet us there."

Dean continued on, making his painful way through the trees. I radioed Jack, and rushed on ahead.

8

THE GIRL HAD DARK HAIR and pale skin, and she wore a red sweater that made tracking her easy enough as she wove in between the trees. Casper wasn't paying attention to her, though. The dog had caught a scent and was working that hard, his nose moving back and forth between the ground and the air. It didn't really matter—the girl was headed in the same direction they were. Whether Bear followed the dog or the ghost, he knew he'd end up in the same place.

Somewhere behind him, he heard his mother talking to someone. The asshole who wouldn't leave them alone to do the search, he thought impatiently. That meant she'd be lagging behind, and right now... He hated to admit it, but right now he wasn't sure he wanted to end up where he was going. At least, not alone.

He tuned out the amorphous figure making its way through the woods, and focused on staying on his feet while Casper dragged him through the underbrush. Bear felt the air around him getting thicker, harder to breathe, and knew they were close. Casper helped focus him, and the dog's find rate was a hell of a lot more reliable than Bear's was. Bear wondered, sometimes, what would happen if he stopped relying so much on the dog and found out what he was capable of on his own.

"Bear!" his mother called from behind.

"Up here," he called back. Wade, the forest ranger, had caught onto what was happening and circled back. He looked on as Bear continued tracking.

Casper came to an abrupt halt in a grove of beech trees up ahead. The dog glanced back at Bear, barked twice, and then ran back toward him. Other dogs had passive alerts—a couple of barks, lie down, call it a day. Not Casper. He wasn't the passive type.

The dog ran straight toward him, full tilt, and punched him in the pocket with a wet canine nose.

"What've you got, Caz?" Bear asked. He'd been fooled by the dog before. More than once, Casper had gotten bored with the search and false alerted just for the sake of getting his reward. Now, Bear knew better than to surrender the dog's prize until he'd verified something had actually been found.

He didn't really need to verify this time, though.

Casper stuck close beside him as Bear approached, the dog whirling ecstatically—his victory dance. Once Bear had visual confirmation, he choked back his own horror over what they had found, and focused on the dog.

"Good boy, Caz. Good find!" He forced enthusiasm into his voice and pulled the tug toy from his front pocket. Instantly, Casper calmed. The dog sat in front of him, every ounce of focus fixed on the prize. Bear could hear others approaching—he'd been expecting his mother, but clearly she wasn't coming alone.

He offered the tug to Casper, who fixed sharp white teeth

around it in an instant with a low growl. Bear obligingly held tight, the two of them pulling like that until something broke Bear's concentration. A whisper in the stillness as they moved farther from Casper's find—a darkness in the air, as much physical movement as it was sound.

"I'm working with Caz," he shouted back toward the site, where he could see his mother just arriving with Wade and Dean Redfield.

Keep that dog away from me, a male voice said. A threat if Bear had ever heard one, but he knew it hadn't been whispered aloud. He let Caz win the game of tug—a prerequisite after a successful find—and let the dog take his prize. Looking back toward his mother and the men, Bear couldn't tell whose thoughts he'd heard.

He remained a good distance away, watching. This time when the thoughts came, he could almost see them working their way through the air—tiny black threads that stitched themselves together in whorls and slashes in the air.

Jesus. God, no.

The father of the dead girl, Dean, sank to his knees by Casper's find. By the body. Bear took up the slack in his dog's lead and approached cautiously. He knew enough to stay back as much as he could to keep from contaminating the crime scene, but the old man obviously didn't know the way this kind of thing ran.

Bear's mother held up her hand to stop him from coming any closer. She was on the radio, presumably with Agent Juarez.

"Yeah, I'm sure," she said. "There's only one body here. Get here quick."

That was the end of the conversation. Jamie told Casper

he'd done a good job, and Casper's tail wagged frantically, the fool grinning from ear to ear. Phantom was an empath who would deflate at every shitty find, but Casper was all about the fun. As long as he won the game and got his prize, he couldn't care less how the rest of the world felt about it.

Bear looked back toward the body—at the sight he'd purposely avoided up till now. The old man was still on his knees.

Unlike the girl in red Bear had seen running through the woods, this one was naked. Blood saturated the site—her front and back had been cut deeply, and Bear's cheeks heated with embarrassment when he realized where she had been attacked. He averted his eyes rather than looking any lower, focusing instead on her hands. They were bound, wrapped tight with a thick woven rope they used regularly out on the island. What confused him, though, was the sight of two loops outside her own hands, frayed and dark with blood.

Someone else had been there.

"What about Ariel?" Dean asked from his place on the ground. He wiped tears and snot away with the back of his arm. When his eyes drifted toward Casper, Bear automatically stepped forward to keep himself between them.

"She's not here," Jamie said.

"The way she's been cut up," Dean said, his voice tentative. "It looks just like Katie and June—" He struggled to his feet. His eyes were bright blue, still swimming with tears. Bear took another step back when the man staggered toward him. "You're going to keep looking, right? You keep looking all night if you have to—Ariel's still out there somewhere. The killer is still out there. You see that rope? Ariel got away."

"We'll need to talk to the police," Wade said. "This proves we have a predator out here—someone who isn't afraid to kill. We need to move very carefully from here on out."

"Fuck careful!" Dean shouted. "She's hurt. You need to find her."

"Dean," a voice called from behind them. Bear turned. Casper got to his feet, but made no move to leave Bear's side. Agent Juarez stood between them, his expression strained. Cheryl and Ren were with him, both of their dogs at a close heel. The lady reporter he'd seen back at base had followed them in, her cameraman tagging along behind.

"You see what they found?" the old man said. He practically ran toward Agent Juarez, gesturing wildly.

Ren handed her dog off to Cheryl and came to Bear, her eyes fixed on the dead body.

"Melanie was here—the same way they found the girls last time when you sons of bitches starting nosing around my land," Dean said. "You need to figure out what the hell's happening. How my brother is doing this if he's locked up."

"You found her?" Ren whispered to Bear, while the old man continued shouting.

"Casper did," Bear said. "He caught the scent."

Ren's gaze remained fixed on the dead woman. Bear noted tears in her eyes. He took her arm and steered her away from the scene.

"Don't look," he said. "You don't need to see that."

"I've seen a dead body before," she said. She shook her arm from his grip and stepped away.

"Calm down and let me take a look," Agent Juarez said to Dean Redfield. His voice was even, but there was no room for argument there. The old man started to fight him nonetheless, but Agent Juarez silenced him with a glance and moved forward, stepping carefully to keep from contaminating the scene.

"Your people are behind this," Dean said.

Agent Juarez ignored him and remained standing, studying the body without ever making contact. Ren watched beside Bear, transfixed.

"I'm sorry you're going through this again," Agent Juarez said to Dean. "But you have to be realistic about what's going on here. The whereabouts of the law enforcement involved in this can be verified—a lot of them weren't even in the Bureau in '09. We'll find out who did this, but you have to let us work."

"You're a bunch of liars and thieves," Dean Redfield said. "A den of degenerates. This is just like with Gordon. He's got one of your people working as his henchman—mark my words. You honestly mean to tell me you think these sons of bitches are innocent?"

He was coming unhinged—Bear could see it in the wildness of the old man's eyes, the tremor in his voice. Agent Juarez turned his attention from the body, seeming for the first time to notice the shift in power that had taken place. He held out his hands, no weapon to be seen, and spoke directly to the older man.

"We'll figure it out, Dean."

"Figure it out?" Dean parroted in disbelief. "Figure it out? You see what they did to my little girl? It's identical to what happened to our sisters back in Mass. Ariel got away, but…that's the only explanation. My brother might be in jail, but he's behind this whole thing. I'm done keeping your secrets, done with all of you. It wasn't my family who did this—it's your goddamn agents."

Bear was aware of his mother off to his right, trying to get his attention. Trying to draw him away from whatever was unfolding. Bear touched Ren's arm. She looked at him, her dark eyes wide. Casper was standing at Bear's side. For the first time since he'd rescued the dog more than two years ago, he heard Casper growl.

"Dean," Jack tried again. This time, his voice was firm. Unequivocal. "We need to get the police in here. The one thing this does prove is that there's a killer loose in these woods. We can't send civilians out under those conditions."

Bear took another step toward his mother.

Casper and Ren both stayed with him, but the thoughts on the air swirling around them were a maelstrom—too dark and too thick to even decipher.

And suddenly, Dean was in front of him. His face was dark, furious, twisted with grief.

Casper turned toward the man, hackles raised, head down low.

Off to his left, Bear heard the unmistakable sound of a bullet being chambered in a shotgun. Terror ran through him in a chilling wave.

"Bear—Ren. Come here," Jamie said. There was a touch of panic in her voice, something Bear hadn't heard in years.

When he turned, Bear saw that Dean had a gun—a pistol, a lot smaller than the rifle he'd been lugging around the woods before. It was leveled straight at Bear.

"What are you doing, Dean?" Agent Juarez asked. There was a threat implicit in the question. He had a hand on his own gun, but other people had materialized from the trees.

Friends of Dean Redfield's, Bear assumed. A lot of them armed. They were outgunned here.

"I've seen the way you people operate," Dean said. "The way my brother operates. You forget, I was there start to finish last time. You've done this to me before. You dick around and double talk me and somewhere out there Ariel is alive, and hurt, and waiting to be found. You're going to find some way to blame somebody here for this, and you're gonna tear us to shreds all over again. I won't let you do it."

"Dean, this is a mistake—" Agent Juarez began.

"The hell it is!" Dean shouted. He closed in on Bear, that gun still leveled right at his chest. He took a step forward, his other hand out like he meant to grab Bear. Before he could, Casper leapt in the way. Bear could see the way the whole thing would play out—he could hear Casper's agonized yelp before it ever sounded.

He pushed the dog aside, dropping Casper's leash.

A sharp crack sounded in the stillness, shaking the ground beneath Bear's feet. He saw Casper turn once, eyes terrified, before he shouted, "Go long, Caz!"

The dog raced away from them, a white streak in the darkening woods. It was only after Casper was gone and chaos broke out around him that Bear realized he was on the ground, Ren beside him. And he'd never before felt the kind of pain that was burning through him now.

9

I WATCHED AS CASPER tore through the woods, putting as much distance as possible between himself and the terrifying noise that had just rocked our world. I wasn't worried about the noise, though. I barely noticed it.

All I could focus on was Bear.

He lay on the ground, eyes open, stunned. Ren knelt beside him, her own eyes wide with fear. I started to go to him, and one of the Neanderthals with the Redfields was stupid enough to raise his gun to me.

"Get that thing out of my face," I ground out.

"Get her away from here," Dean Redfield shouted to Jack. Bear groaned. He tried to sit up, then cried out in pain. It was a visceral sound for me, something I felt go through me in a way I never felt anything before I became a mother.

"Jamie," Jack said to me. He moved toward me and caught my arm. I shrugged him off and kept moving. A shell was chambered in one of the men's guns. Jack caught me again. This time, he held on despite my fighting him.

"What's your play here, Dean?" Jack asked.

"We're taking the boy," Dean said. He nodded toward Bear, now gasping in pain, his face the whitest I'd ever seen it. Meanwhile, the damned reporter—Angie Crenshaw— was taping the whole thing, whispering in her cameraman's ear while he filmed. "I'm guessing by the look of you that this is the motivation you need to get this job done. You find Ariel. Talk to my brother, and figure out who he's got working with him. I'm not going through this again. I'm not losing anybody else."

Bear locked eyes with me. Despite the pain, there was that deeper level of calm that's unnerved me since he was a toddler. *That boy knows things,* an old friend told me when Bear was no more than two. *I've never seen anybody with eyes like that. He doesn't even know, all that's locked inside those old eyes of his.*

"This is stupid," I said to Dean. "You really want to take an injured kid with you? Do you have the time or the capabilities to deal with that? Take me instead."

"We can handle the boy just fine," Dean said. "You don't need to worry about that. We'll figure it out. I don't care who you think might be in these woods—I need somebody to keep searching, and I need them focused on a good outcome. This is the only way I can think to make that happen."

Dean bridged the distance to Bear. Ren knelt beside him on the ground, silent tears tracking down her dark cheeks. The man grabbed my son by his right arm—the one that hadn't been hit. Regardless, Bear gasped in pain. I saw Ren flinch at the sound. With guns pointed directly at me and Jack holding me back, I'd never felt more helpless.

"Let me come too," Ren said suddenly. Dean looked at her, clearly surprised.

"We don't need two—"

"I have medical training," she said quickly. She failed to

mention that her medical training was limited to treating dogs and deer. "Please. I can help him. I won't cause you trouble, but I can help keep him comfortable."

"Ren, no," Bear protested. She stopped him with a single glance, her jaw set.

Dean looked confused. Overwhelmed. He hadn't planned any of this, I realized—that wasn't a good thing. This was a panicked decision, not well thought out, which meant there was no telling what the outcome might be.

"You don't have to do this," I tried with Dean again. "We're committed to finding Ariel. There's no reason to give us any more incentive. There's a young woman missing who needs our help—this is what we do."

"You mean to tell me you wouldn't call off the search after finding Melanie like this?" he asked. He looked at Cheryl instead of me. The handler's eyes gave her away—he was right. With an armed killer loose in the forest, there was no way we could in good conscience risk the lives of our searchers. "That's what I thought," he said.

"Please," I said, pleading now. "Just let them go."

Dean tilted his head and stared at me for a long moment, but I got the sense he wasn't seeing me at all. Instead, he was listening to something. Or someone. The depth of fear I saw on Bear's face stole the air from my lungs.

"Forget it—we're taking them," Dean said. He yanked Bear to his feet. Two other armed men came round to assist, while four others kept their weapons trained on us. Then, Dean looked at his watch. "It's Friday, five o'clock now. I know it's hard to look at night…and I know how big these woods are. You've got till noon on Sunday. If Ariel isn't home with us by then…" He paused and took a breath. "Well, I don't see that I'll have a choice by then but to show you I'm serious. If Ariel's not home by noon on Sunday, I will kill one of these young people. I'd hate to have to do that."

The words made me sick to my stomach. This was happening—there was nothing I could do to stop it. Nothing I could say. Panic set in. It felt like I was drowning in ice water, like I had no say in my fate or anyone else's. I fought to regain control at sight of Bear, whose eyes were intent on my face.

"You'll be all right," I said. Tears stung my eyes, but I blinked them back. I forced strength into the words. "Just go with them. Do what they ask. Ren, make sure you get the bleeding stopped. Fast." I swallowed past the pain in my throat and focused on Dean. "Keep them warm. Keep them safe. Because, so help me God, if something happens to them, I will come for you—"

Dean nodded. He looked strangely moved—kind, almost—when he spoke. "I know you will, ma'am. That's why I'm doing this. Just find Ariel. The faster you do that, the faster your family will be back together again."

Another couple of Dean's men appeared at the edge of the forest at roughly the same time McDonough emerged from the trees with two of his agents and Wade Wright—I hadn't even realized he'd left us. Casper was with the forest ranger now, held tight as the man took in the scene. At sight of Bear, the dog strained to get free.

Jack called to McDonough the moment they all came into sight. "Stay back," he said. "We've got a situation. It's under control."

The hell it was. I heard the sound of an ATV coming closer, and the panic swelled in my chest. The men led Bear and Ren to the vehicle. I looked around wildly, waiting for someone to *do* something.

I just didn't know what.

As they were leading Bear away, he staggered at one point and went down on one knee, and I heard a strangled cry come from somewhere. At a look from Jack, still standing beside me, I realized it had come from me.

"Just hang on," he said to me quietly. "They'll be all right."

I looked away before I beat him.

The Vermont K-9 handlers stood together, McDonough and the other agents beside them. Cheryl and Wade had hold of Minion, Casper, and Festus, Bear's pit bull the only one putting up any fuss. Angie Crenshaw's camera man kept filming, and I noted that more reporters had arrived on McDonough's heels. Jack and I stayed where we were. Only Dean and his people moved, hauling my son and Ren into the woods without another word.

When the armed men had gone and all I could see were occasional flashes of color in the thick trees, I yanked my arm from Jack's grasp. I searched the clearing wildly, looking for any sign that someone knew what the hell to do next.

"Why is no one moving?" I demanded. Phantom shifted beside me, uneasy at my tone. "Two people have just been taken hostage under your noses—what the hell are we doing about it?"

The words seemed to pull everyone from their shocked silence. McDonough strode forward, his gaze fixed on Jack.

"What the hell just happened?" he asked, his voice a dangerously controlled whisper as the reporters continued to film the chaos.

"He just…lost it," Jack said. He looked almost as bewildered as I felt. "Something's going on with him—with Dean. I knew the man before, and he was never like this."

"His family has a history of mental illness, don't they?" I asked. "There was never any sign that something like this could happen?"

Jack shook his head, mute. McDonough took my elbow and tried to steer me away from the reporters who were rapidly converging on us. I shot him a glare that convinced him manhandling me at this point was a very bad idea. It was probably the menace in Phantom's eye, the low growl in her throat, that convinced him to take a step back, though.

"Ms. Flint—" he began.

"We need to get out there and start looking," I said, cutting him off. "We have to find Ariel."

"You're right, of course," McDonough nodded. "Just give me a minute while I tend to something, and we'll get things under way."

I watched with relief as he left us and strode toward the reporters, shooing each and every one of them—including Jack's blonde—out of the area. Only when all of them were out of sight did he return to Jack and me.

"That's better," he said grimly. "Now… What the fuck is going on?" he asked.

"Dean lost it when we found the girl," Jack said. "He must have radioed the family, or one of the others up there must have been watching us—they all just showed up out of nowhere. What can you tell me about the people living up on the mountain with the rest of the Redfields? I thought you were keeping an eye on that whole thing."

"Watch your tone, Agent," McDonough said, his own

voice sharp. "I was told they wouldn't be a problem. Now that I know that's not the case, I'll have someone look into it. Have you checked the body?"

"Briefly," Jack confirmed as he stepped closer. "I didn't want to screw up the scene—we'll need to get CSU in here."

"If they have such a thing in this godforsaken place," McDonough muttered. He approached Melanie's still body with slightly less care than Jack had taken. I remained where I was, watching his every move. Phantom was perfectly still beside me, so close I could feel her warmth through my field pants.

In my line of work, I'm no stranger to death. Violent deaths, natural deaths, people who met their end long before their time or long after. This girl, Melanie Redfield... There was no question that hers had not been an easy death.

The girl lay naked on the ground at our feet. The flesh had been flayed from her breasts and her buttocks. I turned away at sight of the rest of her. It's not my job to look at the dead; it's my job to find the living. I've never been able to stomach the violence humans do to one another.

"This is the same thing you found in Adams?" I asked. I scanned the rest of the area while Jack knelt beside the body, McDonough looming over us.

"Almost identical," he said. "You see this?" he asked McDonough. My back was still to them, but eventually curiosity won out. I stepped closer. Jack pointed to Melanie's left ear, where her head lolled to the side.

I had to take another step to see what he was indicating: a single earring in the shape of a cross at the top of her right ear. It looked like pewter, the ear and the jewelry itself coated with dried blood.

"You think it's the same one?" McDonough asked Jack.

"You've seen this before," I said.

"On the bodies in Adams," Jack confirmed. "And the other victims we think Gordon killed."

"So whoever did this leaves the earring?"

"Jams it through the top of the ear," McDonough said. "And leaves it there. In the right ear of one of the victims, the left of the other."

"There's no chain, though," Jack noted. I recalled what he had told me before about the murders: that the women were strangled with a chain, a purity ring left on the ring finger. "It looks like she was strangled, but there's nothing with the body."

McDonough studied Melanie's neck, brow furrowed. He pointed at an imprint, still keeping a careful distance. "Look at the imprint, though," he said. "I'd say she was strangled with a chain, no doubt about it."

"So someone took the chain and purity ring?" I asked. "Ariel, maybe?"

Jack shrugged. "No way of knowing right now. We'll have the crime scene guys look, see if they can find it."

"How many people know about the signatures—either the chain or the earrings?"

"Us," Jack said, indicating McDonough and himself. "And a couple of other members of the original team. Agent Paulsen, of course. The crime scene guys…"

"If Gordon Redfield wasn't the killer, would he know about this?"

"At this point, a lot of people know about it," McDonough said. "It's in the transcripts of the trial, and I know at least a couple of rags picked up the story and ran with it."

I was fading, barely listening to them any longer. This was their job—all I wanted to do was leave them to it. Right now, I had better things to do with my time.

"What are you doing about getting Bear and Ren back?" I asked McDonough, interrupting their conversation.

He nodded grimly and straightened, as though he'd expected the question. "I'll put in a call to Washington, have them send out a negotiator. If Dean's given us a window as long as he has—forty hours' worth—that means he doesn't want to hurt your son or his friend. He wants you to succeed, and then he wants to let them go; I'd stake my career on that. That's the good news."

"The bad news is that my son has already been shot, so he's wounded," I said. "Dean may not want to hurt them, but if Bear takes a turn for the worse, I'm guessing they don't have the facilities to handle something like that."

"Which is why we'll work on convincing him to let them go now," McDonough said. "I'll do everything in my power to get them back safely—you have my word on that."

"I appreciate that," I said. "But if it's all the same to you, I'm going to keep doing what I can to make sure it doesn't come down to that. You really think he'll return Bear and Ren if we find Ariel?"

"I do," McDonough said, without a moment's hesitation. Despite myself, I believed him.

That was all I needed to refocus me on the matter at hand. Melanie Redfield was beyond our help, but Bear and Ren were still very much alive. And maybe Ariel was, too.

I just needed to find her.

"You all right?" Cheryl asked as I approached her and

Wade, still trying to shake the joint horrors of Melanie's physical condition and the look of terror on Bear's face.

"Not really. Thanks for getting Casper, though," I said to Wade, nodding toward the pit bull. Both Casper and Minion were seated now, looking nearly as shell shocked as I felt.

"Of course. I didn't do much else good while the whole thing was going on, I figured the least I could do was make sure the damn dog didn't get killed trying to get away."

"There wasn't anything you could have done," Cheryl said. I nodded, but didn't have it in me to voice my agreement. "Wasn't your place, anyway," she continued. "The goddamn Feds are the ones who brought this whole thing here."

I rubbed the back of my neck, slick with sweat and rainwater. Tried to think up a coherent thought. Cheryl looked at me reluctantly.

"I know you need to pull the other teams from the field," I told her before she had to break the bad news. "You can't have them out there with a killer on the loose. I'll keep working, and maybe you could work something from inside HQ, if you don't mind."

The thought was terrifying to me. It was already absurd when we had ten teams covering twenty thousand acres. How the hell was I supposed to do it alone?

"I'm not working inside HQ," Cheryl said immediately. "To hell with that. Are you nuts? I'll check in with my teams, but I'm willing to bet there's not many that'll be heading home now."

"Melanie was murdered—" I began.

"No shit, Sherlock," Cheryl said. "Trust me, I saw the body. But whoever the sick son of a bitch was who did that, he's not coming anywhere near a team of two handlers and two strong, healthy dogs with great big healthy dog teeth. He might be crazy, but the man probably isn't dumb."

"I don't want you or your people putting yourselves in danger—"

"That's our call," Wade cut me off. "Cheryl's right. Nobody's gonna jump a SAR team, and I'm definitely not sitting this thing out."

"I'm with him," Cheryl said. "Like I said, I'll give my handlers the option of getting out of here, but I'm not hanging up my hat till we find this girl."

"Thank you," I said. A wave of emotion ran through me, made that much more powerful by fatigue and fear. I let myself drown in it for a beat, then pulled back, took stock, and tried to figure out where to begin. I didn't like where the thought led me:

I would need to call Ren's father. God, I didn't want to make that phone call. If I didn't tell him, though, how long would it be before the press aired the whole story? I couldn't let him find out that way.

"I need to make a couple of calls," I said. "Then I'd like to get back out there."

"I'll meet up with my guys, let them know the score," Cheryl said. Casper shifted on his haunches, his gaze fixed on the patch of woods where Bear had last been seen. "When do you want to head out again?"

"You're sure about this?"

"Have you ever known me to do anything I wasn't sure of?" she countered. A good point. Cheryl might be a lot of things, but pushover is definitely not one of them.

"In that case, as soon as possible," I said. "With Melanie

in the state she was and Ariel most likely tied to her before she escaped, we have to assume she wasn't in the best shape when she got away. I'm not sure how far she would have gotten. We'll use this as the starting point from here on out, and expand from here. I want a grid pattern with a radius of at least ten square miles."

I was at the tail end of the spiel before I remembered this wasn't my search. I glanced at Cheryl.

"Sounds good," she agreed without hesitation. "Let me talk to my people, see what they say. I'll let you know from there who we have to work with."

I surveyed the land around us. The incline wasn't bad here, but it steepened just a few yards north-northeast of us. What did I know about this girl?

Sixteen years old. No hiking clothing or gear with her. Dressed in… I thought back to what Claude had told us originally. Melanie had been in heels or some kind of 'girly' shoes, but, according to him, Ariel was wearing boots. Dean had said she worked out daily; that she loved CrossFit. She was used to challenging herself, then.

"What are you thinking?" Cheryl asked.

"I'm not sure, but I've got a feeling she'd go in the toughest direction she could find," I said. "Even if she's injured… She wants to survive. She's fighting her ass off to do it—did you see how much blood was on those ropes? Once she was free, she would choose a direction she thought the killer would have the hardest time following."

"Up the mountain?" Wade asked.

"Assuming the killer doesn't have her already, I think so. That's our best bet of finding her."

Finding her alive, however, was something else. She

might have been fighting for her life, but Melanie's body had been here for at least a few hours—rigor had already set in. That was more than enough time for the killer to have caught up with Ariel, wherever she might be.

"It's a lot of area to cover," Cheryl noted.

"We don't have any choice," I said. "We each take a partner and we use the dogs to the best of our ability. Phantom's had a rough day—she'll need to sit things out initially. I'll rotate her, Casper, and Minion as needed, though."

"What about you?" Cheryl asked. "I know this is dire, but you'll need to do a little rotating yourself."

"I'll be fine," I said. "I just want to get out there."

Cheryl nodded, her jaw set and her eyes stormy. "Then let's do it."

10

I GOT PHANTOM and Minion settled at the little motel where Rita Paulsen had booked our rooms, made the dreaded call to Ren's father, then grabbed a protein bar in lieu of dinner and was headed back out to hit the trail by six o'clock that evening. I'd already lost an hour since Bear had been shot and he and Ren carted away; I couldn't spare another minute of daylight. Casper was squirrelly beside me, still understandably shaken by everything that had happened. I just hoped he could pull it together enough to do his job tonight.

As I approached headquarters that evening, the place was a swarm of SUVs with government plates, cop cars, and pickups and still more SUVs with the Vermont Forest Service logo. I noticed Jack standing by the white van with the blond reporter—*Angie*—and felt an unexpected surge of resentment when I saw her laugh at something he'd said. At sight of me, he said something to her and a moment later jogged across the parking lot toward me.

"Can I talk to you?" he asked, stopping me at the bottom of the steps to the church.

"I don't have time," I said. "I need to get out there. I've

lost too much time already. I'm just here to check in with Cheryl, then I'm headed out to start looking again." I started up the steps, but Jack stuck close to my heels.

"Without a partner? I thought you and Cheryl were working together."

"She has to manage the other searchers right now, make sure everyone knows what's going on."

"Then I'll go with you," he said immediately.

I paused at the door of the church. "Don't you have other things you need to do?"

His jaw tensed, and I got the sense I'd struck a nerve. "No. Right now, my job is helping find Ariel, and keeping you safe."

"I can take care of myself—" I started, but then caught myself. Much as I hated to admit it, I knew he was right: the buddy system has lasted as long as it has for a reason. I was putting my dog and myself at risk by being stubborn—not to mention the fact that I was losing valuable daylight by arguing.

"Fine," I said. "Get your gear, and I'll check in with Cheryl, see where she wants me."

"Okay," he agreed. "Meet you back here in ten?" I nodded. He hesitated. "Don't leave without me, okay?" I caught the anxiety in his voice, and paused despite myself.

"Why would I leave without you?" I asked. "I just said we're going out together."

"Past experience says some people"—based on the way he said it, I knew by 'people' he meant 'women'—"can be impulsive."

"I do what makes sense, Jack," I said. "And I know this job. Going out in the woods alone makes no sense. Now, will you please go already?"

This time, he went.

Eight minutes later, I had my marching orders and headed out with Jack by my side, Casper tugging eagerly at his leash. We loaded into an SUV provided by the FBI, Jack behind the wheel, and I instructed him to head back as close as we could get to the site where Melanie had been found. We'd hike in the rest of the way.

"How are you holding up?" Jack asked as soon as we were under way.

"I'm all right," I said. The words came out stiff, stilted. He glanced at me.

"I really am sorry about this—" he began. "I had no idea…"

That resentment I'd felt before swelled again. I kept my eyes on the road ahead of us, my hands clenched into fists. "What the hell is going on, Jack?" The words came out harsher than I'd intended, and I realized I'd been holding them in too long. "Who were all those people out there today? If you thought this was dangerous—"

"I didn't," he said immediately. Rain came down in sheets against the windshield, and his hands were tight on the wheel to keep us on the road. The anguish in his voice was too real for me not to believe him. "I don't know who those people were. As far as I knew, Barrett brought up some tradesmen to work on a project he had in mind to make some money up on the mountain. Dean has always been a peaceful man. There were some domestic issues, and the ongoing trouble he had with the IRS. I swear, there's never been any reason to think he would resort to this."

It was agonizingly slow going on the road thanks to the mud and the torrential rains, the horizon getting darker with each passing minute. In the back of the SUV, Casper whined from his crate. Between the two of us, I didn't know who was more eager to get on the trail.

"You've implied a couple of times that there's something you can't tell me about this situation," I said. If we had to be here, I might as well take advantage of the situation to get whatever information I could gather. "You're sure what's going on with Dean now has nothing to do with that?"

"I'm positive," he said quickly. After a second's hesitation, though, he continued. "I told you that Gordon was my mentor in the FBI."

"Yes," I said, and waited for him to continue. We were approaching the point where we would have to pull over and begin hiking in. I took a mental inventory of what we'd need, wishing to God the damned rain would slow.

"He was a good agent," Jack continued. "Well liked, and held in high regard throughout the Bureau. Great with the political side of things that I'm not so good at. I liked him. More than that, I respected him."

"And what happened?" I asked.

"There were a group of agents who used to run together. Gordon and a few other guys."

"The good-old-boys network," I said.

He pulled off the road and looked grimly at the darkened sky and pounding rain around us. "You could say that."

"Dean said he was done keeping your secrets. What was he talking about?"

He sighed. While he was fighting with his damned conscience, I pulled my hood up, put on my gloves, and opened the door. For a second, the wind and the rain knocked my breath away. I went to the back of the SUV, opened the hatchback, and studied Casper.

"You sure you want to do this, boy?" I asked him.

His tail whipped against the bars of his wire crate as he whined at me. I didn't know whether he had any idea what we were out here for, but his answer was clear. *Hell, yeah. Let's get out there.*

Jack joined me at the back while I was securing Casper's harness and raingear. "The higher-ups at the FBI have made it very clear," he said. "I could lose my job if I say anything."

"Yeah, well, I could lose my kid if you don't," I said, the words dripping with bitterness. Casper hopped down from the back of the SUV. "You make the call."

I stalked off without another word, my head bowed against the rain. Jack had to run to catch up with me.

"Would you hang on?" he called after me. He struggled to tighten his hood against the water in what I knew was a losing battle: we could be wrapped in a waterproof tarp cinched with duct tape, and there was still no way we were staying dry out here. "We're supposed to be doing this together."

Right. I gave Casper a little slack on the leash and headed off road and down the trail back to the crime scene. Jack stepped up his pace and caught up quickly. When I glanced at him, I caught a flash of frustration in his eyes as he continued alongside me.

"There were complaints filed against Gordon and the other guys he ran with," he said, his voice raised to be heard over the weather.

"What kind of complaints?"

"Sexual misconduct." We reached a particularly steep grade, topsoil gone and the rocks loose around us. I slipped and lost my footing for just a second, and felt Jack's hand at my elbow. He pulled me up before I hit the ground. "I've got you," he said. The look in his eye made me pause. I pulled away once I was on even ground again.

"Thanks," I said. "You were saying?"

He nodded. "I was married at the time—happy with Lucia, happy with my life. I had no idea what was going on with them... There were rumors circulating, though, that some of the guys would go out in the field and find hookers, have these parties."

"And Gordon was one of the guys who did this?"

"Gordon, and maybe six or seven other guys. I don't know all the names, just a few of them. Some of the agents were demoted. Others fired. But the Bureau kept everything quiet, swept it under the rug as best they could."

"Until Gordon's sisters turned up sexually brutalized and murdered," I said.

"A couple of months before that," Jack said, his focus on the trail ahead of us now, "Rita—Agent Paulsen—had brought to light another series of murders we hadn't been aware of. Four cases where women had been murdered over the past ten years. Prostitutes from around the country. Raped, mutilated, and killed. Each time, the bodies were found in pairs—tied together with box string, made to watch while the killer worked on the first victim, then moved on to them."

I thought of the rope around Melanie Redfield's wrists; the empty loops where Ariel had been bound to her.

"And she told you she thought Gordon had done this?" I asked.

"I didn't believe it at first," Jack said. "There was no denying Gordon was connected to the women, though—some, long before the other guys were involved in the sex ring. Finally, when I'd worked every angle I could think of, I went to Gordon and asked him about it."

"And what did he say?" I asked, drawn in despite myself.

"He didn't deny the connection—by then the investigation into the whole unit's activities was in full swing. Gordon told me this was better left in the past, though. That the women's deaths were a tragedy, but it wasn't like they had anyone looking for them. We had better things to do with our time."

"And that didn't strike you as a little cold?"

"Of course it did," he said, a sharpness to his tone I hadn't heard before. "But Gordon could be that way sometimes. I kept digging, and ultimately couldn't find a single credible alibi to get him off the hook. Not only that, but Gordon had been staying within an hour of each of the crime scenes at the times of death. Logistically, he could have gotten there; he could have done it."

"And then this thing with his sisters happened," I said.

"Right," he agreed.

"Do you think he could be innocent?" I asked.

"I didn't then," he said. "But Rita's been working on this for a while…" He trailed off. I looked at him in surprise.

"Agent Paulsen? You just said she was the one who turned him in, though."

Jack nodded. "All the more reason for her to want to make things right if he didn't do it. The two have a history, so I'm not sure how much that plays into how intent she is on this now."

"A history?"

"They were married," he said, much to my surprise.

Before I could press for more details, I saw the staging lights, tarp, and evidence markers that indicated we were approaching the crime scene. Techs in bright orange raingear were hard at work, but Melanie's body had already been taken.

"How do you want to handle this?" Jack asked me. "Where do you want me?"

"Just keep up," I said. Cheryl had called the other search teams in to headquarters, where they were being briefed on what was happening. From there, they would decide for themselves whether or not they wanted to keep searching. Given the weather and the fact that a homicidal maniac was on the loose, I wasn't optimistic that they'd be joining me. That meant Casper and I got first dibs on the route we wanted to take, though.

Once we were as close to the crime scene as possible, I crouched and let Casper get a good whiff of the T-shirt I'd gotten from Dean before I put it back in the plastic bag. "Find her, Caz," I said, infusing the words with as much enthusiasm as possible. I gave the dog enough slack that he could choose his direction at will, and nodded forward. "Go on, buddy. Find her!"

For a second, the pit bull simply stood there with his nose in the air, rain pouring down on his head and into his eyes. I had a moment of panic: conditions were too bad for us to look. There was no way he could pick up a scent in weather like this. No way he would even *want* to. That thought lasted only seconds before Casper's gaze focused on the incline behind us—the one I'd told Cheryl was my best bet as to where Ariel may have headed after she'd escaped.

I remained still, trying not to inadvertently lead Casper rather than letting his nose do the work. He hesitated one more second, no more, before he bounded forward. His lead rope was almost jerked from my hand, but I held on tight. I gave chase, Jack close on my heels.

Casper had the scent.

For more than two hours, we followed Casper on a blind tear up the mountainside in the rain. It was almost nine o'clock when we crested yet another peak, Casper half-dragging me this time. I struggled to keep up, my body numb from the cold and the damp. Jack had fallen silent beside me, never complaining despite the conditions. Now, though, he came to life, sensing Casper's excitement.

"What is it?" he asked.

"I don't know," I called back over my shoulder. Casper's nose was everywhere now, his body wriggling, head weaving as he moved. The woods had thinned up here, not enough that we had a view of any kind, particularly in the near-dark and driving rain, but I at least didn't feel like the trees were closing in on me.

Casper charged on, practically dragging me into an old maple tree, its trunk mangled on one side. Then, he stopped short. Sniffed at the tree. Paused. His gaze shifted, so he was looking straight up. My heart stopped when he sounded his alert: two clear, sharp barks.

"Ariel?" I called.

No answer. Jack stepped up beside me with his flashlight and trained the beam into the foliage above us.

"You think she's here?" he asked.

I looked at Casper, the dog completely focused above. "Something's up there. I don't know if it's her or not, but he thinks it is."

I handed the leash off to Jack, got out my headlamp, shed my raincoat for better mobility, and reached for the lowest branch.

"Hang on—what are you doing?" Jack asked. "We should radio, get someone up here."

"Go ahead," I said. "But if Ariel is up there, I'm not waiting."

"What if it's someone else?"

I shook my head without hesitation. "Casper wouldn't have alerted if it were someone else. Just make the call," I said. "I'll be careful."

Without another word, I pulled myself up to the first branch. It was actually a good climbing tree, the branches strong and well-spaced, the trunk itself solid.

"Ariel, if you're up here," I called, "my name is Jamie Flint. I'm with search and rescue. I'm here to help you."

No response. I tipped my head and the light from my headlamp cast eerie patterns on the leaves around me. I fought to breathe through a sudden bout with claustrophobia.

"Cheryl and Wade said to mark this spot, they'll come back at first light," Jack called up to me. "What's going on— what do you see?"

"Leaves," I said dryly. I pushed another branch aside, hanging on tight as I stood on the wet branch beneath. The smell of rain and damp wood was strong, and through the foliage I could just make out the path Casper had just blazed through the woods. A gust of wind rocked the tree, and my boot slid on the branch beneath. I clutched at the trunk, my breath knocked loose.

What the hell was I doing?

Just then, out of the corner of my eye, I saw a flash of red on the ground below. I turned my head, still holding tight to the tree.

Fifteen feet below stood a girl in a red sweater—her hair in a neat pageboy, her clothing immaculate. Perfectly dry.

"Jack," I called. It was useless, though—I knew even as I asked the question. "Do you see anyone on the path behind you? About ten feet back?"

I was met with silence, for a second or more. Then: "I don't see anything. Seriously, Jamie—come down."

I didn't move, my gaze locked on the girl in the sweater. I was exhausted, I knew. Half delirious with worry and cold and fatigue.

There was no one there.

The girl seemed to fade into the darkness for a moment, as though some inner light had faded. Then, I watched her turn and walk away—back down the path. When she was out of sight, I came to, realizing I was still in the tree—frozen there, with no idea why I was here.

Casper had alerted at this tree, though.

Why?

I looked around, my body shaking now from the strain of my muscles being tensed this long. And then, farther out on the branch I was standing on, I saw it:

A piece of black fabric, drenched from the rain but clinging there like it had a mind, a will, of its own.

I lowered myself so that I was seated on the branch, then straddled it. Then, I leaned forward with my body wrapped around, and pulled myself forward.

"What's happening, Jamie?" Jack called up to me. The beam from his flashlight hit me in the face. "What the hell are you doing?"

"There's something on the branch," I called down.

He told me to wait for someone else, but I ignored him. Someone would have to do this—it might as well be me. And I couldn't wait until tomorrow to find out what this was. I pulled myself another inch. And another. The fabric was almost within reach now, but not quite. It looked like a T-shirt. I reached forward one more inch.

The branch cracked beneath me.

"Jamie!" Jack shouted. Casper's high-pitched bark split the air. I froze. Thought of Bear and Ren; the look on Bear's face when he realized he'd been hit. The cry of pain. This wasn't me; I'm reasonable. I do things the way they're supposed to be done.

So why the hell was I fifteen feet in the air, clinging to a maple branch just so I could get hold of a T-shirt that most likely wouldn't get us any closer to finding the girl I needed to find?

I took a breath. Closed my eyes. Felt the world still around me, as the thought of Bear's face came to me once more. At ten months old, clinging to our old Newfoundland as he took his first steps. Babbling to field mice. Communicating with a world I couldn't reach—a world few even believe exists.

I moved forward one more inch, until my fingers touched the fabric wrapped around the branch. I held on tight through another gust of wind, then worked the fabric loose until it was in my hand.

Slowly, painfully, I made my way back to the ground.

Jack took my hand when I reached the last branch and held on as I jumped to the ground. Casper leaped up to greet me; I held tight to the dog, still shaking, and handed the T-shirt to Jack.

"Are you all right?" he asked.

I shook my head, stomach rolling, and turned away to gulp a little fresh air and revel in the beauty of the solid ground beneath my feet.

"What is it?" I asked him, waving toward the fabric.

He unwadded it carefully, and came out with a torn black T-shirt with the words *BE THE BEAST WITHIN* across the front. It was drenched, but still stiff with blood.

As Jack examined it, something fell from the sleeve to the ground below. Casper was on it immediately, but took a step back at my sharp, "Leave it!"

I knelt, and examined the items sparkling in the mud.

Two gold chains, and a single silver band.

"A purity ring?" I asked Jack.

He crouched beside me, studied it briefly, and nodded.

"So she did get away," I said. Relief warred with the disappointment still rocking me at the realization that we hadn't found her.

"It looks that way," Jack agreed. The question was, where was she now?

I looked at Casper. His eyes were still bright, tail wagging, but he'd been going too long today as it was. Bear would do me in himself if I ruined his dog by working him too hard. I noted our location on the GPS, and Jack looked at me in surprise.

"What are you doing?" he asked.

"We need to go back," I said. Just saying the words broke something inside me. "Just for a few hours. It will take some time to get back to base, and we both need food. Rest. Casper needs to get dried off, rubbed down, and put to bed."

"Sounds good," Jack murmured. As soon as the words were out, he looked at me in alarm. If he hadn't been filthy and half hidden under his hood, I'm sure I would have seen him blush. "Sorry—that wasn't supposed to be out loud."

I fought a smile, and shrugged. "It does sound pretty good, actually." Our eyes met. Now I was the one blushing. I ran my hand across my dripping forehead and looked away before the tension got any thicker.

"Uh—here," Jack said, handing me my jacket. "I think the rain's slowed, but you'll still need this."

"Right," I agreed. "Thanks."

Casper knocked his blocky head against my hand and whined impatiently—a reminder that he was still here and, as yet, hadn't been rewarded for his find.

We played a quick, half-hearted game of tug as we descended the mountain, but my mind was back on the conversation I'd had with Jack earlier. I thought of the sex scandal he'd mentioned before; of the secrets Dean swore he was done keeping.

"You said you worked with Dean's brother for two years," I said to Jack, calling back over my shoulder.

"That's right," Jack said.

"It seems like the one person who should know anything about this would be Gordon Redfield," I said. "Am I wrong about that? I mean, he was the one who supposedly committed the original crimes in the first place."

"I already thought of that," Jack said. I heard tension in

his voice, and thought of the anger I'd seen earlier when I'd asked if he had anything to do.

"So?" I said. "Where is he? Are you going?"

"He's in a prison in Texas," he said. "Because he was a federal agent, he was too well-known to be held anywhere around here. They found a facility that's been all right, apparently."

"Why aren't you going there?" I pressed. "Either the original killer is back at it again, or someone is copying his crimes. Either way, it seems like we could learn something from Gordon Redfield."

"McDonough doesn't think it's a good way to use our resources."

I stopped on the path and Jack pulled up short beside me. "Seriously?"

He nodded, grim. "It's bullshit, I know. But I'm on thin ice right now. One more misstep…"

"Could mean your career," I said. "I understand that—"

"I don't care about my career," he said quickly. His intensity made me pause. "I care about what's happening with this case. I care about making sure Bear and Ren get out of this all right. I just don't want to make things worse."

I laughed, a strangled sound pulled from somewhere deep, and hit the trail again. I waved one hand around wildly, the other still clutching Casper's leash. "We're stuck in one of the thickest, most desolate stretches of wilderness on the eastern seaboard. One girl is already dead; the other may or may not be alive, and my son has been shot and is being held hostage with his best friend. And if we get any more rain, Glastenbury Mountain will fall into the damned sea before this is all said and done."

I stopped again, fighting hysteria, and turned to look at him. "How exactly could this get worse?"

"Right," he said after a moment. He took another step toward me, his focus on me rather than the ground beneath our feet. "Okay... So, I'll tap some of my contacts and make it happen. Screw McDonough. Like you said, how could this get any worse—"

The words were barely out before his foot hit a patch of loose rocks and soil. He fell backward and landed hard. I gasped and reached for him—but the mountain wasn't done with him yet.

The ground beneath our feet consisted of loose shale held in place by a layer of mud that was anything but stable. In an instant, I felt myself slipping. I managed to grab hold of a tree before the ground came loose completely and I picked up speed, then clung there, breathless, with Casper's leash tight in my hand.

Jack wasn't so lucky.

I watched in horror as he tumbled back down the path, half-buried in rocks and mud, desperately grappling to find a hand hold to stop his free fall.

I followed as fast as I could, making my way from tree to tree, Jack still in sight—just completely out of reach.

He had managed to slow himself as I got closer, but he was still moving when something shining and silver caught the beam of my flashlight. I went still, realizing with horror exactly what it was.

A bear trap.

And Jack was on a crash course straight for it.

"Jack!" I shouted. "You have to get off the path! Grab something!"

Like he hadn't already been trying that for the past fifty feet.

I watched, breathless, as he barreled down, the trap fully visible now: spring loaded, and capable of snapping a human leg straight through the bone. Casper stood beside me, breathing hard, both of us powerless to do a thing.

Not even daring to look, I focused instead on getting down as quickly as possible. Already thinking of the medical supplies we would need. How quickly we could get help out here. Casper stuck close to me for once rather than dragging me down, as though he sensed the danger.

I heard the trap snap shut, an explosion of iron against iron that sounded like a gunshot somewhere beneath the riot of the mountain coming down around us.

Headlamp trained on the scene below, I struggled to make the rest of the trek down to Jack. I waited to hear a scream of pain, but there was nothing. The mudslide had worked itself out, the world eerily still now.

"Jack?" I called.

Nothing, for twenty seconds. Thirty. I called him again, dread climbing higher in my chest.

"I'm here," he finally answered.

His voice was closer than I'd expected, exhausted, but I didn't hear the pain I expected to. I shone my flashlight down.

Ten feet below me, Jack sat caked in mud, staring up at me. No more than a foot away, the bear trap had been sprung—a boulder lodged between its jaws.

"Do me a favor?" he said weakly. I eased down the rest of the way, searching for more traps. Casper reached Jack first, and licked the mud from his face with slow, thorough laps of his pink tongue.

"What?" I said.

"Don't ever ask me how things could get worse again."

I grinned. Hopped over a couple of boulders and another patch of mud, relief making me nearly giddy, and extended my hand to help him up. He took it.

"Deal," I said.

11

THAT NIGHT, it was one a.m. by the time Jack reached the Texas prison where Gordon Redfield was being held. He wasn't at all sure what he would find when he actually met with Gordon—and even less sure how things would play out when he returned to Vermont having disobeyed McDonough's direct order. Despite the less-than-stellar course his career had taken over the past two years, Jack still had friends in high places at the Bureau. He'd called in every favor he had with those friends in order to get a private charter to bring him to Texas tonight.

He just hoped to God all of this was worth the effort.

It was a hot night when he touched down at the Livingston Municipal Airport, the air inside the prison only slightly cooler despite air conditioning. Having spent the better part of the day trekking through the wilderness in the rain, and then falling halfway down a mountain, he was not feeling his best. He was battered and bruised and felt like…well, like he'd spent the better part of the day trekking through the wilderness in the rain and then had nearly been taken out by a mountain. Still, he told himself he was here for a reason. The memory of Jamie's blue eyes, the firm set of her jaw, and he knew that reason was worth it.

For the past nine months, he'd been running from the memory of those blue eyes. There were plenty of other things to run from, of course, but sometimes he thought Jamie was the most terrifying of all. With her blond hair pulled back in a ponytail, the nose ring and the competence and the way she seemed to look straight through him, sometimes... The women he'd dated since his wife's death had been haughty and headstrong, intent on their own goals, but Jamie's level headedness was something he didn't always know how to handle. He flashed back to the sight of her in that damned tree earlier that night, though, and grimaced. Obviously, she wasn't always so level headed.

Inside the prison, Jack surrendered his gun, wallet, and keys while he went through the metal detector, dingy concrete walls closing in on him. The sole guard manning the front desk was a short man with a beer gut and a hard face. He studied Jack from the other side of the desk.

"Gordon in trouble for somethin'?" he asked in a thick Texan drawl.

"It's federal business—I just have some questions."

The guard picked up Jack's ID. "Juarez. You used to work with him, didn't you? You're one of the feds sent him upriver for this thing you say he did?"

Jack looked at him evenly. "The judge and jury sent him upriver, not me."

"Right. Sure. Well, you gotta keep your stuff here. You'll get it when you come back through."

"Thanks," Jack said.

The first guard handed Jack off to a second, this one built like a linebacker. They walked wordlessly down the long, echoing corridors while Jack's thoughts returned to Gordon Redfield—his mentor. A man who had taken Jack under his wing, shown him the ropes, and explained what it meant to be a federal agent. Gordon had appeared to be everything Jack emulated: principled, thoughtful, articulate. It was only later that Jack realized Gordon was just a master at telling people what they wanted to hear. He could be kind and reflective with Jack one minute, then turn around and make the dirtiest joke in the room if that was what his audience was looking for. The man was a born politician.

Jack wasn't sure that made him a killer, though.

Though he'd followed Gordon's progress through the system from a distance since the man's conviction, Jack hadn't seen him in the flesh since the day the sentence was handed down.

And now, here he was.

The guard led him to a thick steel door and punched a code into a keypad on the wall. The lock released with an echo. This wasn't the best prison Jack had ever seen, the technology dated, the interior dingy and gray. Not that he'd ever visited a prison that was overtly jolly, but there were certainly better facilities than this one. And worse, to be fair.

On the other side of the door, Gordon waited at a long table bolted to the floor. The room was carved of more dingy gray concrete, with florescent lights flickering overhead.

Gordon was a good-looking man with dark hair that had gone gray in the years since Jack had seen him last. Like his brother Dean, he wasn't a big guy—instead, he had a lean, wiry athleticism that suggested speed over power. Now, however, Jack noted the powerfully built upper torso of a man who worked out heavily and often. A scar bisected his left eyebrow. It hadn't been there the last time Jack had seen him.

The guard nodded to Gordon as though greeting a friend. "Anything I can get for you while you're in here, Gordy?"

"I'm fine, Rick, thanks. You on all night?"

"Yeah, getting in some overtime."

"Diapers don't come cheap these days," Gordon said with a nod. "Sarah and the baby okay?"

"Sarah's tired, you know how that is. But Retta's growing fast."

"You'll have to show me a couple pictures when you come back through," Gordon said. He looked at Jack. "Rick just had his third daughter—all of them the spitting image of their mom. I told him he's in for a world of hurt once those girls hit their teens."

Rick smiled at that, but Jack could think only of the crimes Gordon was in here for. The women he'd allegedly tortured. The guard obviously must know that—he would have to know what the prisoner had been charged with.

"That's why their daddy's got a whole cabinet full of guns and a crate of ammo," Rick said amiably. "I'm ready about the time any wrongheaded Texas boys wander our way." He paused, glanced at Jack, and appeared to remember what he was there for. "You sure you'll be all right in here?" he asked. The question wasn't directed at Jack, however.

"We're fine," Gordon assured him. "Jack's an old friend. I'll holler when we're done."

The guard left with barely a word to Jack, closing the door behind him. There was no indication that he thought Jack might be in danger. Rather, Jack got the impression he was more concerned for Gordon's well-being.

"He's a good guy," Gordon said once they were alone, nodding toward the space where the guard had just been. There was a certain smugness in the words, and Jack got the feeling the exchange with the guard had been entirely for his benefit.

"He doesn't know what you're in for?"

"He knows," Gordon said. He kept his tone even. "Doesn't believe I did it, but he knows the charges."

Jack felt the tension ramp up in the silence that followed. He sat in a wooden chair on the other side of the table. This, like the table and Gordon's own chair, was bolted to the floor.

"It's been a long time," Gordon said when Jack didn't speak. He studied Jack for a few seconds, and shook his head. "Jesus. You look like hell—what happened to you?"

"Lost a fight with a mountain," Jack said briefly. "But I'm not here to talk about that."

"I've been following things," Gordon continued, as though Jack hadn't spoken. "As much as I can from in here, anyway. Seems like you've had some trouble the last few years."

"Some," Jack said with a shrug. "I'm handling it."

Gordon slid to the edge of his chair, looking at Jack intently. There were no shackles on his wrists or his ankles. His blue eyes were soft, earnest.

"I was sorry to hear about Lucia," Gordon said. "I know it's been a few years, but I've wanted to say that to you for a long time. She was a good woman."

Jack's stomach churned at the words. An image of his wife's smile, the echo of her laughter, flashed through his mind. The four of them used to have dinner together—

Gordon and Rita, Jack and Lucia. Lucia would cook; Gordon brought the wine. Rita gardened, and always had fresh flowers for the table. Jack couldn't remember the number of times they'd laughed together. Broken bread. Rita and Lucia had gotten along well... Lucia had never cared for Gordon, though.

"I'm not here to talk about any of that," he said. The words came out with an edge, a rasp to his voice. He cleared his throat.

Gordon nodded. "No, I figured as much. I've been following it on TV. Dean's gotten himself into some trouble, looks like."

Jack wasn't sure exactly what had been reported on the news, so nodded cautiously. "What do you know so far?"

"I know Dean's oldest was found dead," he said. What appeared to be genuine grief darkened his eyes. "They're not releasing any details, except to say that Ariel's still missing. What happened to her?"

"Same M.O. as June and Katie," Jack said. "Same M.O. as all your victims. Raped, mutilated, strangled."

A flash of anger shadowed Gordon's face. "I think you mean, the same M.O. as all the killer's victims. It wasn't me." Before Jack could reply, Gordon continued. "Who's the agent in charge?"

"McDonough."

"And he let you come here to see me?" The surprise on his face was genuine. There was something else there that Jack couldn't read, though. Maybe anger. Maybe fear.

"'Let' may be too strong a word," Jack said. "It doesn't really matter, though. I'm here now."

A beat of silence passed between them. Gordon searched

Jack's eyes. "You know it was three months to the day after they took me in, that your wife was killed?" he asked. It wasn't what Jack had expected.

"What are you talking about?"

"To the day. And before that happened, do you remember what you said to me?" Gordon's hands were clasped tightly on the table, his whole body tense.

"I don't remember much about that time," Jack said roughly.

"No, I guess you wouldn't," Gordon said. There was sympathy in his voice, but no pity. "You told me we'd get through this. That there was nothing on this earth that could convince you I'd done what they said I did. You remember that?"

Jack thought back to that time. He and Lucia were expecting their first child—a baby girl. Everything that was happening with Gordon had seemed like a bad dream, something he would inevitably wake up from. The rest of life was so good... The charges against Gordon had seemed absurd.

And then, Lucia wanted to go to Nicaragua. There was work she needed to do there, she told him. She wouldn't be gone long... An orphanage there needed help, and Lucia never turned her back on people in need.

"That was before I had all the facts," Jack said. It was hard to get the words out.

"You had all the facts. I didn't do what they said I did. I never could have—not to the women they found, and I sure as hell never could have done that to my sisters. You knew me. You of all people knew I couldn't have done it."

"I didn't know you," Jack said. "The women you slept

with, the lies you told—I didn't know the first thing about you. About *any* of you."

"So why the fuck didn't you look at the others?" Gordon said. For the first time, his voice rose. "We were all involved, none of the agents in that ring were any less culpable than the others. Half of them still have their jobs; others retired, kept their pensions. And here I sit."

"Their sisters weren't found murdered with their DNA on the bodies. They had alibis. They hadn't kept up relationships with every one of the dead hookers."

"And they never claimed to be your friend," Gordon said quietly. "That's what this is really about, isn't it? Your goddamn pride? And anger. You thought you knew me, you thought you knew the world, and then all of a sudden everything gets turned ass over teakettle, and nothing is what you thought it was."

"You lied to me," Jack growled, unable to hold it back any longer. "You say I knew you? Everything I knew was lies, a fairytale. I didn't know shit about you."

"You knew what was important," Gordon said, his own voice tight. "I'm not saying I was right in the way I behaved—I know that. I fucked up, but I was doing the best I could. Don't sit there and judge me for falling off a pedestal I never asked to be put on in the first place. So I paid for company from a few women… That was poor judgment, but that was my only crime. I didn't kill anyone."

"So who the hell did?" Jack said. "All this time, and you still haven't come up with a viable suspect. And now…"

"And now he's killing again," Gordon finished for him. "And you're wondering if you were wrong. If maybe what I've been saying from the day they took me in, is true." He paused for a moment, watching Jack carefully. Studying his face. "Why are you here, Jack? The girls are dead. I can't help you."

"They're not, though," Jack said. Gordon looked surprised. "Melanie is. But the other girl—Ariel, the youngest. She got away. It looks like she's in the woods somewhere. There's a chance we could find her…"

"And find the man who took them," Gordon said. For the first time, there was hope in his eyes. "You have people looking for her?"

"Yeah. There are some SAR folks from Vermont, and a team from Maine that Dean requested—people I've worked with before."

"Who?" Gordon pressed.

"She used to work under a man named Brock Campbell—Dean apparently knew him. After he died, this woman—Jamie Flint—took over the business."

"Campbell was an asshole," Gordon said. "The only kind of man Dean could ever appreciate. This Flint knows her stuff, though?"

"She's the best there is," Jack said unequivocally. He felt his face warm at the way Gordon looked at him, so he rushed on. "But things are worse than that—thanks to Dean."

"What do you mean?" Gordon asked. "What happened?"

"He shot a boy. Jamie's son. They shot him, then took him and another girl hostage. So a scenario that was already dire just got a hell of a lot more so."

"Jesus Christ," Gordon said, half under his breath. "What the hell are they doing? You know my brother—he's a stubborn S-O-B, but he's not a violent man. This has to be somebody else." He frowned. "Barrett?"

"It could be," Jack said. "I agree with you, this doesn't seem like Dean. But this whole thing has done something to him. I don't think he's been well. I'm not sure how much more of this he can take."

Gordon sighed, long and heavy. "What do you need from me?"

Jack hesitated. This was the question he'd been asking himself since he left the ground back in Vermont; since Jamie asked him to come here.

What the hell was he doing here?

"What I said before," Jack finally said. "About you never providing another viable suspect. You've been behind bars for the past seven years. Your lawyer's filed appeals. I know you've been looking into it. I need to know if you have a theory that, for whatever reason, you haven't shared."

Gordon's eyes slid from his. Jack shook his head, recalling the frustration he'd felt when all this first began. The man knew something. "Forget it," Jack said abruptly. He stood, annoyed. "I tried to help you when this thing first happened—you asked if I remember that. Yes, I remember. I remember believing in you. Even with the evidence they kept bringing in: DNA, hair and fibers on Katie and June. Fingerprints at the crime scenes of the other women. I *still* believed you, even when everyone around me was saying I was an idiot to."

"So what changed?" Gordon asked.

"Everything changed. They murdered my wife. They took my world. And if they could do that and I never saw it coming, who the hell was I to say anyone was innocent? Especially if you weren't fighting it yourself."

"I fought it," Gordon said.

"The hell you did. You said you were innocent. That's it. No alternate theories, nothing to absolve you of guilt. Just the same four useless words. 'I didn't do it.' And what I'm asking you to do now is to tell me who did. Because I believe you know. Or at least you have an idea."

Gordon looked away, his gaze shifting to the table.

Jack ran his hands through his hair. He thought again of Jamie, waiting for him to come back with something. Of Ariel Redfield, out there in the woods right now running for her life—if she was still alive at all. Of Jamie's son, bleeding, left to the mercy of Dean Redfield and whatever idiotic plan he might have.

"I don't know," Gordon said.

Jack fixed him with a glare. "You're lying. And this time, I'm not letting you get away with it."

Gordon actually smiled. "Oh yeah? What are you gonna do about it?"

"I'm taking you to Vermont," Jack said. Gordon looked only slightly more surprised than Jack himself was. "We'll work this case together, until one of us comes up with the right solution this time."

"You can't do that. They won't let me leave this place. And there's no way in holy hell McDonough will sign off on it."

"Despite everything that's happened, I've still got a few friends left at the Bureau," Jack said. "McDonough will just have to deal." He headed for the door, forcing more confidence into his tone than he felt. "Pack your shit, Gordon. We leave tomorrow morning."

12

THERE WAS A FIRE going in the woodstove in the old house when Dean brought Ren and Bear there. It was a chilly night, so a fire made sense, Bear supposed. Or it felt chilly to him, at least—he was freezing, sure he'd never be warm again. He heard Dean whispering. Saw other men prowling around them, watching. Like he and Ren had stormed their castle; like being there had been their choice, and now they were the unwelcome guests putting the Redfield family out in their own home.

"You said you can tend him?" Dean asked Ren when they were set up beside the fire. Ren's eyes were wide, but her hands had stayed steady, her jaw set, through this whole thing. If there was ever anyone Bear would choose to be held hostage with, it was definitely her. Though he really could have been happy missing this whole experience.

"I need supplies," she told Dean. Her voice was tight, the anger just below the surface. "He should be at a hospital."

"And he'll get to one," Dean replied. "Just as soon as his mum does what she's supposed to and finds my Ariel, then he'll get everything he needs. In the meantime, I just need you to do what you said you could and keep him alive." He turned to a tall, thin woman in one of the ugliest dresses Bear had ever seen, her long gray hair pulled back in a braid.

"Wendy, get her whatever she needs. Set it up in one of the bedrooms upstairs—they'll stay up there." He hesitated, and Ren rushed in before he could change his mind.

"I'll need alcohol, hot water, and plenty of sterile dressings."

The woman watched Bear, and he sensed genuine empathy there. She didn't want them here; felt bad that he'd been hurt. The thought that they might have an ally here buoyed his spirits. "She's right," the woman said to Dean, her voice quiet. "The boy should be in a hospital. You shouldn't have brought him here."

"Do it now, Wendy," Dean said when she started to argue. She didn't act like Dean's wife, Bear thought. And she was too old to be his daughter. Sister, maybe. With a pinched frown, the woman turned her back on all of them and left the room. A moment later, Bear heard footsteps ascending a set of stairs nearby.

Inside the room, a big guy with red hair stood apart from the others, his eyes fixed on Bear. He was rocking slightly, talking to himself. Three other men remained close to Dean, all of them talking in hushed voices. Bear didn't like any of it, but at the moment he was in too much pain to even try tuning into what they said.

"How are you doing?" Ren asked him quietly. They were on a couch close to the fire, so at least they were warm and comfortable for now. Who knew what the room Dean was sending them to next was like, though.

"I'm okay," Bear said through chattering teeth, the burning in his shoulder dulling everything else around them.

"I don't have to be an empath to know you're lying, you know," she said. She managed a small smile.

Wendy reappeared at the door. "It's ready," she said.

The redheaded man looked up at that. He looked terrified, and Bear felt a spear of dread course through him. Something was wrong. Well… Everything was wrong, but something beyond the fact that he was shot and bleeding and Ren had come along with him and now they were being held captive by a bunch of nut jobs with guns.

Dean came up to them, his gun still in hand, and nodded to Ren. "Help him up. Wendy'll show you where you'll stay."

"What about food?" Ren sked. "We were out searching all day—we haven't had dinner. And he needs some kind of painkiller."

"There's aspirin in the kit," Wendy volunteered. She looked annoyed, but Bear got the sense it wasn't with them. "And I'll bring some dinner up for you once you get settled."

"Is there water?" Ren asked. She was softer with the woman; she'd come to the same conclusion Bear had. Wendy wasn't against them.

"There's a couple of gallon jugs up there with water from the spring—that should do you for tonight. I'll bring more if you need it."

"Thank you," Ren said. Wendy left the room again, presumably to get them food. Ren took Bear's arm and tried to help him up, but a jagged bolt of pain ran through him the second he moved. A cry of pain escaped his lips before he could stop it. Ren's forehead furrowed in sympathy. She crouched beside him. He'd never felt more out of control in his life, and he fought to get himself back where he needed to be. He couldn't fall apart in front of her.

"Just take it easy," she said. Her hand moved to his good arm, but she remained facing him so he could look her in the eye. "We'll move on the count of three. Can you do that?"

He nodded.

Just as he rose, he caught sight of something out the window—a flash of red that remained hazy for a second before it came into focus. A girl stood staring in at him, her face pale, her eyes wide. She wore a red sweater. The red-haired man looked in that direction at the same time, his own eyes widening at sight of the girl.

"That's her!" the man shouted. He lurched toward the window, so unsteady on his feet that Bear thought he would fall. Dean followed his movement with a frown.

"For Christ's sake, I've had enough of you," Dean said. His voice rose as his gaze fell on the window, where the girl in the red sweater remained. The girl recoiled, but Dean wasn't focused on her. Instead, he pulled the red-haired man away. "I don't want to hear anything else about these woods, or the people who talk to you or the things they say. You think we don't have enough to worry about right now?"

"She's there," the man insisted. "Look there—just look. She's got brown hair and a red sweater. She's there. She knows where Ariel is, but she won't tell me."

"Shut the hell up, Claude," Dean shouted. "She's not there, all right? You want me to go out there and show you just how not there she is? She's not fucking there."

While this was happening, Ren looked at Bear. Her eyes followed his to the window and she pressed her lips together in a firm line, though she didn't say anything.

"Come on," another of the men said to Bear, while

Dean was dealing with the red-haired man freaking out by the window. This one was tall and dark-haired. There was a strong resemblance to Dean, but he was considerably younger. A lot better looking, too; Bear got the sense he knew it. Another brother? How big was this family, anyway?

The man took Ren's arm to pull her forward, but she jerked it away. Bear didn't care for the way the man's eyes darkened at the movement. He struggled to his feet, ignoring the pain or the knowledge that there was a ghost just outside the window—and someone other than himself could actually see her for a change.

"It's all right," Bear said to the man. "We'll go. Just keep your hands off her, and everything's fine."

The man smiled. "Said like a boy who believes he's in charge."

Bear glanced toward Dean. Claude had backed down, and the pale face outside the window was gone. To Bear's relief, the old man's attention returned to him and Ren.

"Leave them to me, Barrett," Dean said. "You just keep an eye on the searchers, make sure we've got everybody out there looking for Ariel."

Barrett scowled, but he backed away and Dean took his place. Bear sat down once more, before he fell down.

Outside, the rain had returned and there was a strong wind blowing outside the cabin walls. It was pitch black out there. Bear thought about the girl he'd seen outside the window. He knew it wasn't Ariel Redfield—they'd all seen photos of her before taking up the search so there wouldn't be any confusion if and when she was found. There was the story about the girl who'd gone missing out here back in the 1940s. That girl had been wearing a red sweater. It made sense that her spirit might still be here, he supposed. He couldn't shake the feeling that she had something to tell him, though.

He thought back to the redheaded man's words. *She knows where Ariel is, but she won't tell me.* Was that really what it was? And how was Claude able to see her, when so far Bear had never met anyone able to see the dead the way he could?

"You're too quiet," Dean said, breaking into his reverie. "Come on, let's get you upstairs. How are you holding up?"

Bear looked at his arm. Dean had wrapped it with a rough bandage as soon as they'd taken him and Ren from the clearing, but it still leaked blood and hurt like hell. He frowned when he met Dean's eyes again, but Ren cut in before he could say anything.

"How do you think he's holding up?" she demanded. "You shoot him, kidnap us, don't tell us anything about what's happening. Bring us to this house in the middle of nowhere and then you don't even let me take care of him. He is in shock. We are both afraid. Neither of us are doing well."

Her accent got stronger when she was angry, Bear noted—he'd never really heard that before. Of course, so far he'd managed to avoid pissing her off. Based on the temper she was showing now, he decided that was a good precedent to follow.

"I'm sorry it had to happen that way," Dean said. And he did look sorry, Bear had to give the guy that. The rest of the group had gone off to separate corners, though Barrett remained at the door, watching Dean with Bear and Ren. "I didn't care for the way that dog was looking at me, though. He was getting ready to take me or my family out if I didn't act."

"You're wrong," Bear said. The words came out terse, impatient. Ren glanced at him—warning him to stay calm. Around Flint K-9, he was known for being agreeable, quiet. He rarely talked back, almost never lost his temper. Right now, though, he wasn't feeling all that charitable. He didn't try to conceal the disdain in his voice. "The dog was just reacting to the energy you were putting out. He wouldn't have acted unless he knew we were in danger. Which, it turns out, was pretty accurate."

Instead of being annoyed at the words, Dean smiled. He continued studying Bear for another few seconds, giving the impression that he was in some other place, thinking of something else completely.

"Your mum's old boss—Brock Campbell. I knew him, you know," Dean said.

Bear stilled. He tried to read the man's thoughts as another cadre of black threads began dancing around the room, but it was hard to focus.

"Good for you," Bear said. He kept his voice even.

"I was sorry to hear about him passing," Dean continued. Still watching Bear, poking at him with the words. "It was pretty sudden, wasn't it?"

"It was a long time ago. I don't remember much."

"Brock and your mum were pretty close, then?" Dean continued, undeterred. "How close were they, exactly?"

Ren had wrapped a blanket around him, but Bear was still shivering. His skin was tight with pain and fear, brittle with cold.

When he was little, he used to think maybe he had superpowers that he hadn't discovered yet. Sometimes he could read people's thoughts, right? Did that mean he could do other things that other kids couldn't? Start fires? Throw furniture across the room with the power of his own mind?

He couldn't do anything like that, though. All he could do was see things others couldn't see; sense things they didn't sense. Sometimes, hear things they couldn't hear.

More often than not, he wished the powers—or *sensitivity*, as Ren called it—would just disappear.

Before he could respond, Ren interrupted.

"Can we talk about this later? Unless you want him to die, you need to let me take care of him. Now."

Normally Bear would have piped up, told her it was okay—done anything to keep this asshole from fixing his attention on her. Right now, though, he could barely think straight, let alone come up with the power of speech.

"You're right," Dean said with a nod. He actually looked chastened. "I'm sorry, let's get you two upstairs. Wendy will check on you through the night to make sure you don't need anything."

"Thank you," Ren said. Once more, she helped Bear to his feet. He hadn't prepared himself for the move, and pain rocked through him. He felt himself go pale, a barrel rolling in his gut. Ren caught him before he could sit back down again, and he leaned heavily against her.

They made their slow, painful way up the stairs.

13

I GAVE UP ON SLEEPING by three-thirty the next morning. We were staying in the Serenity Motel in Shaftsbury, a place that was clean, quiet, and cheap... Clean and quiet were a nice bonus, but the biggest selling point had definitely been the price—along with the fact that they allowed dogs, which was obviously key. I got up, took a shower, and then sat by the window and stared into the darkness, waiting for sunrise. Phantom slept peacefully at my feet. Minion and Casper were both in their crates, finally asleep after hours of pacing and whining. Neither of them were happy to be without their people for the night.

I could hardly blame them; I felt the same way. The double bed beside mine was disturbingly empty, Bear's things strewn across the cheap polyester comforter. He'd had just enough time to drop his backpack before we dove into the search earlier that day. I kept staring at that backpack. Ren had sewn patches on it, most of them related to animals: pit bulls and SAR, animal rescue, vegetarian slogans—Bear embraced vegetarianism by the time he was six, forcing me along with him, and Ren had taken things a step further by going vegan not long after she and Carl began working with us.

The backpack was open, a lighter jacket than he'd worn today peeking out the top. I hadn't gone through the rest of the bag. It wouldn't tell me anything I didn't already know about my son, anyway. There would be no iPad, no laptop, no books or journals… Bear has always been a child of action, not contemplation. Part of that is the dyslexia he was diagnosed with at nine, but I think it's also his natural inclination. At three years old, long before we were fighting about schoolwork, he would invariably choose being with the dogs over watching TV or being read to. That inclination has continued over the years, meaning he pays little attention to the technology so many of his peers are obsessed with.

Lately, Bear had been complaining about sharing a room with me when we were out on searches. *No one else has to share a room,* he'd said the last time we had the discussion. *Look at it this way,* I said. *At least we're not sharing a bed the way we did when you were little.* He hadn't been impressed with my response, but it had effectively shut down the discussion. That time.

At four o'clock, with the world still pitch dark outside, I got up and went outside with the dogs. The air was cold and damp after heavy rains the night before, and there was a stillness that didn't sit well with me. Instead of the calm I usually feel when I'm outside, all I felt was claustrophobia and unease—the trees too close, the world too quiet.

Normally, this would be the time when I'd take the dogs for a run, something I've been doing since Bear was small. By five a.m. most mornings, we have the whole pack out running trails together. By the time he was four or five, Bear was running with us—not always able to keep pace with me, but never far behind.

"Come," I called to Casper and Phantom once we were out in Serenity's parklike grounds. So far, Minion had been velcroed to me since we set foot outside. Phantom returned to my side readily, but Casper didn't budge. He stood at the edge of the woods with his nose up, scenting the air. "Caz, come." I slapped my hand on my thigh. He whined, staring into the woods. His white fur was as good as a beacon in all that darkness, and I turned my flashlight in his direction.

"He'll be back soon, Casper. We'll get him back."

Phantom and Minion sat back on their haunches, their attention directed at Casper. If there was something out in the woods, my shepherd at least would still be on her feet—which meant Bear's pit bull was just being difficult. Not an uncommon problem where Casper is concerned.

"Casper!" I said. More sharply this time. He glanced at me, then turned back toward the woods. Rather than stepping into the trees, he started with a slow, loping gait along the tree line.

Annoyed, I looked at Phantom. I'd been wrong about her having no interest in the woods, though—her ears were pricked forward, her body on alert despite being seated, a steadfast gaze directed into those trees. Minion got to her feet. I took a step forward. Instantly, Phantom was up. She put her body in front of mine without a sound, blocking my way.

"Heel, Phan." She didn't move. When I tried to take another step forward, her body block became more aggressive, until she was actively herding me away from the woods. "Casper!" I said, louder this time. Frustration was fast being overridden by fear, though fear isn't something I usually associate with the wilderness. "Damn it, come."

The pit bull took one last look into the woods, whimpered once more, and then turned toward me. The tension still in his compact, muscled body, he returned to my side.

"Have we got bogeymen we should be worrying about out here on top of everything else?" I heard a familiar voice ask behind me. Festus joined the pack with surprising enthusiasm considering the amount of restraint he'd shown around Phantom earlier, and I turned to greet Cheryl. To my surprise, Wade was with her. Both of them still in flannel pajamas. Hmm.

"I don't know about bogeymen," I said. "But something doesn't feel right out there."

Too dignified to join in, Phantom remained beside me while the other dogs played. Minion and Casper were both young dogs roughly the same size, and I was pleased to see how well they got along with the newcomer.

"Something hasn't felt right here since this whole thing started," Cheryl said.

"I'll be glad when we get your kids back and can put this whole thing to bed," Wade said.

"Amen to that," Cheryl agreed.

Festus, as second-most senior dog in the group, left the younger dogs and came over to join Phantom. They touched noses in a brief greeting and then settled down together. Meanwhile, Casper and Minion chased each other through the darkness, Minion having pulled herself out of her funk, at least for the moment. Neither of them seemed even tempted to go into the woods now.

"Did you talk to Ren's father?" Cheryl asked me.

"Yeah," I said. The conversation hadn't been a good one. I thought again of the fear and anger in his voice—anger I knew was directed at me, though he said nothing. I had let something happen to his little girl. In his place, I knew I wouldn't be nearly as calm. "He said to keep him posted."

"He's not coming here?" Wade asked.

"Not unless he's needed. His choice," I added at Wade's expression. "I think if he stays on the island he has enough to distract him that maybe he won't let this eat him up." I paused. "Or maybe he just doesn't trust himself to be near me after I let this happen."

"You didn't *let* anything happen," Cheryl said. "Last I checked, you weren't the sons of bitches roaming the woods with shotguns and not enough sense to keep the thing holstered. Bear and Ren both wanted to be here. I just spent the morning with them, and that came through loud and clear. They both trained to be here."

Behind us, the parking lot's motion-sensitive light came on before I could respond. All three of us fell silent, watching as one of the big black federal SUVs pulled into the parking lot and cut the engine. I couldn't see who got out of the driver's side, but a woman got out of the passenger's side.

Rita Paulsen, I realized after a minute.

Her voice was raised, though we weren't close enough to make out her words. The driver came around to her side of the vehicle, and I came to attention. It was Agent McDonough. The two walked together to the same motel room, voices still raised.

"Hmm," Cheryl whispered to me, voice dripping with sarcasm. "I would've thought the Feds weren't so cheap they'd make their agents bunk together."

"Ssh," I hushed her. The two agents went into the room together, still apparently arguing. McDonough shut the door behind them.

"Same old same old," Wade said, dismissing what we'd seen with a shrug. "Birds and bees do it, why shouldn't uptight federal agents?"

Cheryl's lips tightened, but she didn't offer any further commentary.

We were on our way back to our rooms, the dogs worn out and the chill of the night settled into my bones, when the same motel door opened again. Our entire party hung back, though there was no way we hadn't been seen. I watched as Rita left the room, saying something to McDonough before she turned her back on him and walked away. What caught me, though, was the way he watched her go. Something unmistakably human, almost heartbreaking, in his eyes before he closed his door once more.

•

The girl in the red sweater returned a few times over the course of the night, her pale face appearing in the bedroom's second-story window. Every time she did, Bear heard the rattling at the windows. He saw her just outside, caught in the rain, her mouth open in a silent scream. He'd seen the pictures of Ariel and Melanie Redfield; just as he'd thought, this girl was neither of them. She was older, for one thing. There was something about her, though, that went beyond that—a timelessness that suggested to him that she wasn't part of the search they were doing now.

The third time she returned, it was 4:22 according to the battery-powered clock on the bedside table. Ren was asleep, her breathing even and her body heavy against him.

It was uncomfortable, especially with the pain in his arm, but he'd slept most of his life with something beside him— everything from bear cubs to pit bulls to a litter of skunk kits, once. He was just grateful not to be alone.

"Mary," he said when the girl appeared again, recalling the name of the girl who had gone missing years before. She stared at him, half quizzical, half shocked. She hadn't expected to be heard, he realized. That happened a lot. People, spirits...whatever you wanted to call them, would appear to him. Throw things, scream in frustration, or simply walk past, and when he acknowledged them, it invariably set them back as much as—if not more than—it did him.

"Why are you here?" he whispered to her. He looked down to make sure Ren was still asleep, but she hadn't moved.

Mary looked back over her shoulder, eyes wide with fear. *Something is here,* she whispered to him—the words more sight than sound, appearing on a delicate thread that spiraled through the air.

"What something?" he asked, still whispering. "A person? The man who killed that girl… Is that what you mean? Did you see him?"

She shook her head. *You don't understand. You have to leave this place.*

Before he could respond, he heard footsteps down the hall and then a firm knock on the door. The girl seemed to shimmer in place, fading in and out for a moment before she turned from him and vanished. Dean Redfield let himself in a second later, without waiting for an answer from him. At the sound, Ren jolted awake.

"Who were you talking to?" Dean demanded as he closed the door behind him.

"Each other," Bear said without hesitation.

"She was asleep," Dean said. He nodded toward Ren, who seemed too dazed to protest.

"I don't know what you're talking about," Bear said, unnerved. He'd barely spoken above a whisper. Even if the old man was standing right outside his door, Bear couldn't see how he'd heard a thing. "We were talking to each other." He kept his eyes on the floor. He was bigger than Dean Redfield. Stronger. Even injured, he should be able to take the man out. It made no sense that he should be this afraid, but right now all he could do was sit there, in pain and fighting not to shake like a frightened pup.

"I heard you," Dean persisted. Bear raised his eyes and looked at the man. Those threads were whirling round his head, blacker than the words that spun round the girl. *Don't fuck with me, son.* How the hell had he heard? "You said someone's name. Not hers."

"You're wrong," Bear said, drawing strength from the older man's uncertainty. He kept his head up, staring Dean down. "Maybe you were dreaming."

Dean backed away. He glanced toward the window, and Bear followed his gaze. The girl was long gone. If Bear hadn't already experienced this before, he would doubt he'd seen her at all.

"I want you to stay quiet," Dean said. "Both of you, just shut the hell up. You need to save your strength."

"I'm bleeding again," Bear said—something he'd only just realized himself. "The cotton strips your sister gave us aren't absorbent enough, I just keep bleeding through the bandages. I either need actual bandages or, crazy idea, you could just let us go."

"If I could let you go, I would have done it already." Dean went to the window and stared out, his body rigid. In dogs, that kind of tension meant you backed off or you did something to ease things—throw a ball, offer a treat, make some kind of gesture to indicate you meant no harm. Dogs were easier than people, though. The problem, as Bear saw it, was that right now he wasn't sure he wanted to ease things. What would that accomplish in the long run?

He could almost hear his mother's voice in his head. *It'll keep you alive, Bear. That's what it will accomplish.*

"If you have another sheet, that might be good enough," he said, his voice purposely lighter now. He saw Dean's shoulders relax.

"I'll see what I can come up with. You still think you can take care of him?" Dean asked Ren. She blinked, still trying to get her bearings after just waking up.

"I can, yes. But he's right—if you can get more bandages, that would help."

"Yes, ma'am," Dean said, surprisingly respectful. He stopped with his hand at the doorknob and turned back to them. "That girl you were talking to," he said, focusing on Bear once more. "It's the one in the red sweater, isn't it? The one Claude was going on about?" Bear didn't answer, but Dean didn't seem to require a response. "If she comes back, you tell me. I want to talk to her."

"I don't think it works like that," Bear said.

"I don't care how you think it works. Claude says she knows something about my girls—knows something about where Ariel is now. I need to talk to her."

"Has Claude, uh…" Bear's mind was spinning. Claude had seen the girl—that had been clear earlier. But had he seen that kind of thing before? Dean looked at him without a shred of understanding in his eyes. What would he say if Bear told him that this girl in the red sweater was just one of dozens of dead people he'd communicated with over the years? That sometimes he couldn't sleep for the faces clamoring outside his window, the voices whispering his name?

"Has Claude talked to my mother?" Bear bluffed. "Or have any of you, since you took me? Has anyone told her I'm all right?"

"We'll call in the morning," Dean said. "I want to make sure they don't forget what they're supposed to be doing out there. Time's running out."

Bear thought of the time limit Dean had put on this thing when it had all started. Just over thirty hours now. If his mother didn't find Ariel by then, Dean would kill one of them.

He wasn't ready to die—and he definitely wasn't ready to see Ren die.

Before Bear could ask any more questions, Dean left the room. As soon as he was gone, Ren turned to Bear.

"What was that about?" she hissed. "What was he talking about? Were you talking to someone?"

Bear's gaze drifted back to the window. "I was," he admitted. "But she's gone now."

Ren shivered beside him. For the first time, he saw fear in her eyes. Her thick, dark curls were a mess, and he wondered what she would do if he pushed them back from her face. If he touched her cheek, the way she had his earlier that night. She was in bed by his side, they'd slept together for the past several hours—hell, they were facing death together... And yet, he couldn't bring himself to bridge that last gap between them.

"I need to try and get that bleeding stopped again," she said. She got out of bed, shivering again when her feet hit the cold floor.

Bear couldn't think of anything to say. Instead, he remained silent. What did it say about him, he wondered, that he was better at communicating with animals and dead people, than flesh and blood of his own species?

14

IT WAS ALMOST FIVE a.m. by the time we went back inside the Shaftsbury motel. We fed the dogs, and then I returned Casper and Minion to their crates before heading back to Glastenbury, my shepherd by my side.

As soon as I pulled up, the light went on in several of the news vans that were now parked at the edge of the parking lot. I saw Angie Crenshaw hop out of her van first, already made up and far more enthusiastic than she'd been the day before. Bloodshed, hostages, a madman on the loose... *Now* they had a story.

"Jamie," she called to me. "Jamie Flint, right? What can you tell me about your son? How close are you to finding the missing girl?"

I shook my head and hurried up the steps, Phantom keeping pace beside me. The reporter continued calling questions to me as others followed in her wake. I ignored them all, hauled open the church door, and closed it just before any of them reached me.

McDonough was already in the "war room" at HQ when I arrived. Jack was not, though I hadn't really expected him yet. Had he gotten anything from Gordon, I wondered?

"You get any sleep last night?" McDonough asked me as I came through the door.

"A few hours," I lied. At the doubt on his face, I added, "That might be a little generous. You?"

"I got what I needed." I thought of the look I'd seen on his face when he'd said goodnight to Rita, but there was no sign of that vulnerability now. He returned his attention to the whiteboard. The map was up again, this time with a large red *X* where Melanie Redfield's body had been found. The immediate area around it was circled in blue. "You ready to get out there again?"

"Not much else I can think of doing right now," I said.

He nodded. The tension between us was palpable when he looked at me again. "Have you heard from Jack?" he asked.

"No," I said honestly.

His lips thinned into a grimace, as though he were in physical pain. "Lucky you," he murmured. "I got a call from my supervisor at o-three-hundred this morning. Turns out Jack made an unauthorized trip to Texas to visit Gordon Redfield last night. You know anything about that?"

"I know he believed Gordon could help with this case," I said. He was doing his best to intimidate me, but he could grimace all he wanted—the reality was, he had no power over me. I've dealt with far worse than Gerard McDonough in my life.

"He's wrong," McDonough said unequivocally. "I told him as much, but Jack doesn't listen to anybody but Jack. And this time, it's going to bite him in the ass."

I remained silent, unsure what my role was in all this. What he wanted from me. McDonough took a swig of coffee from his mug, made a face, and set it back down on his desk. He looked at Phantom, then at me.

"I'm sorry about what happened to your boy," he said. Hardly what I expected. "And since occasionally—very occasionally—Jack comes up with a good idea, I approved his request to bring Gordon Redfield up here to consult on this case. Of course, just because he's been given the okay to come here doesn't mean Gordon will actually come."

"What do you mean, he won't come?" I asked, drawn in despite myself. "Make him come. Don't tell me you guys don't have ways of making that happen—"

"We're doing what we can," McDonough said smoothly. "If there's a way to get him here, we'll do it."

I still didn't know what to think about Gordon. Jack believed the man had killed his sisters—or at least those were the words he'd said to me, but there was more conflict there than Jack was willing to admit. He might have gone along with the conviction, but there were seeds of doubt. And now, with Melanie dead and Ariel missing, it was only natural that those seeds should start to grow. The problem was, I didn't know where that got me. Or Bear.

"Thank you," I said. "I know you don't believe this will help, but I've always been impressed with Jack's instincts."

McDonough didn't seem impressed by that, but said nothing. "That wasn't all I wanted to talk to you about," he said. "I wanted to see if you could talk to the other SAR folks that are out there. We're trying to diffuse the situation up on the mountain, but we're no closer to finding whoever killed Melanie Redfield. I've tried to warn the searchers, but so far nobody's paying much attention."

"I don't know what to tell you," I said. "I can talk to

them, but I doubt it will matter." I wasn't at all surprised that he'd had no luck getting VTK9 to leave the search. If it had been another searcher's kid, I would have kept searching regardless of the danger. It's one of the things I like best about the SAR community. We look out for each other, first and foremost. A dog falls sick, the messages start coming in. A handler is injured, and everyone's right there to help out. Dog people aren't known for their interpersonal skills, but when one of our own needs us, we're there.

"Do you really think people are in danger out there?" I asked. The thought unnerved me. "It seems to me that whoever killed Melanie will stay as far from search and rescue and law enforcement as possible."

"True," he grudgingly agreed. "My guess is that the killer's already long gone—high tailed it out of here as soon as the cops moved in. But just because he's not out there doesn't mean you're protected from the other idiots holding court with the Redfields. My men are up there now and report that just about everyone has cleared out after what happened with your son, but I still don't like this."

"And you think I do?" I said. "I'll talk to Cheryl, but I don't know that it will help. The last I knew, she put a call out and expects another dozen teams may show up by this afternoon."

"In that case, I'll put the word out to the Redfield camp," he said. "Let them know the authorities are authorized to arrest anyone roaming the woods with a weapon during this search. Hopefully, that will make a difference." He paused, eyeing me thoughtfully. "You know, Dean got what he wanted. All along, he wanted you here," he watched me as he spoke the words. Unbidden, a chill went up my spine.

"Do you know why?"

"I thought about it last night," I said, shaking my head. "I have no idea. He knew Brock Campbell, my former mentor." I had to fight to keep my tone level when I said Brock's name, but I saw McDonough's eyes narrow. "That's all I know."

"Campbell was a big deal in dog training, wasn't he? Died a few years ago?"

Just as Jack had, I was sure McDonough knew the details. I kept my face impassive, one eye on the horizon lightening outside. "Yeah, he was a big deal," I said. "The macho bullshit that some trainers go nuts for—dominance theory, alpha and omega." Something I expected was right up McDonough's alley, though I didn't say so.

"Something you don't buy into?"

"I think force is always an easier way to get what you want. Not necessarily the right way, but often simpler."

He considered that for a second. "And he was your mentor." He was still watching me. I raised my eyebrows, too tired to play games.

"Do you have a question for me, Agent McDonough?"

"A few of them, actually. This one is pretty simple, though: If you thought his theories were bullshit, why did he leave his business and upwards of ten million dollars to you and your son when he died? Why were you the sole beneficiary on his life insurance policy?"

I tried to remain cool, but my palms were sweating. How many times had I answered these questions before? Schooled Bear on them? I knew what to say. It shouldn't be this hard to get the words out, given the number of times I'd told this lie.

"He didn't have any children of his own. I was young when I went to his training camp—barely fifteen. He thought I had a lot of promise as a handler. Later, a few years after I'd had Bear, we reconnected. He and Bear got along well, and it was a time in Brock's life when he couldn't handle the business on his own. I ran it for him; he was pleased with what I did. And he genuinely cared for my son."

McDonough nodded, still eyeing me speculatively. Before he could ask anything further, Phantom pricked her ears forward, eyes on the door. Outside, I heard vehicles rumbling toward us. McDonough tipped his chin toward the exit.

"You should get going, get everything coordinated. If there's a chance of finding this girl alive, I want to know we did everything in our power to make that happen."

I started for the door with a nod, then paused and turned back. "If you hear anything from Dean Redfield…" I began.

"I'll let you know," McDonough said briefly, dismissing me out of hand. Not the most reassuring man I'd ever met.

15

SIXTEEN TEAMS STRONG by morning, our forces were ready to go by five-thirty a.m. The horizon was already beginning to lighten when we set out. Sunrise wasn't technically until 6:02, but there was enough light to work with in the meantime. I'd gotten word from the island that Monty and Sarah, two of my strongest handlers at Flint K-9, were in the field on another search, but would join us within a few days if they could. If Ariel Redfield was anywhere in that forest, I couldn't imagine how she could possibly stay hidden.

Phantom had rested enough that she was ready to go again that morning, but I knew this would need to be a short day for her. No matter: Casper and Minion were both eager to get out there, and I'd simply swap the dogs out when Phantom had had enough. Cheryl and I teamed up again, Phantom and Festus greeting one another with a brief butt sniff before they regarded one another with polite disinterest once more. Like everyone else, it seemed they were ready to get started.

We started by trekking out to the tree where I'd found Ariel's shirt the night before, the going slow thanks to the washout that had nearly taken Jack down with it. Every dog we brought by tracked the scent to the tree I'd climbed, then nosed around briefly before they lost the scent, looking at us in bafflement. I had no answers for them. It was like Ariel had vanished into thin air from here.

For the next three hours, we searched the forest. I heard occasional barks in the distance, alerts from other dogs on other teams, and I would stand there with my own ears straining as much as Phantom's as I waited for the call telling us the search was over; the girl had been found.

That call didn't come.

We agreed to rendezvous back at the station at eight a.m. to regroup. When the time came, I was reluctant to go. Phantom had alerted twice in the same area, nearly a mile from the tree where Ariel's T-shirt had been found. She even circled back once after I'd examined the place and told her to move on. Shortly afterward, Festus alerted in the same spot. Cheryl scratched her head and eyed me speculatively.

"Your dog known for false alerts?" she asked.

"It happens. Not often, but no dog is perfect."

She nodded. "Strange that Festus is fixed on the same spot, though."

I agreed. The problem was simple, though: we'd checked this area. It was a clearing surrounded by a grove of beech trees and yellow birch and, frankly, there wasn't a hell of a lot to see. I checked the ground for signs that someone had been through recently, but the rains had washed away any footprints that might have been left behind and the plants in the area appeared to be intact. There were no hair elastics lying in the dirt, no snapped twigs, no telltale piles of stones or messages carved into the bark.

There was nothing here.

Regardless, Phantom and Festus sat where they'd planted themselves, looking for all the world like they were saying, *Job done. What the hell are you still looking for?*

I radioed McDonough. "We've got an alert up here we can't explain. Can we get an excavation team out?" The only explanation I could come up with was that whatever the dogs were reacting to, it was out of sight.

There was a pause before McDonough responded, but I couldn't tell if that was due to a delayed signal or something else. "What are the coordinates?"

I read them from my GPS, and waited while he plugged them in on his end and then responded.

"I'll pass it on, but the excavation team's a little busy right now."

"Busy with…?"

"Investigating three other alerts on the mountain," he said. "It seems a few other teams are also convinced they've got something. You can't get a visual or confirm what the dog's reacting to?"

"Negative," I said, trying to process what I was hearing. False alerts happen, but they're typically easily disproved. Something was wrong here, but I couldn't just ignore what Festus and Phantom were trying so hard to tell us.

"Just send them when you can," I said. "We'll do a little more searching around here, then head back to HQ afterward."

"Affirmative," McDonough said. "Be careful out there."

Cheryl looked at me expectantly once I'd signed off, eyebrows raised. "So?"

"Apparently, ours is not the first alert this morning."

She didn't look surprised. "It happens around here—I don't know why, but perfectly reliable dogs go haywire in these woods. Alerting at every clearing or suspicious rock pile." She paused. We were in woods deep enough that getting any sense of our bearings without GPS would have been practically impossible, and I didn't care for the feeling. "Ariel's been gone forty-eight hours now," she said.

"She has."

"And her sister's already been found."

I nodded, thinking again of the bound, eviscerated girl Bear and I had found the evening before. We knew what happened to Melanie Redfield, but where the hell was Ariel? Had she truly broken free at the site where Melanie died? If so, she would have been running for her life for more than twenty-four hours now. Which led me to the next question:

Who was she running from?

My thoughts returned to Bear—a near-constant over the past twelve hours since Dean had taken him. I wanted, more than anything, to just storm the castle and be done with it. I didn't give a rat's ass right now about bloodshed or collateral damage. I just wanted to know my kid was safe.

"Jamie?" Cheryl said. The way she said it, I could tell she'd been saying my name for a while. I looked up.

"Sorry. Yeah?"

"I was asking about Melanie. You still don't know why they left the house on their own that morning?"

"Not for sure. One of the men there said the girls told him they were going to meet someone. His impression was that it was a man."

She frowned. "Out here?"

"Or men," I mused. "If they were both excited about

going, had gotten a little dressed up even, it seems unlikely that they'd both be going for just one guy."

"Unless they were *really* close."

"I guess," I said. "I have four sisters, though, and I can't imagine ever wanting to go meet a guy with any of them."

"So... Two guys, then," Cheryl said. She sat down on a dead log and Festus came over and settled beside her. I sat on a rock opposite her and considered that for a moment.

"They wouldn't have internet access out there, would they? If it was someone they met online..."

"Not unless they've got some pretty fancy satellite equipment, there's no way they were logging on up there. The only way they could've corresponded with a pen pal is good old-fashioned snail mail."

Which was a possibility I was sure McDonough and the others had already explored, but I made a mental note to check all the same.

"There has to be some way to track them down," I said, frustration beginning to burn through. Even if we did, though, would it really matter? Whoever the killer was, we were looking for someone who had killed before—but the focus in every instance in the past had been on prostitutes. What did he have against two sisters, one sixteen and one eighteen?

Unless there was something we didn't know about Melanie and Ariel.

I thought about the men most accessible to the girls, stuck as they were at the top of a mountain in the middle of nowhere. When I'd first come on the scene, the impression Jack had given me was that it was just Dean Redfield and his family up on the mountain. There had been far more than family in the woods yesterday when Bear was shot, though. The folks Dean had at the top of Glastenbury Mountain were a rough crowd.

Most of them men.

On the other hand, there were the FBI agents who'd been trolling this area ever since they'd learned the Redfields had set up camp here.

"How much do you know about the FBI team that's here?" I asked. "The ones who headed up the original Redfield murder investigation in 2009?"

She raised her eyebrows at me, surprised, but remained silent for a second or two. I waited. Finally, she scratched the back of her neck and gazed off into the distance as she answered. "Wade told me some stories, but they're not the kind I'm supposed to be go spouting off to anybody who'll listen."

"You really think I fit that bill?"

She smiled faintly. "Nah, I guess I don't." She looked around, searching for eavesdroppers, and lowered her voice when she spoke again. "Wade says there was a hell of a sex scandal just a little while before the whole thing in Adams went down. A videotape somehow got into circulation, showing a couple of hookers and a group of Feds doing some very nasty things on the taxpayers' dime."

"And Gordon Redfield was one of those Feds," I said.

She looked surprised for a moment, assessing me. "Son of a bitch—you already know all this, don't you? Here I am thinking I've got some big-time gossip…"

"I'd still like to hear your take on it."

"Sure… I don't know that I'll say anything you don't already know, but I'm always happy to talk trash about the men in black." She thought for a second, then continued. "Gordon Redfield was small-time compared to the others who were in there, according to Wade. Couple of high-ranking muckety mucks in the Bureau, couple of politicians, local businessmen… This wasn't just some Bring-Your-Own-Handcuffs, half-assed orgy."

"If that many people were involved, how did they manage to keep it out of the press?" I asked.

"Who knows," she said with a shrug. "Money, most likely. You know about the hookers that got murdered around that time?"

"I heard."

She frowned. "Well, that's no fun. You know the story."

"I don't understand why Gordon Redfield wouldn't have come forward, though," I pressed. "He's in prison for life for murdering his sisters; suspected of killing these prostitutes around the country. He's said all along that he's innocent—why wouldn't he have said something to someone about the men who were part of the whole sex thing with him? Don't tell me they're threatening him—he's already in prison for life."

"Prison is hardly the worst thing that can happen to a person," she said, eyeing me thoughtfully. "He's got a big family—"

"That he's estranged from," I interrupted.

"Doesn't mean he's not going to do everything he can to protect them, when push comes to shove. Besides which, seems to me if the wrong people wanted to make his life worse in prison, they could definitely make that happen." She shrugged again. "I've never met the man, so hell if I know what's going on with any of it. But it doesn't seem like we've got the whole story yet, if you ask me. That's all I'm saying."

I had to agree with that. "We should get back," I said abruptly. "I want to ask Agent McDonough some questions."

We marked the spot where the dogs had alerted so that an excavation team could come back later, then returned to headquarters at ten a.m. The parking lot and the road up were both filled to overflowing, a dozen teams with dogs and handlers of all shape and size headed in at the same time. Overhead, the sky was blue and the leaves were turning, the air warm, all traces of rain forgotten.

As soon as we were back, I gave Phantom water and headed straight for McDonough. He was in a meeting with Agent Paulsen and some other cops, but I didn't wait for him to get out. Instead, I knocked briefly on the door and went in without waiting for a response. The others looked up in surprise when I barged in.

"Have you talked to Barrett Redfield?" I demanded.

"Well, hello to you, too," a well-coiffed agent whose name I couldn't remember muttered.

I ignored him. "What about the others living in the houses up there? What do you know about them? Jack asked if you had followed up—have you done that yet?"

"We've talked to them," McDonough said "What exactly are you thinking?"

"This mysterious man Ariel and Melanie were supposedly going to meet—"

"If you believe Claude's story," McDonough interrupted. "The guy's got rocks between his ears. Not the most reliable witness."

"So you've talked to Barrett, then?" I pressed.

"We talked to him," McDonough said with a placating nod. "And I'll head up there personally today to talk to the others there. I'm sure they'll love to see me coming."

No doubt. I glanced at the others in the room, not pleased that we had to have the next part of this conversation in front of them.

"We'll finish up in ten," McDonough said to his team, reading me well.

"I'm sorry to storm in the way I did," I said when they were gone. "But it doesn't seem like anything is actually happening here—"

McDonough held up his hand. "I can understand where you're coming from on this," he said, in his best politician's voice. "Trust me—my daughter's fifteen. If this were her in your son's place, I don't know how I'd handle it. But we know what we're doing. Whatever we have to do, we will get your son and his friend out of there alive."

I didn't point out that there was no way he could realistically promise that. Based on the look in his eyes, he already knew.

"What did Barrett say when you talked to him, questioned him about the girls? He has a house alone up there, and we already know that the victims in the previous murders were prostitutes. Do we know what Barrett's doing up there? Maybe Melanie and Ariel were headed there that morning."

"We're looking into it," McDonough said, his voice starting to tighten. "We have a few different avenues we're pursuing right now, you just need to let us do that. We know—"

"What about your own men?" I asked, cutting him off once more.

"Excuse me?"

"Are there other agents working this case who were part of the scandal with Gordon Redfield before the murders in 2009? Is there a possibility that one of them might be in on this investigation?" A shadow crossed McDonough's face, his cheeks flaming red.

"Agent Juarez never should have given you that information. Whatever he told you about that—"

"Spare me," I said. McDonough was not an unintimidating man, but right now I had no patience for his brand of horseshit. "This place is crawling with FBI and other law enforcement. Have you done background checks to figure out whether any of them was involved with the case in 2009?"

"That's not your concern—"

"The hell it's not."

"Ms. Flint," McDonough said. His voice was harder now, brooking no argument. "We know what we're doing. *I* know what I'm doing. I am pursuing every avenue to find out who is behind Melanie's murder and Ariel's disappearance. Failing that, I have a SWAT team on standby. We will get Bear and Ren out of this, alive. But, with all due respect, you don't know what the hell you're talking about. You need to back off, get your dogs out there, and keep looking for Ariel. That's what you can do to help your son."

"I'm trying," I said. The fight left my voice, and a wave of exhaustion ran through me. "But all these false alerts, the sheer acreage of this place… If we don't find out who's behind this, I honestly don't know how we're going to find her."

"I understand that," he said coolly, though I thought I saw just a glimmer of humanity in there somewhere. "But you have to leave that to me. If you go off the reservation, it's not going to do a damn thing for Bear or Ren."

I nodded. I'd been telling myself the same thing for more than twelve hours now. Despite his words, however, I knew this time I couldn't simply leave things alone.

●

Once I was done with McDonough, I retrieved Phantom and went back outside. The parking lot was full now, and I noted more news vans parked on the side of the road on the way in. The vultures were circling. Angie Crenshaw spotted me and nodded to her cameraman; I turned and went the other way, hoping she would give up and leave me the hell alone.

I went to a rocky clearing out behind headquarters and knelt on the cool earth beside Phantom. The dog stood patiently, her feet square, as I took her right leg in hand and stretched it carefully behind her. At the point of resistance, I held for a count of fifteen, letting the slow, steady movement calm me as much as her. There was a creak in her left knee when I did the same stretch on the opposite leg, and I made a mental note to make an appointment for her.

"I know, Phan," I said. "None of us are as young as we used to be." She tipped her head to look at me, but otherwise didn't move as I finished the stretch and moved on to her forelegs.

"What are you doing?" a woman's voice asked from

behind me. I tensed.

"Stretches," I said without turning around. "We do them with all the dogs—helps keep them from getting lame during long searches."

Angie Crenshaw circled until she was standing in front of me, her focus on Phantom. "She's a beautiful dog. Full shepherd?"

"Not sure," I said. "I got her from a shelter in Georgia. If she's got a pedigree, I forgot to get the papers."

The reporter had apparently come without her cameraman, since I saw no sign of anyone. She crouched in front of us, still watching Phantom.

"I know you don't want to talk to me—" she began.

"I *can't* talk to you," I corrected her. "Don't want to either, really, but technically I can't. We're all under strict orders."

"From the FBI, right?" she asked. I remained silent. "I'm sorry about what's happening with your son in all this. Do you know what happened with the last case involving the FBI and the Redfields?" she continued. "Considering what went on last time, it seems like they should have had some idea violence like this was a possibility."

I didn't say anything, though I could tell she knew I was listening now. Before she could say anything more, Cheryl came over with Festus. She looked at Crenshaw coldly.

"Scram, Corky. We've got shit to do—be a good girl and crawl under a rock with the other snakes you run with."

"We were in the middle of—" Crenshaw began.

"No, actually, we weren't," I said. "Go on. She's right, we've got work to do."

"If you want to talk—"

"She knows where to find you," Cheryl said. "Now go." She stood with her hands on her hips, a ferocious scowl on her face. Crenshaw finally gave up. Cheryl and I remained silent until the reporter was out of sight.

"Corky?" I asked.

"Sherwood," she explained. I shook my head. "*Murphy Brown?* Sorry. My pop culture references tend to be a little dated."

"Don't worry about it," I said. "I wouldn't have gotten it if it were any more current, trust me."

She eased herself somewhat painfully to the ground and got Festus to sit, then started running through the same gentle stretches I'd just done with Phantom. She glanced up after she'd done his right hind leg. "I hear there were a lot of false alerts out there," she said.

"That's what I hear. Agent McDonough said there were half a dozen all told that couldn't be confirmed one way or the other."

"I've never seen anything like it," Cheryl said. I finished up with the foreleg stretches and gave Phantom the 'down' command, then twirled my finger so that she rolled onto her back. We'd been through the routine so many times the command was purely for my benefit; Phantom knew the drill. As I stretched the dog's shoulders, Cheryl glanced at me again.

"What's on your mind?" I prompted when she didn't say anything.

"Nothing," she said quickly. "Except that I know there are some…things you and your boy see, deal with, that maybe the rest of us don't have a lot of experience with."

I tensed. I don't make a point of shouting my 'gifts' from

the rooftops, and Bear is even more sensitive about it. Word about this kind of thing does tend to get around, though. "I'm not sure what that has to do with anything," I said.

"No," she agreed. "Me neither. But Wade and I were talking last night, and even he thinks there's something going on out here. And you know how sensitive dogs can be. I'm just wondering…"

Her pussyfooting around the subject was getting old. "What, Cheryl? That the dogs are alerting to ghosts? Evil spirits?"

There was a split second where the question hung in the air before she laughed aloud, shaking her head. "Shit. I think I'm going round the bend myself around here," she said. "This place gets to you after a while, but you're right. Whoever killed Melanie Redfield was human through and through. And wherever Ariel is, my guess is she's not running from ghosts."

I nodded. "Exactly."

Cheryl looked embarrassed that she'd brought it up. "Right," she said, recovering. "Doesn't change the fact that this place is a damn sight creepier than most searches we do."

"I expect that has more to do with a forest filled with law enforcement, a murderer on the loose, and an asshole who's taken Bear and Ren hostage," I returned.

"True," she agreed. "That's probably it." Even she didn't look completely convinced, though.

16

"WELL, JACK, no one ever said you weren't a stubborn son of a bitch," Gordon Redfield said as Jack entered the same dank room where he'd visited the man just a few hours before.

Jack hadn't slept well in the small Texas hotel, haunted by images of Jamie trekking through the wilderness in search of a girl Jack was almost certain was already dead. For what it was worth, Gordon didn't look like he'd slept much better himself. There were shadows beneath his eyes and a tension in his shoulders that Jack hadn't seen the last time they'd met.

"Tell me about the women you killed," Jack said without preamble.

Uncertainty flickered in Gordon's eyes as he tried to figure out Jack's angle. "I've told everyone until I'm blue in the face. I didn't kill anyone."

"You were in the same towns where eight women—two women each, every time—were raped and murdered. You've admitted that every one of those women were prostitutes you slept with. You have no alibi to cover yourself during any of the times of death."

"All of which is circumstantial. There's not a trace of hard evidence to link me to those murders."

"Unlike your sisters," Jack said. "We found plenty of DNA there. Their blood in your car. Your skin cells under June's fingernails."

Gordon's face tightened. He looked away, as though struggling to maintain control. "That evidence was planted. Even if any of this made sense and I was the one who killed the hookers you're saying I did, you really think I would have killed them without leaving a trace of DNA, gone to the trouble of burying them out in the woods in cities thousands of miles from my own home, and then murdered my own sisters in cold blood, left behind forensic evidence, and then dug a shallow grave half a mile from my brother's house? What kind of fucking idiot would do that?"

Gordon's voice had been rising progressively. Jack searched the guard for some sign of unease, but the man looked more concerned about Jack than he did the enraged inmate. Jack was reminded of the way Gordon had been treated the day before; the looks Jack had drawn from those on the inside.

He wondered briefly what Gordon had done to engender such devotion, and then recalled what it had been like to work under the man. Everyone at the Bureau had felt the same way, Jack realized. Whatever came up, whatever Gordon Redfield had ever needed, he invariably had a crowd of people lined up ready to give him whatever he asked for.

If they had all misjudged him, though, had all been so completely off-base about the strength of his character, then how much could he achieve here with the ability to get people so readily in his corner?

"You used to believe me," Gordon said. He'd regained control. "If Lucia were alive, she would remind you of that. Would remind you that I'm not this monster you imagine."

"Come to Glastenbury, then," Jack said, never mentioning that Lucia wouldn't do any such thing. He refused to react to Gordon's use of her name, the invocation of her memory. "Prove it to me. Come help me solve this case. Find the person who killed Melanie—and the other girls you've been accused of killing."

Gordon shook his head before Jack had finished the sentence. "I've made my peace with being here. There's no reason to fight it any longer. I'm where I am for a reason."

"You're where you are because you had a rotten lawyer and when push came to shove you refused to stand up for yourself. Come to Glastenbury with me. Help me with this case. Talk to me about whatever the hell is going on, damn it."

There was the barest second of uncertainty before Gordon shook his head. "No. I'm sorry, but I've already told you before: I'm not going anywhere."

Truth be told, Jack had already anticipated this response. He paused for no more than a beat before he stood. "Pack your shit, Gordon."

"I'm not going—"

"Yes, actually, you are. I was trying to do this the nice way, with you feeling like you had some choice in the decision… I see now that you have no intention of cooperating, so here's the score: I've got an injunction. You are legally required to come with me to Vermont."

"And if I refuse?"

"Don't test me," Jack said. He held the man's eye. "Just

get packed. We leave in an hour."

This time, Gordon didn't argue.

•

At noon, I swapped Phantom out for Casper, and Cheryl and I kept searching. The weather was cooperating, which meant less slogging through mud and rain for the dogs and less fatigue for me—though there was no denying I was exhausted by this time. With insufficient sleep the night before and the worry to compound it, I had to push myself to maintain focus. Casper, already a dog with attention issues, was all over the place now that Bear wasn't the one leading him and my energy was compromised. I fought to keep my temper more than once when the dog stopped to eat a pile of deer droppings or, once, gave up on the search altogether and chased a squirrel through the underbrush—something I was sure he would never try with Bear.

By evening, with false alerts dotting the mountainside and still no sign of Ariel, I had officially lost patience. I was dragging, but forced myself to stay focused and on task to at least maintain some semblance of control for the dogs. That focus was disappearing fast, though.

"All right," Cheryl said finally, at five minutes till eight. "Time to head back. I'm starved, and the dogs need to go in."

"I want to check the trail one more time," I said, motioning toward a path to the south where Casper had alerted earlier.

Cheryl grimaced. "The dogs need rest. Hell, I need rest. And food."

I managed to keep my temper, but couldn't stop the impatient glare I sent the older woman's way. "Go on. I'll look myself, it's fine."

"You know that's not the way it's done. Just go in there and do whatever in hell you think needs doing, but I'm staying right here."

She'd retired Festus not long after I'd put Phantom in, so our team for most of the afternoon hours had been Casper and Minion. Despite Cheryl's warning, both dogs were bright-eyed and alert, clearly eager to keep going. We'd stopped for the obligatory breaks over the course of the day, and taken an hour for lunch. They were both young, energetic dogs who, I knew, could safely keep searching for at least another couple of hours. Which meant Cheryl wasn't nearly as worried about their welfare as she was mine.

"I'm all right," I said.

She rolled her eyes. "The hell you are. Just go on. I'll wait here and watch the dogs for a few minutes, if you really want to go in and check it out one more time."

I nodded without acknowledging her kindness and ordered Casper to stay. The pit bull didn't look happy, but he didn't break his stay as I left him behind.

Alone, I went back down the path and into the woods.

The trees closed in immediately. I've been on searches around the world but this was one of the thickest forests I'd seen in the U.S., short of the Cascades in the Pacific Northwest. That combined with the steep upward climb and everything that was at stake were making this a challenge I wasn't sure I was up to.

I followed the half-assed trail we'd broken with the dogs until I found the marker I'd left to denote an area where

Casper, Phantom, and Festus had all alerted before.

Unlike what you see on TV or read in books, dogs don't actually have superpowers when it comes to scent. If there's not some physical remnant to find, most can't simply detect a lingering scent from decades past. And even when there is physical evidence, conditions may hinder the search: other scents masking the target, or things obfuscated by wind, weather, or the dog (or handler)'s own mood. But all three dogs had seemed so clear on this exact area that I couldn't help but pause. Cheryl and I had run the dogs through twice, and then searched exhaustively to try and find…something. Anything.

We'd bushwhacked our way through the area, mindful of where we were laying waste to brush to make sure we didn't inadvertently hack Ariel to pieces in our zeal. We'd checked the ground, which showed no signs of being dug up recently. We'd checked the trees, but no one that we could see was hiding up there. Still, every dog brought through here stopped in the same spot and gave their alert, whether it was Phantom's down followed by two sharp barks; Casper's zealous return to me to punch my pocket with his nose, eager for the treat he knew was waiting after a successful find; or Festus's sit-stay, bark, and calculated glare at Cheryl.

There was something here.

If Bear were here, he'd be able to see it. Find it.

I don't know what I expected to happen. Bear has this inexplicable…gift, curse, whatever you want to call it. I do not.

I sat cross-legged in the dirt and leaves, eyes closed, other senses straining. What were the dogs trying to tell us? Not for the first time, I wished they had the power of speech. Or

I had the ability to read minds.

If there was something else here—something that was not Ariel Redfield—then it was unlikely all the dogs would have alerted in this spot. They weren't trained to find just any old thing; they were highly trained dogs searching for one specific person. While Phantom had trained as a cadaver dog early on and occasionally alerted when she came across older remains, the other dogs hadn't had any such training.

Somewhere in the distance, I heard the cry of a peregrine falcon—higher, clearer, than that of other raptors. Was Ariel out there? Was she still alive, hiding somewhere in terror after what she'd witnessed? Or did the killer already have her? Was he watching the whole proceeding from somewhere close by, reveling in our continued failure?

"Aaaaaariiiiellll!" I shouted. It wasn't like we hadn't tried that before; we'd all been screaming the girl's name for hours. Days.

I shouted her name twice more, then fell silent. That scant amount of activity felt like it had been too much. Then I thought of my son, and chastised myself. What kind of mother gave in to her own fatigue when her child was bleeding to death, held captive by someone, and Mom alone may have the power to save him?

I sank back on my haunches and looked around the darkening forest. No one appeared to me, either living or dead.

Just then, I heard rustling in the brush behind me.

I whirled, fully expecting to find Ariel Redfield emerging from the forest.

Instead, Phantom stood there, her ears pricked forward and her eyes alert. She trotted to a spot a foot away from me, lay down, and barked twice. Her lead dragged behind her, no human to be found on the other end.

"Where did you come from?" I asked her. She barked again, her gaze unwavering. "Yeah, I know. I've heard the story. There's something here."

Her tail swished on the dusty ground, her mouth open in a relaxed, smiling pant at sight of me. I heard the more pronounced crash of a human moving through the undergrowth, and a moment later Jack appeared.

"She got ahead of me," he said, nodding toward Phantom.

"I can see that. " I frowned. "What are you doing with my dog?"

"I heard you were still out here, and Phantom was antsy being left behind. I thought if we weren't actually searching but just out for a light hike, maybe it would be all right to bring her along."

I struggled to my feet. "She was supposed to be resting—I don't even let Monty take Phantom out most times."

"I'm sorry," he said. "I just thought maybe you could use a friendly face, and I wasn't sure mine would fit the bill."

I turned away, trying to quell my frustration. "You should go back," I said. "Thank you for trying. I just want to keep searching a while longer." I turned to look at him again. He looked tired himself, but right now the fatigue was nothing compared with the concern I read on his face.

"I'm not leaving you out here alone. If you're going to keep searching despite what anyone with any common sense tells you, we'll just stay and search alongside you."

Phantom sat watching this exchange, ears up, head going back and forth between Jack and me as though watching a cartoon tennis match. To my surprise, Jack sank down beside her and settled himself on the damp ground. He wore jeans, loose fitting enough to reinforce the fact that he had lost weight recently.

With no more strength to keep going and nowhere else to go besides, I sank down beside him.

"When did you get back?" I asked.

He glanced at his watch. "About an hour ago. I brought Gordon with me—short of the final DNA analysis, we're about seventy-five percent sure whoever killed Melanie was the same one who killed June and Katie."

I looked up at that. "And the prostitutes?"

"We don't know." He shook his head. "All we had was circumstantial evidence linking him to those crimes before… And we were never able to prove beyond a shadow of a doubt that the same man who killed the Redfield sisters was the one who'd killed the hookers. Same M.O., but no physical evidence linking back."

"So if he's exonerated of killing June and Katie, Gordon could be a free man?"

Jack nodded. He didn't look happy about that—or, at the very least, he looked conflicted. He shook it off, though, and refocused on me.

"What do you think you'll find here, anyway?" he said. "You've already looked, haven't you? Cheryl told me you've had the dogs through here three times. They've all alerted. An excavation crew is on the way. There's nothing more you can do."

The words were not ones I wanted to hear. I looked away, still searching the clearing. I was desperate. Tears pricked my eyes, and I fought for control. Losing it now would accomplish nothing.

And that's when I saw it.

It was so slight it was no wonder we'd missed it before: a barely discernible depression in the earth to my left, at the very edge of the clearing.

I swallowed my excitement and shifted so that I was lying on my belly in the dirt. Jack no doubt figured he was watching my final unraveling, but I ignored him. Sure enough, from this vantage I could see the change in topography. I got to my feet and strode to an area two yards from where I'd been lying and studied the ground.

"What is it?" Jack asked. He got up and came to my side.

I pointed to the earth at our feet. He looked at me blankly. "There's something there," I said. I moved forward, bent, and touched the ground in that spot. It felt exactly the same as everything else here did: cool and damp.

I didn't care, though. Something was here. Excitement built in my chest.

"We need to get the excavation team up here now," I said. "This is it. Something is here."

It was all I could do not to start digging with my bare hands. Jack got on the radio and I heard him apprising McDonough of our coordinates. He argued, telling Jack that they already had crews out investigating three other sites where the dogs had alerted. He took one look at me, and the request became a demand.

"Just send them here. Do it now."

17

IN THE DAYS when Glastenbury was first settled, the township faced the same problem any mountain region faces: finding a reliable water supply. In order to do this, wells were hand dug and reinforced with limestone to keep them from collapsing. Once they'd dried up, however—or in Glastenbury's case, the town simply disappeared—those wells needed to be dealt with. Some were simply abandoned; others were covered with slabs of limestone and buried. They were forgotten.

Until now.

Ultimately, Jack and I didn't wait for the excavation crew before we started digging with whatever was available—in Jack's case, a stick and his steel-toed boots; in mine, the survival knife I always carry and my own hands. McDonough and the others arrived before we'd gotten far, armed with shovels and spades.

Sure enough, we found a limestone well cover buried a foot beneath the earth. It took Jack, Wade, and me to pry the thing off. Once we had, I gazed down into a hole that must have extended at least thirty feet into the earth, approximately five feet in diameter.

"You said all three of the dogs alerted here," McDonough said to me. I nodded. "But this thing has been sealed up tight for a good long time. Ariel can't be down there."

"I don't know what to tell you," I said, "except it's worth taking a closer look. If my dogs told us there's something down there, there's something down there."

He frowned, but he didn't argue with me.

To get started, we lowered a camera into the darkness, a flashlight attached to illuminate the space. It was hardly high tech—the flashlight was one I always carry with me, tied with twine to Jack's iPhone. The results were predictable: we couldn't see a damned thing. McDonough got on the phone to order the necessary equipment to do this the right way, but I wasn't interested in waiting around.

"Ariel!" I called down into the darkness. "Ariel Redfield. We're with the police—we're here to help you."

I fell silent. A dozen others from law enforcement were gathered around me. Every one of them seemed to be holding their breath.

There was no response.

"I'll go down," Jack volunteered. McDonough looked at him skeptically, but I shook my head.

"Forget it. I'm smaller, you'll barely fit in there. Besides which, I've been through all the rescue trainings. I've probably done a hell of a lot more work in conditions like these than you have."

Jack had no argument for that. I realized that I should probably say something more about my experience—most notably that I had only done two subterranean rescues in the past, and on the last one I'd hyperventilated halfway down and nearly passed out. I remained silent.

They fit me with a harness, hardhat, and headlamp. I let the rope go slack and eased my way to the edge of the crevice, my back to the opening. There was no graceful way to get down there—no ladder, no gradual incline. There was ground, and then there was nothing. Lacking a better idea, I inched down with my hands tight around the rope and my butt hanging over empty space, boot-clad feet on the limestone.

For seconds that felt like miles, I moved through the abyss. The smell of damp earth and something rotting and long dead closed in around me. Once I'd cleared the opening, I stopped climbing and let them simply lower me, hanging suspended in the darkness.

"Jamie?" Jack called down. "Everything all right?"

"Fine," I said through gritted teeth. "Give me another couple of feet—I can't see the bottom yet."

I strained to hear anything in the pervasive darkness beneath me. There was nothing. I trained my headlamp below as I was lowered another foot. And another. Periodically, Jack, Wade, or McDonough would call down to make sure I was all right. I called back the same thing, again and again: "I'm fine—give me more rope."

The stench grew stronger the farther down I got. My eyes had adjusted to the darkness enough that I could see the stone walls of the old well around me, barely a foot away in all directions. Illuminated by the light from my headlamp, the stones told me no story; they were just stones, grown pale and smooth with age. Occasionally a bug would skitter across my path, trying to get away from the unearthly glow I'd brought with me, but I ignored them.

There was something else down there, though—something I couldn't exactly see, but I could feel its presence, feel it moving around me. Waiting for me, open-mawed, with red eyes and sharpened claws. My breath came harder, my chest tightening in the vice grip of panic. I forced myself to breathe evenly.

"Jamie?" Jack called down.

I couldn't answer at first. I took a breath and held it for a second, then exhaled. They didn't give me any more rope—I hung suspended, the bottom just a couple of feet from me now, and in my growing terror flailed enough to send myself careening into the side of the well.

"Jamie!" Jack called again. "We can bring you back up—"

"No!" I shouted, forcing the word from my mouth. "I'm fine. I'm almost there, just give me another two feet and I'll hit the bottom."

They lowered me until I reached a foot of stagnant water that smelled as bad as any sewer. The water oozed into my boots, since I'd neglected to wear waders down here. I ignored the stench and the sensation and finally stood on my own two feet, grateful to feel the ground beneath me. Then, I looked around.

And I wasn't so grateful any longer.

Around me, the walls closed in. I turned slowly, the headlamp casting its light on the stonework. The limestone was worn and dry, despite the dampness of the air. About midway through my 360-degree turn to examine the space, I paused. The light focused on a single spot, where three words were written in faded, rust-colored letters on the pale stone.

GOD SAVE ME

A chill ran through me. At the same time, my boot hit

something in the shallow water at my feet.

A scream rose up from the ground, so shrill it seemed more animal than human. I froze where I was. It echoed, unearthly, in the narrow confines of the well.

"Jamie?" I heard Jack call down to me.

"It's not me," I called back. My heart hammered in my chest until it seemed my ribcage couldn't contain it much longer. "It wasn't me. Hang on."

I looked around, desperate now. The scream had faded, but it still continued faintly—as though locked in the confines of the earth itself. There was a pause above me, a loaded stillness I could feel though I was thirty feet down and out of sight.

"What wasn't you?" Jack called to me. The scream rose again—shrill, ragged, filling my head until I thought my ears would bleed with the sound. Jack didn't say anything, though, and now I knew why.

He didn't hear it.

Only I could hear that scream.

"I think I found something," I called up again, forcing myself to focus beyond that shattering sound. "There's writing on the stonework." I bent down so my light was trained on the ground and ran a gloved hand through the muck at my feet.

My fingers closed around a long, solid object beside my right foot. Before I pulled it from the mud, I knew what it was.

"There's human remains down here," I called up at last. "I've got a femur here, and someone wrote on the wall of the well. They must have fallen in."

No one said the thing I was sure we were all thinking:

How the hell does someone fall into a well that's covered with a stone seal and buried beneath a foot of soil?

The scream had faded at last, the remnant of the sound just the faintest vibration in the earth beneath my feet. Bear is the only other person I've met who can hear those cries of the dead the way I can. I wonder sometimes if the dogs can, particularly Phantom, but...well, she's a dog. I can't exactly ask her. But there are times when I hear something and Phantom will stop at the same time, head cocked, ears pricked, as though whatever parallel world the spirits walk is clear to her, as well.

"I take it whoever was down there wasn't down there recently," McDonough called.

I looked at the femur in my hand. It was impossible to tell whether it had belonged to male or female, child or adult—or at least it was impossible for me. An expert would probably have better luck. The one thing that was clear, however, was that the bone had been here much more than just a few days.

"No," I said. "The bone's clean. It can't belong to Ariel."

Which begged the question: what had the dogs alerted to here? Though some of the dogs had been cross trained, few were actually cadaver dogs. They were looking for one specific individual: Ariel Redfield. So why were they all alerting above this well?

"Come on back up," McDonough called down. "We'll send a crime scene tech down to recover the rest of the remains, just leave everything as you found it."

I lay the bone back down in the water and grabbed the harness that still hung suspended above me. After I fastened myself in, I tugged on the rope and they began to pull me up.

I'd barely gone five feet before the screams began again. They sounded closer this time—as though whatever barrier had separated us before was thinner now.

I tried to keep my focus, work past the paralyzing fear the sound inspired. I've been hearing the cries and the laughter and the whispered words of the dead for the better part of my life; since eight years old, they have been a reality for me.

"Quiet," I whispered into the air, hoping Jack and McDonough couldn't hear me. "Screaming does you no good… Tell me what you want me to know."

Instead of quieting, though, the scream escalated until it reached a fever pitch, no thin membrane left to separate that world from my own. A headache rang in my temples. I tugged on the rope, shouting over the disturbance inside my own head.

"Stop!" I called. "Wait a second."

Abruptly, my ascent was halted.

I hung in midair once more, and rocked myself until I came into contact with the limestone wall. I clung to the rough surface, bare fingers scrabbling against the stone as I twisted to give myself a better view of the walls around me. The scream continued, a sustained wail that I prayed would end before I went mad.

And then, I saw it.

My light shone on a circle in the stonework, perhaps three feet across.

I inched closer.

"There's a tunnel!" I called up. "It looks like it goes on for a while—it's about ten feet off the ground here."

I thought again of the number of times the dogs had

alerted throughout the forest this morning and last night, seemingly for no reason. The question of how the bone I'd found had come to be here.

The number of disappearances in these woods over the years.

"I'm going in," I called back. "There's enough room, I'll just keep the rope on."

The screaming stopped as suddenly as it had started.

I grabbed hold of the stonework around the opening and maneuvered my way inside.

●

"Do you hear anything now?" Ren whispered, her eyes wide.

Bear listened. His ears were still ringing from the scream that had woken him. "No," he said. He looked toward the window again, searching for a sign of the girl in the sweater. There was nothing, though. They'd been here more than twenty-four hours, the sky now dark outside. He'd heard nothing from his mother. Nothing from anyone. On the bright side, he hadn't bled to death yet.

"So Mary isn't back?" Ren asked. Mary: the girl in the red sweater. They'd taken to calling her that now.

"No," Bear said. "There's nobody there now. Maybe I dreamed it."

She looked doubtful. Anyone else would be doubtful of all the bullshit about seeing dead people; hearing their screams. With Ren, it was the other way around. The second he started denying the things he saw and heard, that was when she got pissed off.

"How do you feel?" she asked after a few seconds. He tried to move his arm and blanched at the pain, though he managed to keep it together enough not to yell. Or cry.

"It hurts," he said. "But I can handle it."

She frowned and scooted closer, her hands cool on his burning skin as she checked the bandages. "The bleeding has slowed, but it's seeping a lot. We need to get you out of here, get you on antibiotics."

"Dean will let us go soon," he said. He saw the doubt in her eyes, and heard it in his own voice. Why would Dean let them go? Just because he'd given his word? The old man was terrified. Heartsick. If Ariel was found the way Melanie had been, that would be the end of them both.

"It's night again," Ren said, nodding toward the window. "You think they've found anything yet?"

He thought again of the scream that had woken him. The girl in red, and whatever she'd been trying to tell him.

"I'm pretty sure they've found something," he said after a few seconds. "I just don't know how much good it'll do us."

●

"How far in does it go?" I heard a voice behind me ask. I was on my hands and knees in the tunnel, inching along at a Basset's pace. At the words, I turned and was blinded by a bright flashlight. Jack's voice directly behind it.

"I'm not sure," I called back. "What are you doing down here?"

"No way am I letting you in here alone," he said. I heard him coming closer. "Since when do you get to have all the fun?"

"If this is your idea of fun, remind me to never go on a date with you."

"I wasn't actually asking. If I were, though, I'm sure I could come up with something a little more original than spelunking in a subterranean prison."

"Well, in that case…" I stopped, and checked myself. I was flirting. What the hell was I doing flirting, in a situation like this? I was the worst mother in the world. "Do you have any idea why they'd have something like this out here?" I asked, steering us back to business.

"Not a clue. It looks like this whole system is hand dug, though, so it must have been done at the same time the well was made."

"I can't imagine the work that must have gone into it. What was the point?" I thought of the scream I'd heard. The bone at the bottom of the well. The words written on the wall.

"You know, they used to say that Glastenbury Mountain was cursed—that Native Americans wouldn't even come up here, because there was something evil about the place," Jack said.

"Old wives' tales," I said. "There are a series of stone cairns at the top of the mountain pre-dating colonial times by several hundred, if not thousand, years. Those cairns follow a line all the way down to Nantucket, possibly one meant to mirror the path of the sun. If they took the time to lug mammoth stones up here to build something like that, they couldn't have been that shy about spending time here."

There was a pause before Jack responded. "When did you have time to research that?"

"Last night. Rita had already given us some info—at

least the disappearances and the folklore associated with the mountain."

"But you don't believe those? Despite…" He paused. "Well—you know."

"Despite whatever it is that goes on with me," I said, aware of what he was implying, "in my experience most things have a logical explanation. I don't know why or how Bear and I can see, hear, or experience what we do, but I think the reality of that is something scientists will one day figure out: a parallel universe or a link to past and present energies that we just don't understand right now. That doesn't mean I believe in alien abduction or the Loch Ness monster."

We'd been following the rough stonework long enough now that my knees were raw from the trek, my hands torn beneath my gloves. I stopped when I reached the end of my rope.

"How much farther do you think it goes?" Jack asked.

"No idea, but I mean to find out." I unclipped the rope from my harness only to feel a hand on my ankle a second later.

"What the hell are you doing? I thought you told me yesterday that you do what makes sense. McDonough's already not happy with the fact that you're down here, but you've got the SAR credentials that mean he's willing to look the other way as long as I'm with you. Now you want to go even further? How does *that* make sense?"

My heart was pounding so hard I was sure Jack could hear the beat echo off the walls around us. He was right. I hadn't felt this out of control for years—in that time, I'd worked hard to become someone people took seriously. But there was that screaming in the back of my head; the memory of my little sister all those years ago, vanished without a trace. And, above all that, there was Bear.

Waiting for me to save him.

"I have to do this. Something's down there," I said. "This may lead to wherever Ariel is now—in fact, there's a good bet it does. I'm not stopping until I figure out where it comes out. We're running out of time."

"Let someone else do it," Jack persisted. "Someone with the right equipment."

"I have all the equipment I need. This is the only thing I can do right now: find Ariel. I'm not stopping."

For all my fighting, the search didn't last much longer. Ten minutes later, I found a small pile of crumbled rock in my path. I shone my light up ahead, and my heart sank.

The tunnel was littered with rock and debris, the path virtually unpassable. Regardless, I continued on. Seconds later, I felt that familiar hand on my ankle. This time, however, there was no room for negotiation in Jack's voice

"Stop. We're going back—we'll get a team in here to make sure it's safe. If you destabilize the tunnel, you could get us both killed. What good does that do Bear and Ren?"

I stopped, still on hands and knees, breath coming faster. Through the rock, a hoarse cry rose, lifting the hair along the back of my neck. Jack tugged gently on my foot.

"Come on, Jamie. I want you to talk to Gordon, anyway. Please."

Reluctantly, I maneuvered in the awkward space until I could turn around. The cry fell off to soft weeping that seemed to move with me; settled into my skin and bones. I kept moving.

I'd gone no more than a couple of feet before I heard something behind me—the sound of someone's breath, the slow drag of a body along the limestone. Instead of a scream this time, for the first time I heard a girl's voice. Her words were unmistakable.

Go faster.

"Jack," I said. I couldn't hide the fear in my voice. He paused. "No—don't stop. Faster. Go faster."

To his credit, Jack didn't question me.

Whatever was behind me had stopped moving. I heard something else, though—something far more terrifying. The sound of a match being struck. From the corner of my eye, I saw the flicker of the flame. Smelled the unmistakable sulfur dioxide.

"Shit. Go, Jack. Go!"

"What's going on?" he called back.

"Just move!"

He went faster, me behind him crawling for all I was worth, suddenly cognizant of just how ineffective crawling actually is. I longed to get to my feet and run, but there was no room.

Something hissed behind me, the smell of the sulfur lingering. I knew an instant before it happened; heard the girl's cry, her words of warning, the air getting heavier and the tunnel more oppressive in that single instant when everything hung in the balance.

In the moment before the charge went off.

There was a gust of hot air behind me powerful enough to push me forward, followed by a deafening roar.

And then, the walls came tumbling down.

18

"HE LIKES US to live underground with him," the girl said to me. She was pretty in a Gibson girl kind of way, with neat features, dark hair, and a red sweater frayed at the edges. She stood in front of me in a darkened cavern, her forehead furrowed and her eyes pensive.

"Who does?" I asked. The air was warm, oppressive, like it was heated by the fires of hell itself. I didn't want to be here.

"The shadow man," she said. "He came for us and brought us here. Wanted us to stay, but we tried to leave."

"You keep saying 'us.' Who's us?"

She looked around. For the first time, I noticed a dozen people—both men and women, young and old—watching us from the back of the cave. They huddled closer, all of them pale, unwashed. Many of them injured.

"He left us here," the girl said. "But now I'm supposed to get us out. Bring us home."

"You…" I stopped. "How long have you been here?"

She glanced back at the others, then looked at me seriously. Her eyes seemed to glow in the darkness. "I don't know. Sometimes I think, not long at all. And other times,

I think maybe…" She swallowed hard, clearly frightened. When she spoke again, she'd lowered her voice so the others couldn't hear us. "I think something has gone wrong. And I can't tell what it is… I only know that the shadows locked us here for what felt like a long, long time. He was gone so long, we'd almost forgotten him."

"And now?" I said.

"And now, someone's here. Running. Hiding. And she brought the shadow man back."

There was a sound like breaking glass in the distance. The girl looked up, fear crossing her face. "I have to go. I have to keep us safe."

"Wait—" I started, but she paid no attention. She turned and limped toward the others.

I looked down, and saw empty space below her right knee, where her leg had once been.

●

"Jamie," a voice whispered to me. Familiar, but hard to distinguish above the roaring in my head and the persistent screams of someone in the distance. I felt a cool hand on my forehead, and started awake at the contact.

Jack peered down at me, his concern plain. His flashlight was in hand, casting an eerie glow over the proceedings. Blood ran down the side of his forehead from a gash that looked deep. "There was a cave-in."

"An explosion," I said. "I heard someone behind us—I could smell the charge, but we weren't fast enough."

He looked baffled. "I just heard the rocks coming down. It felt like there may have been a small earthquake or something. I didn't hear anything else. Didn't smell anything." He moved past that detail long before I had, seemingly dismissing it as inconsequential. "Can you move?"

"Of course," I managed, though the words came out rough. I thought back, pushing past the image of the one-legged girl in the red sweater and the clan of onlookers she'd had with her. "Did you see who did it?"

He frowned. "I don't think it was a who, Jamie. Places like this aren't stable, and there's been some unusual seismic activity throughout New England for the past couple of years… Seriously, just focus for a second, all right? Can you move?"

It was only then that I realized why he was fixed on the question. In the blast I'd been thrown against the wall of the tunnel, my back against the limestone. Like Jack, I must have a head wound—I could feel wet, tacky blood on the side of my face alongside a persistent throb. My hardhat and headlamp had been thrown clear, the light shattered opposite where I sat. When I shifted, it became clear that the head wound wasn't the only thing I had to worry about.

I looked down at my lap.

A Phantom-sized slab of limestone lay across my right leg.

Beyond it, I peered through the still-rising dust and the settling debris. The path we'd been following was blocked off. There was no way we could get any farther. Then, I looked back the way we'd come.

My heart stuttered and my chest constricted at the sight of another wall of limestone and debris.

We were trapped.

"Shit," I said.

"Yeah," Jack agreed grimly. "You can say that again. I'm going to try and move the stone, all right?"

He moved forward without waiting for word from me, but I stopped him with a hand on his arm. That simple movement was enough to send a jagged, wrenching pain through my leg.

"What?"

"I should check for other injuries first," I said reluctantly. It wasn't something I was looking forward to. "I think I'm all right, but if there's internal bleeding, we'll need to handle this a little differently than we would otherwise."

"I didn't even think of that. Jesus."

"Most people wouldn't. I've been doing this for a while." I hesitated as he continued to regard me with a combination of curiosity and overt terror. "Would you mind turning around?"

He looked confused. "This isn't really the place for modesty—"

"Please."

He handed me his flashlight, and turned around. I waited until he was facing away, then carefully lifted my T-shirt up over my stomach to just below my breasts. I put the flashlight in my teeth and searched for signs of bruising, then palpated my abdomen all the way back to my kidneys. My fingers paused at the burn scar that runs along the left side of my body, from my ribcage down to my upper thigh. The skin was rough, but well healed after eight long years. I moved down further still and pressed my fingers to the tender flesh at my lower waist.

The simple act of moving brought on another wave of pain—this one severe enough that I gasped. The flashlight fell to the ground, and Jack turned.

He saw the scar before I could pull my shirt back down. Without comment, he handed the penlight back to me and then, with light, gentle fingers, he pulled the T-shirt back down to my waist.

"Okay?" he asked. His eyes held mine. There were questions there, surprise—pain even, I thought, though that pain didn't seem to cross over into pity.

"Yeah," I said. "Not great, but I think the only injury we need to worry about is my leg. I don't know if you'll be able to move the rock on your own."

As though answering a call I had yet to send out, a shout came from the head of the tunnel, muffled by the layer of debris that now obstructed our path.

"Jamie!" Cheryl's voice. I couldn't even imagine her venturing down here. "Can you hear me?"

"We're all right," Jack called back to her. "Jamie's pinned, but we're both okay."

"Thank God," she shouted back. "You scared the ever-loving shit out of all of us." Her voice was getting louder—she was coming toward us.

"What happened?" Jack called.

"Earthquake. I about shit my pants when I realized what was happening," she said. "You owe me a new pair of Carhartts, Jamie Flint."

"Get us out of here and I'll buy you a gown," I said. My voice was strained, the pain now radiating from my leg through to my entire body.

"They need to make sure things are stable before we start digging you out, make sure we don't do more harm than good," Cheryl said. "Things seem pretty steady in there for now?"

Jack shone the flashlight through the cramped space. The reality of the situation dawned yet again, my chest tightening as understanding took hold. We were trapped. Bear was counting on me, and I was going to fail him.

"Jamie?" Cheryl's voice came through again.

"We're okay," Jack said, answering for me since I seemed to have lost the power of speech myself. "It's tight in here, but I think it's stable for now. Just get us out as fast as you can."

"We're on it," came Cheryl's reply. A moment later, the scant beam of light from the other side vanished, and I heard her leave us.

When she was gone and we were alone, the world fell silent. My fingers tightened reflexively in the darkness. I thought of Phantom, wishing for just a moment that she were here. There's something about animals that's always been inherently soothing for me; in the worst of circumstances, the presence of nonhumans—whether dogs or cats, hares or horses—has kept me going. There was nothing like that now, and the lack was notable and profound.

"We'll get out of here," Jack said, breaking the silence between us.

"I know," I said. My unspoken question hung in the air: *But will we get out in time?*

"How's your leg?"

"Fine."

"Circulation is okay?" he asked.

I wiggled my toes in my boots, then twisted as much as possible to feel the pulse behind my knee. It hurt like hell, but in this case that was a good sign. "It's all right—blood's still flowing, anyway."

"Good. I should probably try to move the rock."

I resisted the urge to groan, knowing how much it would hurt. But he was right: the ideal in this kind of situation would be to get the rock off within fifteen minutes of the injury. I wasn't sure how much farther past that we were, but the clock was definitely running. "Okay. Go ahead."

He set his flashlight on the floor of the tunnel, but it was a piss-poor excuse for illumination. I picked it up and held it above us in my left hand, the beam concentrated on the slab over my right leg.

"Better?"

"Better," he agreed. "Far from perfect, but better."

I watched as he stretched his long legs out in the small space, trying to brace himself to get a sure hold on the rock. In the right circumstances, this would have been a breeze—it wasn't like a building had fallen on me, after all. It was a big slab of rock, but I doubted it weighed more than thirty pounds. It was the positioning that was the bitch of the scenario.

"You'll need to lift it clean off," I said. "If you drag it, you'll do more harm than good."

"If I lift it, do you think you can move out of the way?"

"Yeah. Just get it off me."

It took two or three agonizing tries before he was able to lift it up and I scrambled sideways before he let it fall again. The restored blood flow felt like razorblades racing through my veins and my knee was already bruised and swelling. Crush syndrome—when the kidneys shut down as a result of a traumatic crush injury—was a distinct possibility, but I was trying to ignore that thought.

Fluid loading was the recommended treatment for

this kind of scenario, preferably sodium bicarbonate given intravenously. They'd want to take me to the hospital.

Christ. I didn't have time for the hospital.

Jack checked the leg, but I could tell he didn't really know what he was looking for. "Is there anything else I can do?" he asked.

"Besides dig us out of here?"

"Besides that."

I shook my head.

He turned out the light in order to save batteries, but the darkness was oppressive and the air already growing stale. I felt as much as heard him shifting beside me, though he didn't touch me. Seconds became minutes. Finally, Jack cleared his throat.

"You do what makes sense, huh?" he said.

He sounded more weary than angry, but I felt terrible regardless. "I'm sorry," I said. "You shouldn't have followed me in."

"I'm starting to think you're right, actually."

"Yeah. Probably so." I paused. "I'm just trying to save my kid."

"I know," he said quietly.

Silence fell once more. More time passed. I heard digging nearby, and wondered how much progress they'd made toward getting us out.

"Talk to me," Jack said finally.

I turned my head toward his voice, but couldn't see anything in the absolute darkness that surrounded us. "What do you want me to say?"

He paused. I felt the weight of the questions I knew he had about my life: the scar he'd seen, my past with Brock

Campbell, the childhood I never spoke of. Instead, he went with something simpler.

"Why did you name your kid Bear?"

I laughed despite myself. "I was young," I said. "Old enough to have a kid…young enough to think naming him Bear was a good idea."

Usually, that put an end to the conversation when other people asked. Jack remained quiet, though, waiting for me to give him something more. I considered the question and, ultimately, opted for the truth.

"I was fifteen when I got pregnant. Scared out of my mind. My folks were…not happy with me." Tossed me out on my little Georgian behind, actually, though I didn't tell him that. "I was pretty much on my own for a while there—moved out West, and managed to take care of myself all right. Not long after I got there, I had this dream." I paused, remembering it. How alien the whole experience had been: this thing growing inside me that I didn't want, hadn't asked for, and yet…desperately wanted to keep.

"What was the dream?" Jack prompted.

"It was pretty straightforward, actually," I said. "I went into the delivery room, had the baby—the whole process felt so real in those dreams, I swear I could feel the contractions even then. So, I had the baby, and the doctor took it away for a minute and I remember being so afraid they wouldn't give him back. But finally, they brought him over."

"And it was a bear," Jack guessed.

I laughed again. "Yeah. I had the dream almost every night for most of my pregnancy. Sometimes it would be a black bear, sometimes a panda, sometimes a polar bear. So…"

"You named him Bear," he finished for me. He paused for a moment. "It could be worse, I guess. You could have dreamed he was an aardvark."

"Yeah. You've got a point."

Silence had descended for only a minute more before I gathered the resolve to ask my own question.

"Why didn't you call me?" I asked. "Last year, after you left Littlehope... I know we didn't have anything in writing, but I thought we had a plan. I wouldn't have been mad if you told me you wanted to do something else—I'm glad you got your job back. It would have been nice to hear something from you, though."

The words came out needier than I'd intended, and I hated the vulnerability I heard there. Jack cleared his throat. I imagined him there in the darkness, wishing for some way out of here. Finally, he spoke.

"You remember last year in that blizzard, when you told me...that thing?" he asked, more hesitant than I'd ever heard him.

Last year, when the entire town of Littlehope was in grave danger and a blizzard was blowing strong and it seemed at times that none of us would make it out alive, I'd made one of those mistakes I try to avoid where the opposite sex is concerned: I'd been honest.

"I told you I'd had a premonition," I said, "that somewhere along the lines, I'm supposed to save your life."

"Right," Jack said with a sigh. He didn't say anything more.

"I'm not sure how that's a problem," I said. "I didn't say that somewhere along the lines I'm supposed to murder you or bear your children or something. Saving your life should be a good thing."

"It should," he agreed. Somehow, however, it wasn't. "I can't really explain it—I'm sorry. The whole thing just makes me uneasy. I don't know how to handle the idea that I'll put you in danger somewhere down the road. That you'll have to make some kind of sacrifice, for me."

"How do you know it will be a sacrifice?" I said. "Maybe it will be as simple as me pushing you out of the path of an oncoming car. Or giving you the Heimlich maneuver over sandwiches."

A beat of silence followed. Then: "Do you really think that's the way it will play out?"

My non-answer was all he needed: we both knew it wouldn't be that simple. This premonition I'd had, some fuzzy impression I still couldn't completely define, didn't speak of something as innocuous as choking over stirfry some evening. Whatever linked us, there was something weightier than that in store for the two of us.

"I didn't mean to freak you out when I told you that," I said. "I thought we were in imminent danger of dying. I figured if I was going to save your life, it would probably have been then."

"But it wasn't," he reminded me.

"No," I agreed.

I sighed. The air was getting stale, the cramped space damp and too warm now. My head ached; my leg was on fire. Neither of us spoke again. If I'd given him an opening, made the request, I thought Jack would probably comfort me. Hold me, maybe—he seemed the kind of person who would fall easily into that role. The great protector. I considered that for a moment: what it would be like to have his arms around me, my head against his broad chest. His hands in my hair; his lips at my ear.

Steady, girl. Definitely not a road I wanted to go down—and certainly not now.

That light no one else could see still shone over his left shoulder. Lucia. I wondered if it would always follow him, the way my own ghosts followed me. I was fairly sure she had his best interests at heart, but it still made me wonder why she remained there. Was there something that needed to be resolved? Her killer brought to justice, maybe? There is a darkness that follows me as surely as the light that kept pace with Jack, but I know that will keep following me for a very long time. Only one person to be brought to justice in that case; only one way the spirit that follows me will have peace. I'm not willing to give myself up to make that happen.

I felt something light against my arm, sweeping down with surprising tenderness. Far from ghostly, that touch.

"I'm sorry I didn't call," Jack said. His hand remained at my arm, a comforting weight.

Before I could reply, there was movement again on the other side of the barricade. A voice came through—this one belonging to Agent Paulsen.

"You two still in there?" she called.

"No, we popped out for coffee," Jack returned.

"Funny, Juarez," she said. "We're going to start moving the rocks, see how we do getting back through. You okay with that?"

"We're more than okay with it," I said. "Just get us the hell out of here."

"Hang tight. Another thirty minutes, maybe an hour, and you'll be out."

I leaned my head back against the limestone again, trying

to shift my body to ease the pressure on my leg. Jack started to take his hand away, but a sound escaped my throat—not quite a whimper, but uncomfortably close. I felt the cool pressure of his hand against my face, his knuckles a light caress slipping past my cheek. Through the rock, somewhere far off, I heard the haunting cries that I'd heard earlier. They sounded farther away now, as though whoever—whatever—it was had been carried far from here. Not willingly.

I closed my eyes. Despite the desire, I never leaned into Jack's touch.

●

"Something's going on out there," Bear said, his gaze locked on the darkened night outside the window. Not that it did any good—he couldn't see a damned thing. But he could hear, and what he heard was definitely not good.

After Phantom's howl, Casper had started up. Bear could tell because he'd memorized the barks of all their dogs: Phantom's deep-throated shepherd bark; Casper's high-pitched, almost deafening bully bark; Minion's feminine *woof*... They were as distinct as human voices to Bear. On top of those dogs, he heard a dozen others he didn't recognize. The forest had to be filled with searchers as far as he could tell, the dogs' voices carrying well in the quiet of this creepy damned cabin.

None of them sounded happy tonight.

"Maybe they found something," Ren suggested. She stood beside him but not touching, both looking out opposite sides of the same window.

"If they found something, they would have alerted.

These definitely aren't alerts—they're freaking out. Besides, it's too late for them to be searching by now."

It was just after eleven, according to the clock. Still, Ren shook her head. "Your mom will keep looking for Ariel as long as it takes, as long as she knows we're in trouble."

Bear didn't say anything to that. He wished he could be so certain, but the truth was that his mom was a handler first. Always had been. You didn't overwork the dogs—that was the first rule of this whole business. Everyone benefited if you acted in the K-9's best interest whenever possible, and Jamie had always lived by that.

"You think I'm wrong?" Ren asked. He shrugged, but didn't say anything. He watched Ren's reflection in the glass, and saw her roll her eyes. "Jamie would do anything for you."

"I don't want her to do anything for me," he said after a long few seconds. "I just want her to do her job, and take care of the dogs in the process. If she does that, I'll know she did everything she could to find Ariel and get us out of here."

Outside, another couple of dogs howled in the wilderness. Bear didn't recognize them—did they belong to the Vermont K-9 teams who'd come in? He would have thought they'd have gone by now, knowing there was a killer out there somewhere. Phantom answered the call, and that started a whole new string of canine wails across the forest. Then, he heard Dean's voice outside the door. Both he and Ren froze.

"What the hell's going on out there?" Dean demanded. The tension was strung so tight in his voice, Bear thought the man might snap. A second later, the door slammed open.

Dean stood in the doorway with Wendy beside him.

Neither of them looked good, but it was Dean who worried Bear. The nearly legible threads he'd seen on the air around the man earlier were nothing but tangles now, blackened and rotting. Bear was reminded of worms left to bake alive on the concrete on hot summer days.

"What's happening? What's going on out there?" Dean demanded of them.

"How should we know?" Ren asked. Her voice held some of the old spirit, something Bear was only briefly happy to hear. "How are we supposed to know anything if you lock us in here and refuse to let us go?"

"You saw something earlier," Dean accused Bear. "You know the same kinds of things Claude does. I could tell the second we started talking. What's happening out there? Why would the dogs be barking like that?"

"I don't know," Bear said. Dean took a threatening step toward him, his face twisted with anger. Bear held up his good hand and stepped sideways just enough to block the man from reaching Ren. "I swear!" he said. "If I knew something, I'd tell you. As it is, all I can say is that something is happening. But I can't tell anything without talking to my mom or the others."

Dean nodded. His gaze drifted to the window, and Bear had to resist the urge to look as well. For a few seconds, the old man just stared. Beside him, Wendy looked tired. Afraid. Ready to quit—which Bear figured might work in their favor, or might not.

"If you know something…" Dean began.

"I'd tell you," Bear said. He didn't know whether or not it was a lie, but he figured it didn't really matter. Right now, he didn't know shit.

Dean looked out the window again and shook his head. "It's a goddamn nightmare," he muttered under his breath. He turned around and left the room without another word.

Wendy stood there for a minute after he was gone, like she wasn't sure whether or not she was supposed to follow him.

"Are you hungry?" she asked.

Earlier that day, Bear had explained to her that both he and Ren were vegetarians. The woman had looked almost baffled at the news at first, before she'd dutifully nodded. That evening, she'd brought them homemade vegetable stew.

"We're all right," Ren said. "We just want to go home."

Wendy nodded. Her eyes were shadowed, her skin sallow. Half the ghosts Bear knew looked better off than she did. "I know. You're not alone—that's all I can tell you."

She turned and left without another word.

19

AT TWENTY MINUTES PAST midnight, an hour after rescuers had broken through to set us free, I sat sideways in the front pew of the Glastenbury Church so I could keep my foot elevated, an ice pack against my knee. Phantom was asleep at my feet, while Casper and Minion had retired for the night after what I knew had been a long day for both of them. Both were now fast asleep in their crates for the night.

Beaten and sore and with no end in sight, I wished I had a crate I could crawl into myself.

After McDonough had briefed the swelling ranks of law enforcement and searchers on where everything stood, he had dismissed everyone but Jack and Rita Paulsen. Despite my fatigue, I wasn't budging till I knew what our status was now that the tunnel had been discovered, so McDonough escorted Jack and Rita into his cramped office in the back of the church for a little privacy. I could hear him giving them both a dressing down, as clear as if I'd been in the room with them. The gist of the trouble, as far as I could tell, was that Jack had gone over McDonough's head in order to make the trek to see Gordon Redfield, and then had done that one better by getting them to bring Gordon—accompanied by

U.S. marshals—out here. He'd forced McDonough's hand, and McDonough was not a happy man as a result.

I perked up my ears, listening shamelessly as the conversation continued.

"At this point, we don't have a lot else to go on," Jack said. Based on the tension in his voice, it was taking a lot for him to stay calm. "Dean has two hostages—one of them injured—and so far he's shown no interest in letting them go if we don't find Ariel. This may be our best chance of not only finding her, but of figuring out who the killer is. We've got less than twelve hours before Dean's deadline. Bringing Gordon in was the best idea I could come up with."

"The best *we* could come up with," Rita interrupted. "Jack wasn't the only one responsible for going to Texas last night. If you're going to give someone hell about it, at least include me."

"Trust me, Jack's not the only one who'll pay for this," McDonough said. "But he was the one who booked the charter and made the trip. You may see a reprimand in your file, Paulsen, but it's Juarez's ass in a sling."

I winced. Jack hadn't been in a great position before all this, but now I couldn't imagine how he would be able to save his career. Though based on his actions and some of the things he'd said lately, I wasn't sure he cared.

The conversation went on like this for a while, going nowhere, until McDonough was the one who finally drew the whole thing to a close. "I'm done fighting. If we're doing this tonight, let's get him in here already. First light tomorrow I want search teams out looking for the other end of that tunnel."

It was almost one a.m.; first light would be in five hours.

Bear was spending his second night with Dean and his family. McDonough had told me he'd spoken with both Bear and Ren over Dean's radio at one point that afternoon, but I hadn't been in on the conversation. The lack of connection to Bear, that feeling that he was lost and I had no way to reach him, hurt more than my aches and pains from mudslides or collapsing tunnels.

Jack and Rita emerged from the office then, both of them dragging. Paramedics had bandaged Jack's head, but neither of us had had a chance to get cleaned up yet. He looked like half the dust and debris from the tunnel had saturated his skin by now, seeping down to the bone.

"Everything all right?" I asked him.

McDonough came out before he could answer, saw me, and frowned. "I thought I told you to go back to the room and get some rest," he said.

"And I told you, I'm not going anywhere until I know what the plan is for tomorrow. The clock is winding down. If we can't find Ariel by noon, what are you going to do about it?"

"We have a plan in place," McDonough said. "It's not your job to worry about that. This is on us."

I grimaced, but was too tired to come up with a rational argument. "Well, regardless—I'm staying while you talk to Gordon. He could have information I need to help us find Ariel." Even as I said it, I knew it was a longshot. He'd been in prison half a country away for years now. Whatever connection he'd had to the case back in 2009, what could he possibly know now?

A few minutes later, two U.S. marshals brought Gordon

Redfield in wearing handcuffs and leg irons. He was an attractive man likely in his late forties, short and lean and dark-haired, with thick arms and a muscular chest. His eyes were clear and intelligent, and they lingered on each person in the room by turns. He stayed a beat or two longer on Rita before he moved on. Frowned at McDonough, who glared back at him.

"McDonough," he said gruffly. The tension in the room was palpable, and I sensed something red, festering, in the air between the two men.

Phantom had been lying peacefully beside me, but she awoke at Gordon's entrance and was instantly on alert. I couldn't tell whether her reaction was to Gordon himself, or if she was responding to the tension between him and McDonough.

Gordon nodded to me with a grim smile. "You're Jamie?"

"I am."

At the shift in attention, Phantom sat up and watched the man intently. While she wasn't growling, I could tell she wasn't comfortable with something.

"Jack told me about what's happening with your son. I'm sorry about that. Dean doesn't always make the best decisions under pressure, but this isn't like him. I don't know what the hell he's thinking."

"I don't think anyone does," I said.

Gordon had a brief consultation with one of the marshals who'd brought him in, and they led him to the pew beside me. Once he was seated, he shifted his attention to the others. "So, what are you waiting for? I'm assuming they won't just let me stay here forever. What have you got?"

Rita was the one who spoke up. She pulled up a folding

chair and set it directly opposite Gordon, close enough for the two to touch, which surprised me. "We were hoping you might have something for us, actually."

"Oh yeah? Well, then I think you're going to be disappointed. I don't have any theories."

"That's not what you said the last time I was at the prison," she said. Gordon frowned.

"Damn it, Rita," he said.

"You really want to rot in prison for the rest of your life for something you didn't do?" Rita pressed. "Just tell them what you think already—stop trying to protect a man who never deserved your compassion."

"What man?" McDonough interrupted.

"I don't have any proof," Gordon said, his expression darker now. He glared at Rita, the weight of his anger a tangible thing. Phantom sat up beside me, taking in the exchange.

"I'm not looking to convict at the moment, I'm looking for a goddamn theory," McDonough said.

Gordon didn't say anything.

"Gordon," Rita prompted.

"The past eight years thinking about it," Gordon said slowly, "I've narrowed it down to one suspect who could have killed the eight prostitutes around the country, and then had the opportunity to come back and murder Katie and June."

He kept his gaze on the ground, but there was something calculated about the posture that didn't sit well with me. As though he were an actor in a play. Rita touched his arm. "You have to tell someone, Gordon."

A moment of silence passed in the room. The clock read

1:13. Less than eleven hours to find Ariel and figure out who murdered Melanie. Which meant Bear could have less than eleven hours to live.

"Please," I said when Gordon still didn't speak. "You know your brother. Can you honestly guarantee my son's safety if we don't deliver on our end of the deal? Whatever theory you have or don't have, now isn't the time to hold back."

He scratched his head, the chains on his wrists jangling with every movement, and took a long, deep breath before he began. "Like I said, it's just a theory. But my brother Barrett was a salesman back then, and he traveled for his job. I haven't been able to get records on where he was during his entire stint with the company, but I ran into him while I was working in Cleveland. He had regular clients there."

"Which is where the first murders took place," Jack told me before he shifted his attention back to Gordon. "But Barrett's name came up in the original trial. It went nowhere. He had alibis for every murder."

"Alibis can be bought," Gordon said shortly. "You know that. All the alibis you've got from him are from low-rent women who wouldn't think twice about lying to the cops for the right man. Barrett can be a charming son of a bitch under the right circumstances."

"We'll look into it," McDonough said. He nodded toward the marshals. "If that's what you've got for us, I think we're set. You start the long trip back, you can make it back to Texas by morning."

"That's not all he has," Rita said. Gordon's jaw was so tense I was sure he'd crack a tooth. He shook his head, but she took his arm. I saw her press her nails into the skin there, an urgency about her that was frankly a little unnerving to see. "Tell them, damn it."

Gordon shifted in his seat. He shook his head. Rita sighed in frustration.

"If you won't say it, I will," she said. "There's someone else who was known to be in the immediate vicinity of two of the prostitutes killed, and there are rumors that he met at least three of the other victims personally. And he was onsite during the investigation at the Redfield homestead in Adams."

A profound silence had fallen over the room, all eyes on Gordon now. His eyes remained on the floor as Rita continued.

"No one ever knew about your connection to the victims, did they, Gerard?" she asked McDonough.

"You're not serious," McDonough said. The shock in his eyes appeared genuine.

"Trust me—I've never been more serious in my life," Rita said.

"Would you excuse us for a minute?" McDonough said. His focus shifted to Gordon, still sitting silent on the pew. "I'd like to have a word with Gordon."

"Forget it," Gordon said. He lifted his eyes for the first time. "You're not leaving me alone with him. You do, and I can all but guarantee I won't make it out of this place alive."

"What the hell are you talking about?" McDonough demanded. He stood, but then remained frozen in place, his fury a physical force in the room. "You can't just come in here and make baseless accusations." He looked at Rita. "What the hell did he tell you? Before he starts spouting his half-assed theories, just keep in mind what this asshole put you through. You may remember, I was there for the whole thing. I never gave you any reason not to trust me... I know firsthand that you can't say the same thing about him. The man is playing you."

I watched Rita's expression shift, a shadow of doubt in her eyes. She might have changed her tune about Gordon, but she still didn't trust him completely.

"What did he tell you?" McDonough pressed. "That I was part of the sexcapades Gordon and his crew had going when you two were married? Because I can tell you right now, I never was. Not once. And if he's trying to feed you that bullshit, think about what else he's lying to you about." He shook his head. "You're so intent on busting him out, so convinced you pinned him wrong all those years ago... I'm telling you, you were right. He's never been worth a damn."

The intensity of the exchange between him and Rita surprised me—it felt like we were all horning in on something intimate, a conversation between two people who knew each other better than anyone had ever expected. I certainly hadn't, until I'd seen the exchange at the motel. Based on the look on Gordon's face, it was a surprise to him, too.

A beat of tense silence passed before Rita's gaze shifted to Gordon. "You told me you had proof."

A pulse in Gordon's jaw ticked. McDonough stood there, poised for violence, but there was a righteous indignation there that I believed. Gordon, not so much. And for her part, every ounce of Phantom's energy was fixed on Gordon. Her reaction told me more than any court transcript ever could, about the kind of man we were dealing with.

She didn't like him. And I sure as hell didn't trust him.

"Not physical proof," Gordon said. Backtracking now.

"Because I was never part of it, you son of a bitch," McDonough ground out.

"What kind of proof, then?" Rita pressed. "You were there, right? All these…trysts the agents had, you were in the room with them. You either saw him there, or you didn't."

"I wasn't there every time," Gordon said. "There were rumors that other agents were involved. Men who kept a lower profile than we did." He was grasping at straws, spinning the story even as he sat there. It would have been pathetic, if I didn't find the whole thing so damned terrifying.

McDonough shook his head, turning his back on the man. "Christ. You're the same man you always were, Gordon. You open your mouth, and the only thing that comes out are lies." He nodded toward the U.S. marshals now standing watchful off to the side, then looked at Rita. "Make sure they keep an eye on him. If you still believe any of the horseshit he's handing you, go over what you think he can tell you about this case tonight. I want him gone tomorrow."

And with that, McDonough strode down the aisle and out of the church without another word. The heavy double doors slammed shut with a clatter, and the room fell silent.

Rita stood stiffly and went to a folding table at the back of the room lined with files and photos. She gathered them and brought them back to Gordon, setting them on the pew beside him.

"You should take a look at these. See what you make of them."

"Rita—" Gordon began.

She shook her head quickly. I saw the glint of tears in

her eyes. "Don't."

He fell silent.

Awkward as the exchange may have been, I pushed past it—aware once more of the minutes flying past. I studied the 8x10s Rita had set down. I hadn't looked closely at the scene before, too shocked at Dean Redfield's reaction and the fallout that came after. Now, I watched as Gordon stood, awkward with the shackles around his ankles, and spread them across the old wooden pew.

The scene was as I remembered it: Melanie Redfield lying prone and naked on the ground, flesh flayed from her buttocks and breasts; the tree branch between her legs; the ligature marks around her neck. Gordon paused at one of the photos. Melanie had been rolled onto her back for the shot, the focus on the tree branch that had been shoved inside her. I looked away, sick, thinking of Gordon's words. What if Barrett truly was the killer? Bear and Ren were locked up there, in a place where I couldn't get to them. But Barrett could.

Gordon studied the photos dispassionately, his gaze keen. "Have you got the autopsy results yet?" he asked.

"Here," Rita said. She handed a manila folder to him. He opened it and read in silence for a few seconds before he shook his head.

"What about the others?" he asked. "Do you have the autopsies for the other girls? Katie and June? The prostitutes?"

Rita dug into a satchel propped against the wall and came out with a stack of files. She hesitated only a second before she handed them over.

Gordon took them and sat back down stiffly. The marshals remained at attention at the door, both of them young and blank-faced as we continued. Phantom finally settled back down beside me.

"It's the same guy," Gordon said after less than five minutes of silence.

"It's in your best interest to say that," Jack pointed out. "There are some differences here. A different kind of rope, for one thing."

"That's purely cosmetic," Gordon said. "You give this to any M.E. who knows anything at all and they'll tell you the same thing. Petechial hemorrhage points to strangulation; bruised—not broken—hyoid means the victim was choked multiple times before finally being killed; penetration with a foreign object. Flaying of the buttocks and breasts, strokes consistent with a right-handed perp. Left ear pierced for one victim; presumably, the right ear pierced for the other. They may have been tied with a different kind of rope, but the knots are the same."

"What about the force?" Jack asked. "The penetration is wrong."

I focused on Phantom rather than the words being said after that, but I caught the gist of it: there hadn't been enough force this time. Whoever had tortured the prostitutes prior to the Redfield murders had done considerably more damage than had been done to Melanie Redfield. I pet Phantom's head and tried not to think of Melanie Redfield's final hours, or the fact that somehow whatever had been done to her was perceived as less severe than what the victims before her had suffered.

"What about June and Katie?" I asked.

Gordon looked up from the files, as though he'd forgotten I was there. "What about them?"

"Was the force used with them the same as with the

prostitutes, or was it more like what's been done here?"

"The same," Jack said. "With them, it was to the letter. The judge may not have tried him for the murders of the prostitutes, but we were all certain: whoever did June and Katie was responsible for the other murders, as well."

"This is seven years later," Gordon noted. "Maybe the killer is trying to mix it up now, plant doubt—make it seem like it's not the same killer so I don't go free. Or maybe something happened to him, he's not as strong as he was back then."

"Barrett's been dealing with health issues," Rita said. "He was hospitalized twice last year, though I couldn't find out what the diagnosis was."

"He looks fine now," I said. "And McDonough certainly doesn't look like he's had any problems, if you're still thinking he could be a suspect."

"Where was McDonough when Melanie and Ariel went missing?" Gordon asked Jack.

"He's been here since I got here," Jack said. "He was the reason I got pulled in in the first place."

"Would he have had opportunity for something like this, though?" I asked. I was hardly a big fan of McDonough's, but pinning any of this on him seemed like too much of a stretch to me. "The media's been watching this place like hawks, not to mention all the other cops, wardens, and agents roaming around. It isn't like he has a low-visibility job."

"He could have snuck away," Gordon said. Rita looked away, eyes hard now. "There must have been diversions over the past few days. Maybe he has somewhere nearby where he hid the girls."

"We've still got a ticking clock here," Jack said, "so we don't really have time to debate any of this. I'll go up and talk to Barrett, see if I can find out where he thinks the girls were going the other morning. And feel out from there what his involvement might be."

"What about McDonough?" Rita prompted.

Jack hesitated. "We'll look into it—just do it quietly. God knows I'm not McDonough's biggest fan, but my gut says it's not him."

Gordon frowned, clearly not impressed with Jack's gut.

"I'll keep it quiet, don't worry," Rita said. "In the meantime, you two are running on fumes. There's nothing the searchers can do in the dark. Gordon and I will stay up and go over the files. At first light, I'll get the marshals to take us to the crime scene while everyone else continues the search for Ariel."

"Sounds like a plan," Gordon agreed. He didn't look enthusiastic, though. Based on the look in Rita's eyes, I was guessing the conversation they were about to have wouldn't be a pleasant one. By the time this was over and done, he might just be begging to go back to prison.

"I still have another couple of hours in me," Jack argued. "I could at least help go through the photos."

Rita shook her head. "Forget it. You nearly got crushed to death in a tunnel today, and you were in a mudslide the day before. That means you've earned a few hours' down time. You two go on," she said, including me in the nod. "Get cleaned up, and get some rest."

I didn't bother to argue. It would have been pointless, and the fact of the matter was that she was right. If I planned to be any good to anyone come morning, I needed at least a few hours to recuperate and get my head screwed back on straight.

I stood with some effort. "Come on," I said to Jack. "You look like hell, and I can't even see straight. We'll be back on by five."

Reluctantly, Jack agreed. As I limped to the door with Phantom at my hip and Jack at my other side, I looked back at the pew where Gordon was still seated. Rita had sat down opposite him in the folding chair again, both of them hunched over the files and photos. I'm not naïve: I know people do horrible things to one another on a regular basis. All I have to do is look to my own past to know that's fact. What happened to these women who'd been tortured, defiled, their lives snuffed out by this killer, though, seemed beyond evil. This wasn't something a human being did.

"Come on," Jack said quietly when he saw that I was fixating on the scene. "I'll drive you back to the hotel."

We walked back out into the cold night together, my mind locked on one thing only: the time. It was one-thirty a.m.

I had ten hours and thirty minutes left, and no idea how to find Ariel Redfield once morning came.

20

JACK DROVE US BOTH back to the motel in one of the oversized, government-issued SUVs. I sat in the passenger seat and stared out the window, thinking about everything that had happened over the course of the day. Ultimately, it all led me back to the conversation we'd just had in the conference room.

"Do you agree with Gordon?" I asked.

Jack turned to look at me, his face cast in a strange glow courtesy of the dashboard lights. "About what?"

"The suspects—that it was either Barrett or McDonough. That's a pretty narrow playing field."

"He's certainly had a lot of time to think about it."

That was true. Something still bothered me about the whole thing, though. "Why do you think he didn't say anything sooner? If he had this theory, these suspects, he could have put someone on the trail and maybe gotten the whole thing overturned."

"Family loyalty—"

"Only applies if it was Barrett," I pointed out. "If it was McDonough…"

"I think the McDonough thing is just wishful thinking

on Gordon's part," Jack said. "The man's a power-hungry ass, but just looking at opportunity alone, he didn't have time to do something to Melanie and Ariel over the last few days. There's no way it could be him."

"Was he with the Bureau when the whole sex thing broke?" I asked.

"He was." He fell silent. I read the pause, and waited for him to say whatever was on his mind. When he didn't, I filled in the blanks.

"Do you think he was involved?"

"I'm not sure," he said. "Like I said, McDonough is an ass. This doesn't really sound like him, though."

"So why would Gordon say something that could so easily be discredited?" I asked. "To make an accusation against McDonough while the man's right there, if he's wrong—"

"He didn't make the accusation, though," he pointed out. "Rita did."

"So maybe Gordon was spouting off theories with no basis in fact for some other reason," I ventured. I thought about the night before, considering what I'd seen. "Do you know if there's anything going on between Rita and McDonough?"

"They're friends," Jack said, shrugging. "I always got the sense he was fond of her."

Fond seemed like an understatement considering the way I'd seen McDonough watching her as she left his hotel room last night, though. I kept that thought to myself, unwilling to start yet another rumor that, at the end of the day, wasn't anyone's business.

"Why didn't you say something when the whole thing

was happening?" I asked instead. "The sex thing, I mean."

"I would have lost my job," he said. "Who would have benefited if it went public, anyway? We were taking care of it."

"How? By promoting degenerates and potentially railroading one man for murder?" I couldn't keep the scorn from my voice. To my surprise, I caught a glimpse of a smile when Jack glanced at me again. "You think that's funny?"

"Not at all. You just surprise me sometimes, that's all. I met you and thought you were so Zen, so together. But it turns out you've got more of an edge than I expected."

"Not usually. It's been an edge-inducing week."

He grunted at that, which I took as affirmation. "As for what you were saying: I don't think they promoted degenerates. As far as I know, they either fired or demoted those involved, sent everyone to counseling, and did their best to handle things in-house."

"So you really don't think McDonough was involved."

"No. I guess I don't." He sounded surprised by the realization.

"So, that brings us back to the original question," I said. "If you don't think it was McDonough, do you really think it could have been Barrett? I mean… First off, how did he even know the hookers his brother knew?"

A brief, uncomfortable silence followed. "Jack?" I prompted, when he didn't say anything.

He glanced at me, then back to the road. "Barrett used to travel with Gordon sometimes when he was younger. Or they'd get together if they were doing business in the same town."

"Get together?" I asked. I had an uneasy feeling I knew

where this was going, but it was too late to stop now. "As in…"

"Yeah," Jack said. "As in… Barrett was apparently around sixteen the first time it happened, according to Gordon."

"So, they would…" I stopped. I'm no blushing virgin, but I was having a hard time getting my head around this. "Would he just buy the hookers for his little brother, or would they actually…um, together?"

"Both, depending on mood and circumstance," Jack said.

Silence fell. "Wow," I finally managed. "Okay, so Barrett…*knew* the prostitutes who were killed. Do you think he could have done it?"

"I don't know," he said. He turned into the parking lot of Serenity Motel and found a space beside the cargo van we'd been using for our crew. The motel's motion-sensitive security light came on outside, but otherwise the place remained dark. He put the SUV in park, and left it idling as he turned to face me.

"We worked up a psychological profile before," he said. "We came up with a white male, late twenties to thirties, obsessive-compulsive, with above-average intelligence and a deep-seated hatred of women most likely rooted in mother or a maternal figure. He would have a job with a certain amount of autonomy and in which some travel was required, and some knowledge of crime scenes as well as anatomy."

"So, you're right," I said. "I don't know how well it fits Barrett, but based on the profile, I can see why Gordon looked good for the murders of the prostitutes—though not really of his sisters. He got too many things wrong that time, it makes no sense."

"Unless someone was setting him up," Jack said with a nod. "I know."

Phantom whimpered in the seat behind me, and I realized we'd been sitting there too long. It was late, and the day had been exhausting for everyone involved.

"We should go in," I said.

Jack agreed, but for a split second made no move. A sudden tension filled the air when he turned to look at me. His eyes held mine fleetingly before I retreated, wordlessly opening the passenger side door.

It was cool but dry for the moment, though more rain was predicted by morning. We walked in silence for a few seconds while I continued thinking about the case, Phantom at my left side, Jack at my right. The darkness was so complete that the trees were nothing but a walled shadow against a blackened night. Was Ariel out there right now? Still alive, desperately waiting for someone to find her? Or had the killer already silenced her, too?

I thought of Clara, the sister I had lost. Wondered how long she had been alone in the woods—or had she never been there at all, instead taken by some stranger and never heard from again?

After Phantom had peed and sniffed and stretched her legs, Jack walked me to my room. Silence had fallen, and neither of us seemed sure how to break it. Against my will, my mind drifted back to the tunnel. The feel of his hand on my face; his fingertips skating along my side.

What the hell was wrong with me?

"It's okay to need comfort sometimes, you know," he said, as though he'd read my mind.

"What?"

"I'm not saying it should be me. But you should be able to admit weakness to someone. Talk to someone."

"I run a business," I said. "I've got mouths to feed—human and otherwise. Bills to pay. There's no time for admitting weakness in my world."

He stopped walking and turned to face me. We were just outside the hotel, the darkness overwhelming. I heard no voices for the moment, the world blessedly quiet. Except for Jack, of course —whose silence was nearly as loud as the screams I'd heard in the well that afternoon.

"What?" I said.

He took a step closer and looked down at me. He was frowning, something tumultuous in his eyes. A question he didn't know how to ask. I didn't jump in to help him. If he wanted information, I wouldn't volunteer it.

"We should get to bed," I said after a second, when he still hadn't said anything.

"Yeah," he agreed with a nod. His eyes were still dark with indecision. "You sure you'll be all right?"

I wondered what he would say if I said no. Would he come in with me? Offer to hold me until I slept? Make love to me until all thoughts slipped away? I thought again of his fingers sliding along the scars at my side; the weighted silence that had fallen between us once he'd seen.

There were so many answers I couldn't give him, if he ever got the courage to ask the questions.

"I'll be fine," I said.

I turned my back on him, snapped my fingers for Phantom, and went to bed alone.

•

There were too many thoughts in Jack's head for sleep. Melanie Redfield was dead, but he wasn't convinced that Gordon was right. It could have been someone else who had done this—someone other than the guy who'd done the killings in '08 and '09. Why would the killer come out of hiding and risk reopening the case if he'd already gotten away with everything and had someone else doing his time?

If it were the same man, this had to be a compulsion. He could have mixed things up a bit to at least throw them off the trail—at the very least, he could have left out the earrings this time. The fact that he hadn't been able to spoke to a deeply obsessive-compulsive personality. Everything had to be exactly right. To the letter. How disturbed must the killer have been when Ariel got away, then? Had it haunted him when she took the chains and purity rings from the scene?

Jack rolled over in bed and stared at the flower-print wallpaper on the hotel wall. His thoughts drifted from the victims to being trapped in the tunnel earlier that day. Jamie beside him. The electrified blue of her eyes in that dim light. The way her hand had closed over his arm when she'd asked that he turn around. The fear, the shame, on her face when he'd seen…

Those scars.

What the hell were they from? Clearly burn scars. He had so many questions about her. She'd gone to Brock Campbell's dog-training summer camp when she was only fourteen, and had returned to the camp the following summer. Jack knew that much because he'd looked it up. He told himself it was simply being a responsible agent; he should know the people he worked with. There was something more to it, though. He didn't have it in him to deny that.

Jamie had moved out of her home in Georgia shortly after that second year of summer camp—presumably because her parents had learned she was pregnant, and hadn't approved. Just as she'd told him in the tunnel, she'd moved out West then. She had Bear while she was there. She'd remained in Washington State for the next eight years. That information had been hard to come by, and Jack still wasn't convinced it was completely accurate. For all intents and purposes, she'd gone off the grid for the first several years of Bear's life.

And then, in 2008, she'd resurfaced. Jack had no idea what precipitated the change, but she moved cross country the summer of that year and returned to Maine.

At which point, she went to work for Brock Campbell.

Campbell was thirty years her senior.

Jack was certain the man was Bear's father. There had never been any public statement to that effect, but Campbell had left Jamie his business and a ten million-dollar trust for Bear. Jamie had been the sole beneficiary of his insurance policy, worth millions. Why else would he do something like that?

And then there were the circumstances surrounding Campbell's unexpected death. The picture of health, he had dropped dead of a supposed heart attack at fifty-five.

Bear and Jamie had been the only ones at home at the time.

There was a story there. Had she gotten the scars somehow while she'd been with Campbell? Or were they the result of some childhood accident? Jack didn't think so. The way she tried to hide them suggested she was ashamed; Jamie wasn't the kind of woman who would be vain enough to hide something like that. Unless there was a reason she didn't want Jack to know how she'd gotten them.

He rolled over again on the overly firm hotel mattress, and yawned. He was exhausted.

Still, there were so many things to think about. Someone else had killed Melanie Redfield and possibly the other women—not Gordon.

In which case, Jack had been complicit in putting an innocent man behind bars.

He wasn't sure how he was supposed to deal with that.

A branch scraped against the window outside his room, and he pulled his blankets up to his chin. He thought he heard a voice in the hallway outside his door, but when he closed his eyes and focused, there was nothing there.

Suddenly, the voice returned—louder this time. A gust of wind swept through the room. He looked to the window, and his heart lodged in his throat when a girl's pale face peered in at him. She opened her mouth as if to scream, but he heard no sound.

Jack jolted awake, heart hammering. He looked at the window. It was closed tight, the filmy curtains still. No face stared at him from behind the glass.

It had just been a dream.

Regardless, it took a long time before he was able to close his eyes and sleep again.

●

After Jack disappeared behind his door, I rethought things before retiring to my own room. Phantom looked at me with long-suffering eyes, but she followed me as I limped back down the hall, down the stairs, and out the front door, my knee in agony the whole way.

On my way out to retrieve Casper and Minion from the van, I was surprised to see Rita getting out of the driver side of a little sedan in the parking lot. She looked up when I approached, her weary face cast in shadow from the light of the motel.

"I didn't expect to see you back here tonight," I said. "It looked like you were all gearing up for an all-nighter."

"I needed a break," she said. Her dark hair was pulled back from her face in a ponytail, and I noted again the power and natural athleticism in her movements. If I were a bad guy, I would hate to come up against her in a dark alley.

"I can't imagine spending much time with those photos," I said. "Particularly when they're reminders of the kind of past someone I love has had."

"Someone I loved," she said. The words came out dully, her eyes dead. "Gordon and I had a past—it's over now."

"Because he lied to you about McDonough?" I ventured.

She studied me, but she didn't look particularly surprised that I'd figured it out. "Because he lied to me about everything." To my surprise, tears sprang to her eyes. She looked away. "I've given up everything to get him this far. And he…" She shook her head, wiping the tears away with the back of her hand. "Forget it. Just…watch out for Gordon, all right? He'll go back to prison tomorrow. Maybe that's the best place for him after all."

She pushed past me without another word, but I was uneasy with just how profound her grief was as she strode away. I actually considered going after her, concerned about what she might do if she were alone tonight, but stopped when I saw her going toward McDonough's motel room door.

I might be incapable of leaning on someone in my hour of need, but maybe she wasn't. The idea gave me unexpected hope.

Casper and Minion had been relegated to crates in the van during the whole debacle with Jack and me in the tunnel. I opened the cargo doors at the back of the van, and Casper's shrill bark pierced the night.

"It's okay," I whispered. "Easy, it's just me."

He and Minion both stood in their crates, tails and bodies wagging, Casper whimpering frantically as he pawed at the door. I opened the crates and snapped leashes to collars. Casper's body never stopped moving as he wound his way around my legs, butting his thick bully head against my thighs, his whip-like tail sending a jolt of pain through me when it slapped against my bruised knee.

Minion, on the other hand, remained quiet and subdued, the little yellow dog almost mournful as she followed me back into the hotel, her tail between her legs. She'd come to the rescue younger than most of our dogs did—barely four weeks, far younger than any pup should be separated from its mother. She'd been the sole survivor in a litter of five after the mother died giving birth in a little shelter in northern New Hampshire. Ren had only been twelve at the time, and new to the rescue—new to America. She barely weighed eighty pounds herself. Hardly spoke English. But she volunteered for the task of keeping the little mutt alive.

For the next month, things were touch and go for Minion. Ren kept at it, though, hand feeding the pup when she wouldn't eat; keeping her warm at night by sleeping beside her; investing every ounce of her energy into ensuring that her charge pulled through.

And she had. Now, at five years old, Minion was one of our most reliable search dogs. Assuming, of course, that she had Ren at her side to lead her. Without the girl, Minion seemed lost.

"They're coming back tomorrow," I whispered to the dogs as I led them back to my room.

I stripped off my clothes on the bathroom floor and left the door open as I ran the shower, scrubbing off the dirt and grime left behind from the day. Everything on me ached. Hell, my *skin* hurt. My knee was purple and twice its normal size, but I've had worse injuries over the years. I ran the miniature bar of hotel soap over the scar at my side, tracing the rough skin all the way down to my thigh.

I didn't think of Brock Campbell, though on some level the man is always in the back of my mind, the memory of cruel eyes following me into sleep.

Instead, I thought of our son. I thought of Bear's shy smile when he was little. The way he'd somehow always seemed more animal than human to me, even as a baby. That probably said more about me than it did him—hell, what do you expect from a kid named Bear?

I got out of the shower, toweled off, and didn't bother to dig through for a clean T-shirt. Instead, I went to the bed and crawled beneath the covers naked. Phantom was sleeping soundly on her dog bed by the window, and paid no attention to me. Casper, on the other hand, hopped right up beside me the moment my eyes were closed. I opened one weary eyeball to find myself nose to nose with the mutt.

"Fine," I muttered. "Chill." He gave a goofy little whimper, body still wagging, and circled three times—trampling me soundly in the process—before he finally lay down at my right side. I looked over to my left. Minion stood disconsolately at the edge of the bed, her head hanging low.

"Come on, Min," I called. I patted the mattress. She hesitated only a moment before she hopped up beside me.

For the next few hours, I slept without waking, without dreaming, sandwiched between two mutts while we waited for the reckoning day to dawn.

21

I WAS UP by quarter past four the next morning. I met Cheryl, Wade, and the other handlers outside, but no one said much as we watched the dogs go through their morning routines. Phantom stayed by my side as usual, and Minion remained aloof and withdrawn until Casper finally drew her out with his typical persistence. If something happened to Ren, how would Minion handle it? I've seen dogs wither from grief before, so bonded to their human that they seem unable to shake the loss. It seemed to me that Minion could be one of those dogs.

It was cold and drizzling outside, with heavy rains in the forecast for the day. Not great conditions for a search. No matter, though—we'd all worked in worse.

After the dogs had played and eaten, everyone returned inside to gear up. I handed Casper off to Wade, but kept Minion and Phantom with me as I returned to Glastenbury. The place was chaos when I arrived, news vans lit up and parked for a quarter of a mile along the road to headquarters. More law enforcement had arrived, including half a dozen more federal vehicles and a couple of cruisers. The only good thing I could see out of all this was that the cops were keeping a tight rein on the press, and for once I didn't have to deal with Angie Crenshaw or her cohorts as I walked the now-familiar path to the war room.

Gordon was in McDonough's office, though Rita was gone now and Jack had taken her place. His hair was wet and he smelled of aftershave, but his face was drawn and his eyes heavily shadowed. I wondered if he'd slept at all. McDonough seemed to have vacated the premises completely.

"How's the leg?" Jack asked me.

"Fine," I said briefly. I felt like ants were crawling under my skin—I didn't want to be here. Didn't want to be anywhere but out in the field. "I just came to check in, see if there's anything new I need to know. I need to get out there, though."

"I understand," he said with a nod, though his eyes kept slipping to my leg. My knee was wrapped and I'd iced it all night, but anyone with any common sense would know I shouldn't be traipsing around a mountain on it right now. Jack didn't say anything, though. "McDonough hasn't come in yet, but he called in and said the searchers should be good to go at first light."

I nodded, relieved. I considered asking after Rita, but didn't want to spend more time in conversation than I had to. If McDonough hadn't come in yet either, maybe they were still together. Either way, though, I didn't have time to worry about it.

Over the course of the evening while Jack and I had been trapped, a few more dog-and-handler teams had joined the search. Now, armed with new information and a clear objective, a crew of twenty teams hit the dark and stormy

Vermont wilderness at five-thirty that morning. Winds were high and rains were heavy, lashing each of us in turn as we plowed forward, heads down.

Our starting point was the well I'd discovered the day before. We fanned out from there, each team of two handlers and their dogs taking a different direction. Cheryl and Festus stayed with Phantom and me, our focus on the trail I'd followed underground the day before. It seemed like our best chance at finding the other end of the tunnel.

"You're sure you're up to this?" Cheryl asked before we'd gone twenty yards. She had to shout to be heard above the rain and the wind.

"I'm up to it," I said.

The fact was, if I had been in charge, I would have benched me in a heartbeat. My knee had ballooned up overnight to nearly twice its normal size, and every step sent pain through me so fierce I was fighting to keep my breakfast down. Phantom kept a slow pace beside me, pausing every time I stumbled. She'd look up at me, body still, as though searching my face for some indication of what was happening. Why we were out here when I so clearly shouldn't be.

I focused on putting one foot in front of the other as we climbed higher. Phantom kept her head down, water dripping off her raincoat. I slipped in the mud as I was climbing through a ravine about half a mile from the site where the cave-in had taken place, and gasped as a lightning bolt of pain shot through me. Phantom stopped moving and turned, watching me warily.

"You all right?" Cheryl asked from up ahead.

I straightened, teeth clenched. "I'm fine."

She shook her head. "Sure you are," I heard her mutter.

We kept moving.

•

Jack was pleased but frankly a little stunned when Barrett Redfield contacted him before he ever had to go looking for the youngest living Redfield.

"I just think you should know some things," Barrett said. Somehow, he'd gotten Jack's cell number—which meant he couldn't possibly be calling from Glastenbury Mountain.

"Where are you right now?" Jack asked.

"Close," Barrett said. "I can be there in twenty minutes. Will you wait for me?"

Jack assured him that he would wait, despite the fact that time was passing all too quickly. Whatever Barrett had to say, Jack couldn't imagine it would prove irrelevant in this whole mess.

Twenty-five minutes later, Barrett pulled into the parking lot in a black pickup and strode to the front steps of the old Glastenbury church with his head down. Jack greeted him and checked for a weapon, but Barrett was unarmed. He wore top-of-the-line raingear, but was missing his trademark smirk. He didn't even look up when reporters called for him, and kept his head down as Jack opened the church door and ushered him past the threshold.

Barrett followed him in silence through the church sanctuary, where McDonough and several other members of law enforcement were meeting. They looked up in interest when Jack and Barrett walked through, but made no comment. Jack stopped at the side office McDonough had been using, and held the door open. Barrett looked around uneasily, lowered his head, and walked inside.

"Can I get you anything?" Jack asked, closing the door behind them. He noted that Barrett looked tired, and not necessarily well.

"You got coffee?" Barrett asked.

Jack nodded. He went to the coffeemaker and poured Barrett a mug. The younger man took a sip, grimaced, and set the mug back on the desk that stood between them.

"Jesus," Barrett said. "You have any idea when the last time was I had a decent cup of coffee?"

"One of the dangers of moving to the middle of nowhere, I guess," Jack said.

"Yeah," he agreed. "I guess so."

"One of our agents did a little research," Jack said. "He said you haven't been doing all that well the last year or two. How long have you been out of work?"

"The company downsized last year," he said. "No more corporate account, no more paid travel…"

"And that's when you got sick?" Jack asked. He leaned back in his chair, keeping things casual.

"I wasn't feeling great before that. Stress, doctors said." He paused. Jack waited him out, curious where he would go next. "Anyway," Barrett finally continued, "that's not why I'm here. I need to know what you're going to do about getting those fucking kids away from my brother."

Jack couldn't hide his surprise. "Didn't you help him take them in the first place?"

"Hell, no!" Barrett said. "I didn't know he was gonna lose his shit like that. We went down there because one of our guys was keeping track of you and said something was up—but I sure as hell didn't know he'd freak out and the kid would get shot."

"Did you talk about anything like what happened?"

Barrett nodded reluctantly. "Not that specifically. Dean said you needed more motivation to get the job done, but I just figured we'd put the fear of God into you. Nothing like this, though."

"And now you want us to step in and get the kids back," Jack clarified.

"Exactly," Barrett said. "That's what I want."

A second passed, then two, while Jack tried to digest the request. Finally, he shifted position and leaned forward at the desk. "Do you know where Melanie and Ariel were headed the morning they were taken?"

Jack read a flash of surprise, then possibly a beat of fear before Barrett shook his head. "I've told you all how many times before? I've got no idea."

Jack studied the man for a second. A shine of moisture had formed on Barrett's forehead. "That's a nice jacket," he said, nodding toward the raingear Barrett still wore. "Is it new?"

Barrett looked confused, glancing down at the jacket. "What? Yeah, I got it a couple of—" He stopped, aware that he'd been led into a trap. "I still have a discount from my old job."

"Really?" Jack said. "You don't mind if I confirm that, do you?"

He saw panic this time in Barrett's eyes. Jack remained still, waiting. Barrett's gaze fell to the still-full coffee cup on the desk in front of him.

"When June and Katie died," Jack began, "it came out that they'd been hooking. We never did figure out who was handling the business side of things, though."

Barrett's hands curled around the coffee cup, clenched until his knuckles went white.

"Do you know what I think?" Jack continued.

"What?"

"I think you make a good show of being a shallow, relatively harmless womanizer without a whole lot of sense or ambition." Barrett didn't say anything, tensed now. "You know Gordon thinks you're the one who killed your sisters?" Jack asked, keeping his tone conversational. Barrett's head came up. "And he thinks you did those prostitutes, too—that you were traveling for work, so you could have pulled it off."

Barrett stared at him. Genuinely stunned, Jack thought. "Gordon said that?"

"He did. He's spent a lot of time in prison because he didn't want to turn you in—"

"What the fuck are you talking about?" Barrett demanded. He pushed his chair back and stood, vibrating with anger and confusion. "He knows me. He knows I wouldn't do that—"

"But you could sell your sisters to the highest bidder though, couldn't you?" Jack said. Still calm, still casual. "And do the same thing with your nieces. It must have been easy—I've seen the pictures, they're good looking girls. This community you're setting up on the mountain, there are probably more than enough buyers. But then what happened, Barrett? You could sell them, but you couldn't actually stomach it once they'd done—"

"It's not the same thing!" Barrett shouted. "It's not even the same goddamn universe. They needed money. So, yeah, I set that up—I managed things, and got a cut for it." *Bingo,*

Jack thought. Barrett wasn't done, though. "But why in hell would I kill them?"

Jack waited a beat, while Barrett sank back into the chair across from him. "Melanie and Ariel were going to your place that morning," he said. It wasn't a question.

The whole ugly story came out from there. According to Barrett, there were enough men and enough demand in the camp, that he figured he could make a tidy profit if he convinced his nieces to go into business right in Glastenbury.

"Did you see them that morning?" Jack pressed.

"No," Barrett said. His eyes widened at the doubt on Jack's face. "I swear! They were supposed to swing by my place at 6:30, and I had a couple of buyers all ready to go."

"Who?" Jack asked. Barrett didn't answer. "Goddamn it, Barrett. You want me to believe you, you need to give me an alibi."

Reluctantly, he provided the names of three men living in the camp. Jack wrote down the names, his pen clutched tight in his hand. Then, he looked up at Barrett. The man sat back in his chair, eyes closed.

"What do you think we should do here?" Jack asked quietly, once they were done. "How do you suggest we get Bear and Ren away from your brother?"

"I don't know," Barrett said with a sigh. "All I know is, this isn't going to end well. Dean used to be a reasonable man, but he's been off the last few years since June and Katie died. And now with Melanie dead and Ariel missing, he's fucking certifiable. Those girls were the only thing he had to live for. You need to get in there and get those kids away from him before he finds out Ariel's dead, too."

Jack looked at him sharply. "What makes you say that?"

Barrett offered a weary smile, and lurched to his feet. "Cause I already lived this shit once," he said. "I know how it ends."

Jack saw Barrett out a moment later. He'd entertained the idea of holding the man in exchange for the return of Bear and Ren, but he knew that was precisely the thing that would push Dean over the edge. And as for Gordon's theory that Barrett was the killer... Jack would keep checking, but his gut told him it was a mislead.

He watched Barrett go, and thought of the story the man had told. So, Melanie and Ariel were getting ready to sell themselves—something their grandmother had done long before them, and something their aunts had died for.

And now, Melanie was dead, and Ariel had vanished. A wave of exhaustion washed over him as he turned, and prepared to give McDonough the latest news.

Before he could say anything, however, McDonough reclaimed his office and gave Jack some news of his own.

22

"WHAT DO YOU MEAN, he wants to call a press conference?" Jack demanded, seated in the office across from McDonough, now in his rightful place behind the desk.

"Does that really require an explanation?" McDonough asked wearily. "Dean told the negotiator he wants a press conference. Apart from having his daughter delivered to his doorstep by noon, it's the only demand he's come up with."

"Where does he plan on having this press conference?" Jack's head was spinning, but he at least made the effort to maintain focus. "If we can get him away from the others—"

McDonough shook his head. "I already thought of that, sorry. Apparently, so did he. We tossed around a few ideas before I finally came up with a compromise."

"Which is?" Jack prompted when he volunteered no further information.

"Beside the point at the moment. My biggest concern right now is the fact that he's about to go public with some things we sure as hell don't want public."

Jack didn't say anything to that. McDonough studied him for a moment, reading his mind. "Which you're not really that sorry about, clearly."

"I thought staying quiet was the best move at the time," Jack said. He thought of the days when he'd first started with the Bureau. When Lucia was still alive, and he still believed in so many things that seemed like fairytales now. "That was when I thought we were actually dealing with it in-house. But we never did, did we? I did some checking. We got rid of a couple of them, sure, but Marty Crescent, Jim Maroney, Jeff Swift... Hell, they're doing better than ever in this goddamn organization, and I know for a fact none of them have changed their ways. And you..."

McDonough's eyes hardened. "What about me?"

"What Gordon said last night—"

"Is a lie, and you fucking know it," he said. "He knows Rita and I have been getting...close, and he's handing her as many lies as he can think of so he can keep her wrapped around his finger, even while he rots in prison. Because he's exactly that petty. And frankly, I don't care what the two of you think: when we nailed Gordon for his sisters' murders, we got the right man. He's playing all of you."

"Okay, so you weren't getting coked up and having sex with hookers on the clock," Jack said. "Good for you. But what about those other guys? How did they keep their jobs? Hell, two of them got promotions not long after news broke within the office."

"They owned up to what they did, and they got help."

"And rolled over on whoever was running the thing, is my guess," Jack said. He tried to keep the scorn from his voice. Jesus. How gullible had he been all these years?

"They helped with the investigation, yes," McDonough said. He paused. "They've done what they could to make up for what they did. They were sorry about the women Gordon killed, but they had no part in it."

"No, they just slept with them," Jack said.

"Save your holier-than-thou bullshit," McDonough said. Any humanity Jack thought he'd glimpsed before vanished. "You know how the game is played. If you couldn't deal with it, you shouldn't have come back here."

"You're the one who asked me back here!" Jack shouted, finally losing that tenuous peace he'd maintained so far. "Why the hell did you call me if you didn't want me on this case? I was fine where I was."

"You were eating yourself alive where you were," McDonough said evenly. "And you're a good agent, despite what's gone on with you over the past couple of years. That's why I called you."

Jack had to fight to keep from rolling his eyes. "Right. So this was all done out of the goodness of your heart—and not because I'm the only agent Dean Redfield would talk to by the time he'd buried his sisters and we'd kicked him off his land."

McDonough stared at him, seething. Jack shook his head. They could fight about this forever, but he suddenly knew where he stood. The dream he'd had of being a federal agent, of making a difference in the world, had died when his wife had. It seemed he'd just been trying to resuscitate it all this time.

Jack pushed the realization aside for the moment and refocused on the most pressing issue at hand. "I don't want to fight anymore, all right? What's our play? If Dean is holding a press conference in his living room, that means at the very least he'll be distracted. You've got SWAT here now, right? What if we moved in?"

McDonough fixed dark eyes on his, frowning. "He's got the woods up around his house crawling with armed men.

No matter how you slice it, he's got us."

"So let's cut to the chase," Jack said. "What's this compromise you came up with for Dean and his press conference?"

Before McDonough could answer, there was a knock on the door. It opened before McDonough could respond, and Angie Crenshaw stuck her perfectly coiffed blond head through the door. She flashed a dazzling smile at Jack before she turned her attention to McDonough.

"No way," Jack said immediately, shaking his head. "Forget it."

"Sorry, Jackie," Angie said. She stepped into the room without an invitation. "Not your call."

"She's right," McDonough said to him. "Close the door, please." Angie did. For a second, Jack read anxiety on the reporter's face, then it vanished.

"Dean wants a camera crew up there to record his statement at nine o'clock today," McDonough said. Jack glanced at his watch. It was 8:40. "Ms. Crenshaw here volunteered her services in exchange for an exclusive once we've had an opportunity to view the footage."

"We get final say over what airs, though," Angie said quickly. McDonough stared at her for a second. Anyone else would have withered under his gaze, but Angie remained steadfast.

"*We* get final say," McDonough corrected her. "If anything is deemed dangerous to the lives of our agents or the public, it's off-limits."

"But that's it, though," Angie said. Her blue eyes were clear, her makeup perfect, and her jeans and North Face jacket made her look like a cover model for *Outside* magazine. Jack knew better, having known her on the political beat in D.C. Angie was definitely not bred for the backwoods. "Unless it poses a clear threat of harm, we run the story."

McDonough hesitated. They were over a barrel, and they all knew it. Angie waited patiently, unrelenting. Finally, McDonough nodded.

"Fine—but we view everything first, and you air things on our timeline."

"No dice," Angie said immediately. "I agree to that, and you guys have this thing tied up in your annex for three years. You get six hours, then we're running it—with or without your approval."

McDonough scowled at her. "I invited you here—"

"Because you're stuck, and I'm the only thing you've been able to think of to keep this nut job from killing the two kids he's got up there," Angie interrupted. "I know the score. You're not in a position to negotiate."

She was right. From the look on McDonough's face, the agent was all too aware of that. Finally, he nodded. "Just go," he said.

"This is a bad idea," Jack said. "The whole situation is too volatile—Dean is out of his mind right now."

"I don't care," Angie said immediately. "I'm aware of the danger. I'll sign something if I need to, release liability, whatever. But I'm having this meeting."

He looked at McDonough, hoping for a little backup, but the senior agent said nothing. "Then I'm going too," Jack said.

Angie looked surprised; McDonough did not.

"I assumed," McDonough said. "Find out how the kids are doing. Keep Dean talking. See if you can find anything else he wants."

"I know how to do my job," Jack said.

Angie started to say something else, but McDonough interrupted. "Get your camera crew ready. We leave in five minutes."

"What else—" Angie began.

"You can ask your questions on the way," McDonough said. "Just go. Give me a minute with Jack before you leave."

Surprisingly, Angie agreed. Jack and McDonough remained silent until the reporter had gone.

"I'm telling you, this is the wrong move," Jack said when they were alone again.

"Maybe," McDonough said. "But I haven't come up with anything better."

"Who do we have up at the cabin?" Jack asked.

"We have SWAT standing by, just in case we completely run out of options," McDonough said. "I hope to hell that doesn't happen, though. Forest service is still out looking for the girl, but a few staties are backing up our agents up on the ridge. If it comes to a shootout, we can outgun them."

"Not without bloodshed on both sides," Jack said.

"Which is why we'll do everything in our power to avoid that." He paused. "The other vultures are still circling," he said, tipping his chin in the general direction of the news vans outside. "There's an army of them out there now. As far as I can tell, no one knows what's happening, though."

"What about Rita?" Jack asked. "Have you seen her yet this morning?"

"Not yet," McDonough said with a shake of his head. "My guess is, she needed a break from Gordon. She's probably just taking a breather."

Jack didn't like it. Based on the look on McDonough's face, he wasn't thrilled with the news himself.

"I'll keep trying to reach her—we need all hands on deck right now," McDonough said. He paused for a long moment, then looked at Jack. "What do you think the chances are that someone will find this girl alive by noon?"

The thought made Jack's lungs burn and his stomach twist. "We need to come up with another plan," he said. "These kids' lives can't come down to whether or not we find Ariel Redfield alive in time. Because honestly? It's not going to happen. I'd bet even money on that."

McDonough nodded slowly. "Yeah. That's what I was afraid of. So you better hope to hell this meeting between Dean and Megyn Kelly 2.0 goes well."

"Yeah," Jack said dryly. "What could possibly go wrong?"

Jack considered trying to reach Jamie before heading to the house with Angie and her crew, but ultimately decided against it. She would be more help in the field, and he didn't want her to decide she should tag along with them instead.

"So, do you have any words of wisdom for me before we do this thing?" Angie asked. They were in the SUV, Wade at the helm with Trevor—Angie's cameraman—in the passenger seat. Angie and Jack sat in back, Angie's attention fixed on her compact as she did her makeup.

"Would you listen to me if I did?" Jack asked.

"Definitely not," Trevor shot a look over his shoulder at them. "She doesn't listen to anyone."

She considered for a moment, then nodded. "He's right, actually. What can you tell me about the kids who are being held hostage? What are their names? Bear and Robin?

Sounds like a D.C.-Disney crossover."

"Ren," Jack corrected her. "Bear and Ren. Short for Urenna. She's Nigerian, immigrated to the U.S. a few years ago."

Angie nodded, but continued re-applying makeup with a remarkably steady hand as they bounced along the steep incline, rain pummeling the roof of the vehicle.

"Father was a soldier, right?" she said. So whatever she was asking him was just her way of digging deeper. Angie had never been a slouch when it came to doing her homework.

"Right," Jack agreed.

"What about the relationship between this Bear kid's mom and Brock Campbell—that old-timey dog trainer who died a few years ago? There are some rumors—"

"Why don't you focus on the story with Dean and his family? That really isn't juicy enough?"

She pouted, but didn't argue. "Okay, fine. How about we shift gears and talk about the big sex scandal and subsequent cover-up at the FBI instead."

Wade choked on a laugh, while Trevor shifted in his seat up front. The cameraman flashed them a grin over his shoulder. He was young, probably not more than twenty-five. Jack tensed. He'd never had a good poker face, and right now he couldn't begin to hide everything going through his mind. Angie beamed at him.

"No comment," was all he said.

By the time they reached the Redfield house and the cabins surrounding it, Angie was in full makeup and completely in charge.

"Trev, go on ahead and check out the location," she

instructed the cameraman. "Make sure this fucking monsoon isn't going to wash us away. Or, worse, make me look bad. Just make sure you watch your back while you're out there."

"I'll take him around," Wade said. The older man seemed as uneasy with the situation as Jack was, which strangely enough made Jack feel better about things. At least someone was giving this thing the weight it deserved.

"Thanks," Angie said. "Just keep him out of trouble, would you? He's still a pup."

Trevor started to protest, but Angie held up a hand. "Don't argue with me, puppy. Just get out there and make sure you can light me right."

Despite himself, Jack felt a twinge of appreciation. He respected a strong work ethic, and people who were good at what they did. Angie was one of the best.

"Yes, ma'am," Trevor agreed. The young man zipped up a salmon-colored EMS rain slicker and pulled the hood over his head. If possible, it made him look younger.

Once Wade and Trevor had gone, their bodies bent into the wind and the rain, Jack turned to Angie once more. "You ready?"

"Ready as I'll ever be," Angie said with a nod.

Pickups lined the dirt road in all directions, and Jack realized with a start that McDonough and the others really had no idea the number of reinforcements Dean had brought in.

If they didn't find Ariel and bring her home safely, they could have a war on their hands.

Even if they did, how would he react if Jack tried to arrest Barrett once all was said and done?

"Looks like there's a lot going on out there," Angie noted.

Her slicker was blue—a color particularly well suited to her—and the garment made her look smaller, more delicate than she might appear otherwise.

"It does look that way," Jack agreed. He pulled up her hood and tightened the drawstrings until she batted his hands away.

"I can do it—you'll mess up my hair."

"No one can see your hair; you'll have the hood on."

"If I have bad hair, it shows on my face—whether my actual hair is showing or not. Shows what you know." She paused. "You look worried."

Jack's attention was drawn to her hand on the door handle: her nails perfectly manicured, her fingers long and fine. He had a brief flash to that one ill-advised night they'd spent together, a couple of months before. Angie's teeth at his earlobe; the gleam in her eye; the feel of those nails down his back.

"I am worried," he said, pushing the memory aside. "You're going into a charged situation—"

"Won't be the first time," she said with a shrug. "How about you just gird your loins, and I'll buy you a drink when this is all over."

He looked away uncomfortably, Jamie's blue eyes unexpectedly flashing in his mind. Angie shook her head. "Relax," she said. "I'm not making another play for you—I know you've got somebody else on your mind these days."

"I don't—"

"Spare me," she said. "It's pretty obvious that you've got a thing for the dog trainer, Jack. I wish the two of you the very best… But in the meantime, I need to get out there and make this thing happen."

"You're not taking this seriously—"

She fixed him with a level glare. "Actually, I am. I always do. But sitting here pissing myself won't get the job done, and this is one hell of an opportunity for me. So suck it up, Juarez, and let's get out there."

He tried to think of another argument to keep her from going in, but he couldn't. McDonough had signed off. Angie had signed off.

This was happening.

He just hoped to hell it didn't come off as disastrously as he was afraid it would.

23

WE SEARCHED THE FOREST until the sun was fully up—not that you could tell the way the rain was pouring down. Searched as the minutes and then hours ticked by. Searched through mudslides, thick brush, downpours so torrential it felt like we were drowning on dry land. Searched so long that it felt like this was the end of the road for all of us. And we would keep searching until time ran out and the world ended, as far as I was concerned.

It was almost nine o'clock and I was soaked to the bone when Phantom and Festus both took off into the forest together. Moments later, I heard the dogs' distinctive alerts.

"We've got something!" Cheryl called to me. She'd gone on ahead, but I could still see her blaze-orange vest through the trees.

"What is it?" I asked. The question was met with silence. "Cheryl?"

"Just come," she finally called back. "I don't know what in hell it is. Just…come."

Phantom returned to my side. "I know, I'm coming," I said. She sat down in the mud and yawned at me. "Well, you try doing this on one leg and three hours of sleep and tell me how well you do."

She tipped her head, but I was beyond caring about her judgment.

Twenty yards later, through two-inch-deep mud and thick brush, I finally caught up to Cheryl. She stood beside a huge stone structure, and she looked baffled.

"It's a cairn," I said. "They're supposed to be all over the mountain out here."

"I know it's a cairn," she said with a frown. "You think just 'cause I've got the body of a supermodel I've never cracked a book?"

"You asked what it was."

"Not that," she said. She nodded me to a spot beside her while Festus and Phantom waited on the sidelines for us to confirm whether or not it was a successful find.

The cairn was about six feet tall, built of stones covered in moss so heavy it would have been easy to mistake it for a simple hillside if seen from a distance. It had been built into the mountain, making it that much more difficult to find. At the front, there was a narrow entrance. Phantom trotted toward it, her nose up. As though ensuring I hadn't forgotten, she lay down and barked twice, eyes on mine.

I've done my job, now do yours. And where the hell's my reward?

"What am I looking for?" I asked Cheryl.

"Can you get in there? My ass was smaller once upon a time, but there's no way it's clearing that door now."

I started to kneel, then realized the move was impossible with my knee in its current state. Instead, I bent at the waist and peered inside.

"You see what I'm talking about?" she asked me.

I did. It barely registered for me, though—the moment my head cleared the door, a chill climbed my spine and settled at the base of my skull. A familiar scream echoed in my brain.

"There's a tunnel," I managed, staring at a black, gaping chasm at the back of the cairn. "Have you heard of something like this before?"

"I never have," she said. "I know about a dozen archaeologists and historians in the area who'll blow their loads when they hear about it, though. There's already plenty of mystery surrounding these old rock piles, but this takes the cake."

It seemed the folklore had its roots in truth after all: Glastenbury really was a special place. Extraordinary, really. This was far beyond a few coincidental disappearances in a 47,000-acre forest, though. I crouched down as best I could and twisted myself through the narrow opening. The inside of the structure was barely five feet high, so I had to stay down once I was through.

"You should wait for backup," Cheryl called to me from outside. "Didn't you learn anything from the damn cave-in yesterday?"

"Call Jack," was all I said.

A moment later, Phantom joined me. She bumped against my side, glancing up at me with what I took as resignation more than camaraderie. *This is the person I've chosen. Might as well do what I can to make sure she doesn't get herself killed.*

"Thanks," I said. She bumped against me again, and I brushed her wet head with my hand. That simple contact was enough to steady my heart.

"Ariel!" I shouted.

There was no answer. I took out my flashlight and turned it on before Phantom and I continued, deeper into the bowels of the earth.

It smelled like damp soil and pine needles when we first began. This was no limestone tunnel, but rather something carved from the dirt itself. Had it been here as long as the cairn had been, or was this more recent?

The scream started again, but it seemed farther away than it had when I'd been in the well. Phantom whimpered beside me. I should send her back, I realized. Wait for Jack to come. I glanced at my watch, though, and knew I couldn't do that.

It was ten minutes past nine a.m.

Bear and Ren had less than three hours left.

•

By the time Jack and Angie reached the Redfield house, both of them were already soaked. Jack noted that Angie's carefully applied makeup was already running, and he wondered how she would deal with that out here. As soon as the house was in sight, Angie started forward. Jack caught her arm and pulled her back.

"You said you wouldn't interfere," she said, wheeling on him.

"I also said I'd keep you alive," he said. "Just wait here while I get things set up. Unless you actually *want* to walk into an ambush."

She scowled at him, but nodded her agreement.

The perimeter was lined with Dean's men—some family,

some just followers. All with guns; all looking none too pleased at Jack's approach.

"Dean?" Jack shouted toward the house. "I brought the reporter and her cameraman, like you asked."

"Send them in," Dean called from behind the front door, his voice barely audible in the driving wind and pouring rain.

"You know I can't do that," Jack shouted. "The negotiator talked to you about this—the reporter doesn't go inside. You can do your interview on the porch. You've got men all over the place here. You're safe."

"Like that matters," Dean shouted back. "I get out there and I'm dead the second you've got a clear shot."

Jack hesitated, hoping that wasn't a thought any of his fellow agents were entertaining. He glanced around the clearing. McDonough and a contingent of law enforcement had arrived a short time ago, but were keeping their distance. Meanwhile, Dean's men remained steadfast, watching their every move.

"What does that get us, Dean?" he asked. He took a hesitant step closer to the house. "We kill you, and the kids are still inside the house. We still have your militia to contend with. What good does that do us? Now come on—we've kept our end of the bargain. Let's do this already."

It was a gamble, attempting to take charge in this way. Jack waited a tense second, then two, before the front door slowly opened. He glanced over his shoulder, where Angie and Trevor stood at the ready.

Dean appeared on the porch with his sister Wendy beside him. Despite the house's general state of disrepair, the porch was covered and certainly provided more shelter than anyone else was getting from the elements. Regardless, brother and sister bent slightly into the wind. Dean's face was slick with perspiration, his skin an unhealthy shade of pale yellow. He was definitely sick, Jack realized with a start.

The older man stood unsteadily for a moment, Wendy supporting him with one arm. He pushed her away once he was in the open.

"Where is she?" he demanded of Jack. "The reporter and her crew?"

Jack nodded to Angie. For the first time, she looked nervous. Trevor had already started filming; now, he stepped forward as well. Dean straightened at sight of them, though it appeared to take some effort.

"Good," he said with a nod. "That's good. For once, somebody kept their word."

"We've done something for you," Jack said. "Now, how about you do something for me?" He plowed on even as Dean tensed. "I want to see the kids. Talk to them. Make sure they're all right."

Dean scowled, but Jack held his ground. "You knew you weren't getting something for nothing here, Dean. I just want to see them."

Dean whispered something to his sister. She frowned, but nodded and went back inside. Angie was getting anxious behind Jack; he watched as she scanned the trees, and he could all but hear her narrating the story in her head.

Thirty seconds of taut silence later, the door opened again. The girl—Ren—came out first. She held out her hand, supporting Bear as he followed her into the open. Jack struggled to keep his horror at bay, grateful that Jamie wasn't here.

Bear's complexion had taken on a deathly pall, deep circles etched beneath his eyes. The bandage at his arm was stained with blood, and sweat dripped down his face.

Even if Dean let them go, Jack wasn't sure the boy would survive the trip to the hospital.

"You two hanging in okay?" he asked them, struggling to keep his voice even.

"We've been better," Bear said. His voice was barely audible. He wavered where he stood, and Ren leaned in to support him.

"They're feeding you?" Jack asked. "You're keeping warm? Got the bleeding stopped?"

"He needs to go to hospital," Ren said, in heavily accented English. "They have been fine, but he needs antibiotics. Possibly a transfusion. Things I cannot give him here."

"He doesn't look good," Jack said, directing the statement at Dean. "It's not too late to let them go—"

"Bring Ariel back, and I'll do just that," Dean said. His voice was laced with venom. "But that's the deal. I don't have any other terms. Just that."

"Listen to me, Dean—" Jack began.

"No, you bastard," Dean cut him off. His body all but vibrated with suppressed rage. "There's no deal. You saw them. They told you, we're doing what we can do. You bring Ariel home by noon, and all this ends."

Jack started to say something more, but Dean shook his head. "I'm done talking to you." He said something to Wendy that Jack couldn't hear—presumably telling her to get the kids back inside, while he continued with the interview. She attempted to usher Bear and Ren inside, but Bear fought her, twisting back around to look at Jack.

"This isn't safe," he said. "Coming in here right now—there's something wrong with him—"

"Get him back in there!" Dean shouted at Wendy. "So help me god—"

"I don't know what it is," Bear persisted, "but something isn't right."

Wendy's attempts to silence the boy were futile, and Jack watched in horror as Dean turned his gun on the kids. "Goddamn it, I said get back in there!"

"It's all right," Jack said quickly. "Bear, it's okay. I'll take care of it. Just get back in the house. We'll get you out of this."

Ren looked ready to break at the outburst, but remained strong. Jack was moved at the sight of the two of them. All he wanted to do was storm the place and pull them out of there, but Wendy was already pushing them back through the door.

Their time had run out.

Jack just hoped it wasn't for good.

When they were gone, Dean announced that he needed five minutes before the interview could begin. As soon as he was back in the house, Jack turned to Angie and Trevor.

"Okay, that's it," he said. "Interview's off."

"The hell it is," Angie said. She and Trevor were already gearing up, ready to charge ahead.

"Didn't you hear what the kid just said? There's something wrong. Dean isn't all there—"

"Really?" Angie asked, eyes wide in mock surprise. "You mean to tell me a man who kidnapped two kids, a man who's gone off the grid to live at the top of a haunted mountain

with his family and a bunch of half-breed mountain men…
You're saying he might be unbalanced? Hang on, let me get
my producer on the phone. We could have a whole new
lead."

"Listen to me—" Jack began.

She ignored him, returning to her cameraman. "Come
on, Trev. Let's do this."

Trevor looked at Jack helplessly and took a step toward
the house. Jack grabbed Angie's arm. This time, there was no
humor in her eyes when she turned on him.

"Let me go, Jack."

"I can't do that—"

She jerked her arm from his grip at the same time that
she pulled her foot back and kicked him squarely in the shin.

"Ow—Jesus!"

He reached for her again even as she moved forward,
but she stopped him with a killing glare. "It's not your call,
Jack," she ground out. "This is the kind of shot that comes
along once in a lifetime. I'm not blowing it. You want to
come up there with me, that's fine. But keep your mouth
shut, and let me do my job."

This time, he made no move to stop her as she strode
away.

24

JACK CALLED MCDONOUGH and put in one last plea to put an end to what he was now sure was a bad idea, but McDonough dismissed him out of hand.

"Forget it, Juarez," he said. "You're there, Crenshaw is on board to follow through... Just get in there and talk to Dean, see what you can figure out."

Against his better judgment, Jack agreed to let Angie move forward with the interview—on the grounds that Dean allow him to sit in on the whole thing. Neither Dean nor Angie was enthusiastic, but both reluctantly agreed.

They were on the porch for all of sixty seconds, rain dripping down on both of them through the leaky portico, before Dean nodded toward the door.

"Come inside. I'm not doing this out here, it's too open. I told you before: they'll pick me off the second they get a clear shot."

"You don't think they've gotten a clear shot yet?" Jack said. "It won't happen."

"Come in, or go the hell home," Dean said stubbornly. "Doesn't matter to me."

Jack was about to call his bluff—in point of fact, he knew that it mattered very much to the man. Before he could say anything, Angie nodded amenably. "Sure. We'll go inside. The lighting will be better in there, anyway."

She followed Dean through the front door without another word. Jack followed, silent, gut churning.

The house was nothing like what he'd expected. Flowered draperies hung at the windows, a fire burning in the woodstove at the center of the room. Bear and Ren sat on a futon by the stove, the furniture covered with an intricately sewn quilt. There were pictures on the walls, and the smell of homemade stew filled the small space.

"It's nice here," Angie said, obviously with the same surprise. "Whoever decorated has a real flair."

Dean nodded to Wendy. "My sister did all of it. Always had a good eye, a nice touch."

Wendy blushed slightly, looking away, but said nothing.

"How did you find out about this place?" Angie asked. "And why set up camp here?"

Dean nodded them toward a well-built kitchen table. Trevor surveyed the room to figure out the lighting, while Jack and Angie took seats next to one another. Dean sat across from them. Wendy remained standing.

Dean launched into a diatribe about the government laying claim to his land in the past, and how he'd wanted to be as far as possible from humanity and all its trappings. Unfortunately, he hadn't had the funds to get that far.

"I saw the ad for this place and everything around it, and I knew what they were advertising was a doable price."

Angie nodded. Trevor continued to film them, while Jack took stock of their surroundings. The door to the outside remained open as per Jack's stipulation. Bear and Ren were silent on the futon, their faces pale. Both looked shell shocked; they needed to get out of here soon.

"So why make the decision to take these kids?" Angie asked, pulling Jack back to the interview. "You've lost family before—you know how painful that can be. Why inflict that on someone else?"

Dean scowled. He sat erect at the table, shoulders back, but it looked like the posture was wearing on him.

"These people don't work unless they've got a stake in the game," he said. "I can't have them giving up now."

Angie glanced in Jack's direction, a silent question in her gaze. Jack nodded, a barely perceptible movement. *Keep pushing.*

"It seems like they've gotten the picture," Angie said. "And I can tell you, everyone is taking this very seriously now—there are people searching all over this mountain. Maybe you should think about letting them go—"

"Did you tell her to say that?" Dean demanded, looking at Jack. Jack shook his head but didn't answer, taken aback. Dean got to his feet unsteadily. "You told her to say that, didn't you? You brought her here to poison me—to kill me." His voice rose with every word, becoming more and more unhinged. The other brother—Claude—appeared in the doorway, his own eyes wide.

"Calm down," Angie said smoothly, without a trace of fear. "I say what I want to say, don't get your knickers in a twist. I don't need anyone to *tell me* that what you're doing is a pretty shitty idea, and everyone would be better off if you just let the kids go."

Dean sat back down and settled himself, if only slightly.

"I'm not letting them go."

"Suit yourself," Angie said with a shrug. The briefest dart of her eyes to Jack was his only indication that the outburst had unnerved her. "What else would you like to talk about, then? You asked me here for a reason, clearly. Now that your brother's been proven innocent—"

"Who told you that?" Dean asked. "Nobody said that son of a bitch was innocent."

"Word is, whoever did the previous crimes is the same person who killed your daughter," she said. "Since Gordon was in prison at the time, I'd say he has a pretty good alibi."

"He could have told them how to do it," Wendy said, to Jack's surprise. Trevor turned the camera on her, and she looked away quickly.

"Do you have any ideas of who his partner might have been, in that case?" Jack asked. Angie shot him a glare, annoyed at his interference.

Wendy didn't say anything, jaw clamped shut now and her fists clenched at her sides. Dean took in the reaction and frowned.

"Why don't you go on in the other room, Wendy—put some tea on." His tone was surprisingly gentle. "We've got things covered here."

She nodded, eyes still lowered, and left without another word.

"She doesn't like being involved in these things—doesn't like talking to outsiders," Dean explained.

"She started to say something, though," Angie said. "Do you have a theory about who might be working with Gordon?" She paused. "What about your other brother: Barrett?"

At this, Dean's face darkened again. "Who told you that?" he demanded.

"No one," Angie said quickly. "I just—"

"You want to know who did this, look at everybody else in the goddamn FBI. They were all having sex, hiring prostitutes, doing drugs, all on the taxpayers' dime."

Angie's eyes widened. She checked to make sure Trevor was still filming, and the man nodded at the unspoken question.

"What do you mean by that?" Angie asked. "Who was hiring prostitutes on the taxpayers' dime?" Dean rose, pushing his chair back from the table roughly.

"Ask them," he said. "Ask them about the big cover up just before my brother went to trial." He turned on Jack. "Didn't think I knew about that, did you? I knew! Rita told us all about the whole damn thing. She knew the score— knew all about my brother's whores, the things that'd been done to them. Truth be told, I don't think she was sorry what happened to them."

Jack watched with growing unease as Dean paced the room, caged energy tight in every move. "Dean—"

"Don't fuck with me!" Dean growled at him. "Don't lie to me anymore."

"What did Rita say about the victims?" Jack asked, suddenly calculating. Recalibrating what he knew of the crimes. "When did she talk to you about this?"

"Years ago!" Dean said. Spittle flew from his mouth with the words. "Before any of this, before June and Katie—she knew. All along, she knew."

Angie glanced at Jack, as though sensing something major had just been revealed. Jack remained focused on

Dean.

"Did she know about the prostitutes Gordon was sleeping with, or did she know about the murders?"

"All of it," the older man said. The outburst passed as suddenly as it had come on and Dean sank back down, deflated. "She knew all of it. The only one of you worth a damn, and she was treated like shit. But she knew. She said they were paying for their sins, and she was right. This world, you pay for the crimes you do. It's only right."

Jack's radio crackled at his side just then. Everyone in the room jumped. "It's just my radio," he said, hands raised to calm the others. "Okay if I answer?"

Dean nodded without hesitation, eager for news of Ariel. Jack went to the corner to respond. Claude remained in the doorway, transfixed. Terrified.

"Jack here," Jack answered into the radio.

McDonough's voice crackled on the other end. "I just got word that Jamie's asking for you. Says she found something."

Jack glanced up to find everyone's attention fixed on him. "Tell her I'll be there as soon as I can. We're just wrapping up here."

"Roger that," McDonough agreed. When Jack looked up again, the focus had shifted once more. Wendy had returned to the room, and Angie and Dean were deep in conversation.

"McDonough," Jack said quietly into the radio. "Have you located Rita yet?"

"She's still MIA," McDonough said. "We've got bigger fish to fry right now, though—I'll read her the riot act when she gets back."

"I think maybe you should find her," Jack said. He tried

to remain as cool and understated as possible, but didn't want him to miss the importance of the statement. Behind him, voices had risen once more. He caught a snippet of conversation, Dean's voice strained.

"You think you can just ask somebody something like that?" he demanded. Unlike the way he'd reacted before, there was something restrained in the tone. Jack signed off, the hair rising at the back of his neck as he turned around once more.

"I didn't mean—" Angie began.

"Who are you working for?" Dean demanded. Jack's gaze locked on the gun the man held in his hand.

"I work for WABI," Angie said. Her hands were raised, the coolness gone from her voice. "You know that—you've seen me on TV."

"You think people on TV aren't in on it?" Dean asked. There was something tormented in his eyes, as though he were in physical pain. His knuckles were white around the gun, his index finger resting on the trigger.

"Dean," Jack said. "You got your interview. Everyone will know the truth now—you've seen to that. But now you need to let them go. Angie and Trevor came here on good faith."

He nodded. It seemed to Jack that the man was hearing his voice from somewhere far away, and it took a second for the words to get through. His hands shook as he lowered the gun. The barrel pointed toward the floor. Jack took a breath.

And then, an explosion rocked the room.

A second followed on its heels even as Jack was flying across the room to get to Angie. It took him a split second to comprehend what was happening. Dean had hit the floor, his gun beside him. Unfired. From the wooden floor, Jack looked around.

In the doorway, Claude still stood.

A rifle in his hands, pointed into the kitchen.

Jack looked across the room. Trevor lay on the floor, the camera beside him. The front of his salmon-colored slicker was dark with blood.

"Claude!" Dean screamed, the sound ripped from the depths. Claude dropped the rifle, turned, and ran away. Dean stood there, stunned.

"Get them out of here," Dean said to Jack. There was genuine terror in the words. "Get them out now. He didn't mean it. Oh, sweet Jesus." Tears rolled down his cheeks as he rocked in place. He raised his own gun and pointed it at Jack.

Jack pushed himself up off Angie. Ren and Bear were huddled on the futon, stark terror in their eyes.

"Come on," Jack said to Angie, his gaze still fixed on Dean. "Are you hurt?"

There was no response.

He looked down, and his stomach lurched.

One glance was all it took to tell him that she was gone: the upper quarter of her skull had been blown away, an expression of shock still on her face.

He got to his feet on shaking legs and moved to Trevor. The cameraman was still alive, his eyes wide with pain and fear.

"Can you walk?" Jack asked him. He didn't seem to understand the question.

"Get out—now!" Dean screamed the words this time. Wendy came over and helped Trevor to his feet, the camera cradled in his arms. She wouldn't look at either of them, eyes on the ground, something muted and terrible in her silence. Trevor leaned heavily on her, while Jack hefted Angie's body in his arms.

Stunned, bloodied, they walked away.

25

I'D BEEN WALKING through Middle Earth alone for nearly forty-five minutes when I heard gunshots somewhere above me. Phantom whimpered, and fear shook me for a moment. I shoved it back down. If something was wrong, the police knew where I was. They would find me; they would tell me. Right now, I needed to continue with the assumption that Bear and Ren were still alive. That Ariel was still out there somewhere, waiting to be saved.

The space had gotten progressively smaller as I'd gone on, until I was forced to my hands and knees if I wanted to keep going. Putting pressure on my injured knee brought tears to my eyes. I straightened it as best I could to protect it, and dragged my right leg behind me as I continued on.

Maybe twenty minutes after the gunshot, Phantom barked behind me. The sound echoed through the narrow chamber. I was so used to the ethereal screams I'd been hearing since the day before that they'd faded into the background. It took a second to realize the sound had changed.

The screams shifted to voices—not just one but many, though I couldn't make out the words. Far ahead in the tunnel, my light hit a form close to the ground that stood apart from the deepest black of the packed earth.

Almost there, a girl's voice whispered close to my ear.

I looked to my left and then my right, though I knew I would see no one.

"Jamie!" I heard Jack call somewhere behind me, far in the distance.

"I'm here!" I shouted back. "Just keep following the tunnel."

I took the flashlight from my mouth but struggled to keep going, driven by the girl's voice; that shadow up ahead.

"Slow down, damn it!" Jack called.

I was reminded of the gunshots. Was he here to tell me Bear was dead? Surely I would know if that had happened. The voices would tell me; the girl in the red sweater would give me the news before Jack ever reached me. Wouldn't she?

"I've got something," I called back to him. "Tell McDonough to call Dean. Tell him something's here."

I kept going, no longer mindful of the pain in my knee, my fatigue or my fear or the staleness of the air. Something was there, up ahead—waiting for me. I just prayed to God it was Ariel. Alive, and ready for rescue.

●

"What do you mean, 'something's there,'" McDonough demanded on the other end of Jack's radio. Jack scrubbed at the stubble on his chin, the damp seeping into his bones as he made his way deeper into the tunnel. An ambulance had come for Trevor, and the cameraman was on his way to the hospital in Bennington. The local M.E. had been called to tend to Angie. Jack felt raw, shaken. Gritty and rung out.

"I don't know," he said. "I don't know what the hell she's talking about."

He looked back toward the entrance to the cave. When he'd left the scene, Wade Wright was there in his giant yellow raincoat, Gordon in shackles beside him, the U.S. marshals still by his side. No one had been able to find Rita yet.

"We've made contact with someone on the inside," McDonough said on the line, and Jack felt a surge of hope. "There's a chance we can get them out without any shots fired. If not, SWAT is on standby. Whether we have Ariel or not is immaterial—they've already killed someone. There's no turning back now, and no telling what they'll do next."

The realization hung heavy on Jack's shoulders. "I know," he said. "I've got enough blood on my hands as it is—you're right, you need to do whatever you have to and get Bear and Ren out of there. If someone doesn't do something, there's no way in hell they're getting out alive."

McDonough signed off then. The shooting at the Redfield place had shaken him, Jack could tell. *Good,* he thought. He had no doubt he'd be losing sleep at the memory of Angie's death; he hoped to hell McDonough did, too.

A chill crawled up Jack's spine as he refocused on the path ahead of him, alone now. He swallowed hard, kept his eyes ahead, and returned to the dark, damp bowels of the earth.

●

The space in the tunnel widened as I continued to move forward. The screaming had stopped, but there was a low murmur, a moan, like a wounded animal. I was aware of

Jack speaking somewhere far behind me, but I couldn't begin to focus on the words.

I was close.

When the tunnel was finally tall enough for me to stand, I steadied myself with a hand against the dirt wall. My bad knee screamed in protest. As though she'd been waiting too long for the opportunity, Phantom trotted around me and reclaimed the lead. I couldn't tell how far down we were, but whatever I had seen up ahead was only a few yards from me now.

Before I could take a step, I started at the feel of someone's hand at my shoulder.

"Easy," Jack said. "Where the hell are we?"

"No idea," I said. I kept my eyes locked on Phantom, waiting for her to alert at the object—the body, I was sure of it—up ahead. Instead, she sniffed at it idly and moved on.

My heart sank.

"What is that?" Jack asked. We continued on, through the dark and the damp. The object was only a couple of feet away now. Gray, with a few loose red threads all that remained of the sweater Mary Wieland had worn seventy years before.

"It's her," I said. I tried to kneel, remembered that I was bordering on crippled now, and remained where I was. "The college girl who went missing in 1946."

Bitter disappointment ate at me. I just wanted this to be over.

Jack knelt in my place, studying the skeletal remains at our feet. He paused at the femur and glanced up at me, the significance clear. Beneath what was clearly the patella—the knee bone—something was missing. Neither the tibia, the fibula, nor any part of the left foot were anywhere in sight. I thought of the screams I had heard. The bones at the bottom of the well. The girl who had appeared in my dream, and the empty space below her knee as she'd limped away from me.

What the hell had happened to her? Who had done this?

"We should keep going," I said. "Phantom's still tracking. Ariel is either down here now or she was not that long ago."

Jack nodded.

We walked on in silence. Jack was off, pain radiating from him—not physical, but a deep mental cry that seemed to echo in this underground world we now inhabited. I was afraid to ask the question, but knew eventually I would have to.

"I heard gunshots…" I began.

I glanced at him, but he didn't look at me as he continued walking. "Bear and Ren are okay," was all he said. "We've still got time."

Relief weakened my aching bones, but I didn't stop.

The tunnel was wide enough now that we could walk side by side without stooping, which meant it had to be well over six feet tall and three or four feet wide. Parts had been reinforced with limestone, others with rotting wooden beams. It seemed solid enough. Even if it wasn't, there was no way I could go back. Even knowing I was risking Jack's life, Phantom's life, I kept going.

"What time is it?" I asked after another minute or two passed.

"Ten minutes till twelve," he said with a glance at his phone. "I told McDonough to get in touch with Dean," he added. "They know we're onto something. He'll wait."

I didn't ask how he knew that. I just kept moving,

clinging to that last desperate hope.

I caught sight of Phantom a few yards ahead before long, though she was still on the move. Jack and I passed another skeleton, still articulated and, like the previous, missing the left leg below the knee. As with the other one, this body had clearly been here a very long time.

Another twenty yards on, we found another.

And another.

And then, out of the darkness, I heard Phantom's distinctive double bark.

"She found her," I said, suddenly unable to take a full breath. "She's got Ariel."

I started half running, half limping, my gaze fixed on the tunnel ahead. "Ariel!" I shouted. The tunnel twisted to the right and I slipped, went down on one knee, and cried out in pain as I struggled to get back up again. Jack grabbed my arm and pulled me to my feet, and we continued on in silence.

Finally, after what felt like a lifetime, I saw Phantom lying on the ground up ahead. A figure, shadowed and inert, lay in front of her. I felt Jack's hand on my arm as we continued.

The world around me fell silent for the first time since I'd entered the tunnel. I took the final two steps to bridge the distance between us, and gazed at the ground.

And the lifeless body of Ariel Redfield, an iron bear trap clamped to her right leg.

26

DEAN REDFIELD PACED the front room, rifle in his hands, staring out the window at the pouring rain. Claude sat on the floor in the corner rocking slightly, mumbling to himself. The look in his eyes was haunting, something deeply rooted and terrible seeping from him like tar. It was ten minutes till twelve. Dean's radio was on the table. It crackled, someone on the other end trying to reach him.

He didn't pick up.

Ren squeezed Bear's hand. He squeezed back.

"They could have word about Ariel," he said out loud, trying to get Dean's attention. The old man shifted, spirals of blackened chaos whirling in the air around him. He stared at Bear blankly.

"Whoever is trying to get in touch with you might have found Ariel," Bear tried again.

Dean just looked away.

Bear hadn't seen Mary again since early that morning. Had she given up on them? He still wasn't clear on what it was she wanted. Was she trying to tell him something? Or was she expecting him to do something for her? If that was the case, she was bound to be disappointed. He couldn't even save himself and Ren.

"They're doing the best they can," Bear said, keenly aware of the minutes that kept ticking by. Was the deal the same, now that Claude had killed the reporter? "You killing one of us won't change anything. It won't make losing your daughter any easier."

"But it'll make it even," Dean said. Claude glanced at Dean and then Bear and Ren, lifting his eyes but not his head. The kind of look you get from a beaten dog too scared to fight anymore.

"They could have found her," Bear repeated. "Just pick up the damn radio and talk to someone. Whatever happened, you can't change that. But why make it worse?"

"These people have a job to do," Dean said. It was like he hadn't even heard Bear. "They made a promise. I let the feds get away with this before—taking my sisters from me, and I barely put up a fight. They think they can do it again?" He shook his head. "They won't do it again."

"Maybe you should lie down," Wendy said to him. She looked as tired as Dean did, but Bear sensed determination there, strength she'd kept hidden. "Let them go back to their room, and you rest."

"I can't sleep now," Dean said, frantic. "They killed my Melanie—and probably Ariel, too. You think I can just go lie down somewhere, close my eyes, and everything will be better?" The man was unraveling before their eyes, and Bear didn't want to be at his mercy when that last thread came undone.

Claude's mumbling got louder, the rocking more violent, but Bear couldn't make out the words. He looked at Ren. Her eyes were red, watery, but she hadn't cried. She'd just gone quiet.

"We did not kill your daughter," she said suddenly. She hadn't spoken for more than an hour.

"You're with the—" Dean began.

"We're not with anyone who had anything to do with it," Ren cut him off. Her voice was tight, raised now. Bear touched her arm, tried to get her to be quiet, but she shook him off. "We came here to help you, because this is the job we choose to do. We choose to help people. I am sorry about your daughter, but what happened to her is not our fault."

"Doesn't matter," Dean said—his own voice just as tight, something unyielding, dangerous, in his eyes. "It doesn't matter who you're with or not, this sends a message. You think after what happened here, they're going to let any of us get out of here alive? Least I can do is send a message. Maybe next time they'll think twice before they fuck with another family, steal their children from them in the night."

His voice rose on that last, his hand curled tighter around the rifle. He took a step toward them, and Bear saw fear flash on Wendy's face. She stepped in front of him.

"Please, Dean…" she began.

Dean raised a hand to her, backhanding her across the cheek. Claude cried out when Wendy flew back against the wall, but Wendy didn't say anything. A charged silence fell, those threads turned to knots that seemed to be choking Dean from the inside out. Wendy just stood there, her own hand raised to the rising welt on her cheek, shock in her eyes. Dean looked at her, his forehead furrowed. Tears coursed down his stubbly cheeks, and she went to him. Bear watched as she gently took the gun from her brother, and guided his head to her shoulder.

"Claude, take them back up to their room," she said, while Dean wept on her shoulder. Claude didn't respond, didn't stand, still rocking in the corner. "Claude," she said again, sharper this time. He looked up. "Take the gun, and bring these two back up to their room. Then come back down, and I'll make a snack."

Claude nodded, silent, but didn't move until Wendy had led Dean up the stairs and turned the corner. The gun was where Wendy had left it, propped against the wall. Bear glanced at Ren. He didn't need to be psychic to know she was thinking the same thing:

This was their chance.

Still mumbling to himself, Claude's eyes locked on the gun. Bear took a step toward the man, not even sure what he would do—what he *could* do, as weak as he was. But he had to do something.

Before he could act on that thought, Wendy returned. Bear saw their one chance of escape—of survival—vanish before his eyes. He froze. Wendy took the situation in at a glance, and lay a hand on Claude's arm.

"Why don't you go upstairs and clean your room," she said, in the same gentling tone Bear used when working with injured animals. "I'll take care of Bear and Ren."

"But Dean said—" the man began.

"Dean told me it's all right," she said. "Go on, Claude. I think your coins spilled…"

An almost comical look of horror crossed his face. "I didn't know," he said. "I should fix it. Make sure I didn't lose any."

He went to the stairs still mumbling to himself. As soon as he was gone, Wendy went to the window. She peered out the edge of the flowery curtains.

"We have to move fast," she said. Bear and Ren both stared at her, uncomprehending. "I don't know how long Dean will stay down. The police can't be far after everything that happened—they should be just outside, out by the trees."

"Have you talked to them?" Bear asked.

"They found Ariel," she continued. It was like she hadn't even heard him. "She's alive—that's what they said. I need to get to her. The police said they would take me to her, if I let you go."

She glanced up the stairs, completely spooked. There was a welt on her cheek where Dean had hit her.

"You're letting us go?" Bear asked. He couldn't make the words make sense.

"She is," Ren said.

He didn't ask any more questions. Bear felt like he'd been run over by an ox, but he forced himself to move.

Wendy grabbed her raincoat from a hook by the entry, opened the front door, looked around, and nodded them forward. Bear hesitated. What if it was a trick? Or they got shot by the cops, if Wendy hadn't made it clear what she was doing? Ren squeezed his hand.

"We have to trust her," she said, half under her breath.

She was right, he knew. He took a deep breath, ignoring the pain in his shoulder—the pain in his whole body, for that matter. They stepped outside. Rain poured down, the world dark and soaked through. Wendy had her jacket, but Bear and Ren were still in the clothes they'd been taken in. Bear wasted no time thinking about the water. He and Ren made their shaky way down the front steps, following

Wendy. Bear half expected Dean to come charging out the front door after them, but it stayed closed.

There was no one in sight.

Ahead of them by fifty yards or less, an old truck was parked on the side of the road. Bear knew there were other people living in this settlement, but where were they? Did they even know what had happened? Were they even still here? He thought of movies he'd seen about alien invasions, mass abductions. Whole towns that vanished. That was what this felt like. He searched the horizon, but he didn't see a soul. Even the dead were gone.

Wendy paused as they approached the truck. She looked around, in much the same way Bear had. "They told me to take this truck," she said. She spoke quietly, like she was afraid of being overheard. "They just want me to get away from the house, so no one else gets hurt."

"Okay," Bear said. Instead of getting in, though, she just stood there for a second—frozen, about to take a flying leap into nothing. Bear could practically see her weighing the arguments in her head. Finally, she took a deep breath and nodded toward the truck.

"Get in," she said.

Ren helped Bear into the cab, then pulled herself in. Wendy got behind the wheel. She still had her dress on beneath the raincoat, the welt on her cheek ugly and red from where Dean had hit her. The woman sat there for another second. She looked back at the house, swallowed hard, and turned the key in the ignition. The engine roared to life.

Behind them, Bear saw Dean emerge from the house, his rifle in hand. The old man shouted after them, his words lost in the rain and the wind. Wendy put the truck in gear. The gearshift grated for a second before it took hold. Her knuckles were white on the wheel, her whole body rigid. *Go, go, go* Bear chanted in his head, willing the vehicle forward. The engine caught; the tires spun in the mud, found solid ground, and they lurched forward. A gunshot sounded behind them. The rear window exploded. Wendy gave a small, terrified yelp, glass shards flying in all directions. She kept driving. Another couple of gunshots followed, the impact enough to make the truck shimmy on the road. They didn't stop.

Ren clutched the dashboard with both hands, bracing her body as they bounced over ruts, rocks, and debris. There was glass in her hair from the exploded window, a cut in her neck seeping blood from a stray shard.

"It wasn't supposed to be this way," Wendy said, half to herself. "None of this was supposed to turn out this way."

She barreled over the rough terrain, every bounce tearing through Bear like he was being shot all over again. Ren glanced at him, the fear in her eyes clear. "Just hang on," she said. "It's not much longer—just hold on. You can make it."

His vision blurred at the edges, darkness closing in. He fought to stay conscious. If he closed his eyes, he was terrified that he might not open them again.

Wendy glanced at him, her hands still tight on the wheel. "Your friend is right," she said. "I'll get you out of this."

"I'm all right," he said. Or tried to say. He wasn't sure the words ever actually made it past his lips.

Wendy nodded, about to say something. Her focus on him instead of the road, so Bear saw it before she did. Another pickup—this one red, and headed straight toward them.

"Look out!" Ren shouted. Bear caught sight of the other Redfield brother—Barrett—in the driver's seat. Wendy twisted the wheel a split second before they hit his vehicle, their own truck going up on two wheels as they careened to the side.

Bear looked behind them. Dean's battered SUV wasn't far behind, and closing in fast. The road was narrow, and Barrett's truck stood solidly in the middle, barring the way. Bear expected the man to close the gap and box them in, but at the last second he seemed to catch Wendy's eye, and Bear saw understanding there. The man nodded, fast, and Wendy slid past. With Barrett now in their wake, Bear turned and saw the man turn the truck until it was perpendicular to the road—cutting Dean off completely, making it impossible for him to follow.

They barreled on.

27

"IS SHE BREATHING?" Jack asked me as I crouched next to Ariel. Phantom hovered beside me, and I was reminded of her treatment of the fawn a couple of days before. I slid my fingers over Ariel's neck, pausing at the chain that hung loose around it. A silver purity ring shone on her left hand.

A second passed, perhaps two, before I found her carotid artery. A weak pulse fluttered beneath my fingers.

"She's alive, but I don't know what kind of condition she's in. We need something to cut the trap off," I said.

He shone his flashlight around like a pair of bolt cutters might magically appear in a corner, and his sudden intake of breath caught my attention once more.

"What is it?" I asked.

"Get hold of Phantom," he said, his voice tight. The dog was right beside me, but I grabbed her collar regardless.

"What?" I asked again.

He shone his flashlight just a foot or two deeper into the tunnel, and I cringed.

"Oh my God," I said, barely able to find my voice. I straightened, and stared at the same spot where Jack had trained the light. There were at least a dozen animal traps of varying sizes. Some had already been triggered, and my stomach turned at sight of the whitened bones caught in those traps. Others still hadn't been sprung.

"We have to get out of here," Jack said. "This isn't good. This feels very, very…" He paused, still staring at the traps. "Not good."

I focused my own light on the trap Ariel was caught in. Two bolts at either end of the chain had been solidly driven into the rock floor beneath us. One look at it and I knew there was no way in hell it was coming free without intervention.

"You need to go get bolt cutters," I said. "It's the only way." Jack looked back down the tunnels, weighing his next move. "Jack," I began.

"I know," he said with a nod. "I just don't want to leave you here—"

"I've got Phantom," I said. "You're wasting time. Go!"

He hesitated another second, then removed his sidearm and handed it to me.

"I don't want that," I said.

"I don't care. I'm not leaving you here unarmed." He left the gun on the ground beside me. "You know how to use it?"

I nodded briefly. He looked conflicted for a second more before he finally went, jogging back the way we'd come. When he was gone, I stroked the hair back from Ariel's forehead, cataloging her injuries. It looked like she had a fractured cheekbone. Bruises and cuts on her face. Her right arm hung awkwardly, and I expected her shoulder was out of joint. She was naked, her feet badly cut and bleeding. Bruises, scrapes, a couple of deep cuts in her thigh that looked like they'd been carved by a knife of some kind. The same that had cut Melanie, I assumed. I took my jacket off and draped it around her.

She was smaller than I'd expected, and I remembered that she was only sixteen. She had the muscle tone of someone naturally athletic who obviously took pride in that fact. Except that now, she was broken.

Phantom whimpered and lay down beside the girl, licking her cheek with great care.

"We've got you, Ariel," I said. "No one's going to hurt you again."

In the distance, the screams I'd heard before began again—far away at first and then, suddenly, moving forward as though on a wave. They barreled closer still, until they were almost upon us. Phantom lifted her head and stared into the darkness, her ears pricked forward.

Ariel didn't move.

Goose bumps pricked my skin when a figure appeared in the distance.

The girl in the red sweater.

She limped toward me, her eyes serious, her mouth set in a grim line. She seemed to move with the screams, propelled forward on that wave of anguished cries.

"He trapped us down here," she said.

"I know," I said. I couldn't get a full breath. This had happened how many times for Bear? The dead had come to him from the time he was small; shared their realities, their individual truths. It was all new to me, though. I had no idea how to handle it. What to say.

"Do you know how long?" she asked. She limped closer. My attention was riveted to the empty space below her knee. I shook my head, not clear what she was asking. "What year is it?" she pressed. "How long have we been here?"

"You're Mary?" I asked. "Mary Wieland?" She nodded wordlessly. I told her how many years had passed since she'd vanished without a trace from Bennington College. She stopped moving. The screams faded as she stared at me.

"In my dream, you said something had woken," I told her. "Something bad. Do you mean because this girl was in the tunnels?" I nodded toward Ariel. Phantom remained where she was, her eyes fixed on the girl in the red sweater. Neither the dog nor the spirit seemed particularly disturbed.

"I think so," she said with a nod. "We were here alone for a long time. At first, he ruled the tunnels. He brought us here. Set us loose. Waited for us to get caught in his traps, and then he added us to his collection. He loves the blood—lives for it."

"His collection?" I asked. I wondered where Jack was. How long it would take before he returned. Whether or not Bear was all right. Whether I'd gone insane, and he would find me blank-eyed and mad, mumbling to the walls.

"That's what we called it," Mary said. "His collection. That was what we were to him… Just things, designed to amuse him. He brought us here. Hurt us. Took… everything." She shivered.

"This was a man," I clarified.

"He was a man," she agreed. "Now, he's more than that. More powerful—and so happy to have new flesh here."

Was he a ghost now too, then? And if so, what kind of danger did that mean for us? I thought of the match I'd smelled; the rock that had trapped Jack and me. Fear crawled through me, gathering tight in my sternum. Phantom sat up. Her gaze shifted from the girl to a cloud of darkness beyond. Mary froze. Terror shone in her eyes.

"It tried to trap me yesterday," I said.

She nodded silently, still unmoving. The fur stood up along Phantom's spine. The dog got to her feet. The screams stopped—didn't fade, didn't merely quiet. They stopped, and silence fell. I'd never heard anything more disturbing, including the screams themselves.

Beneath that blanket of deep wet stillness, Phantom growled. I reached for the gun Jack had left me, though I had no idea what good it would do.

The cloud of darkness moved closer.

28

WENDY TORE DOWN the mountain like the devil himself was chasing them. Bear blacked out twice, the pain excruciating, but each time Ren brought him back. He didn't want to die—he knew all about what he could expect, that plane of nonexistence that awaited him. But, God, he wasn't sure he could hang on much longer.

They could have been driving ten minutes or an hour before Bear spotted a car up ahead. Totally at odds with the surroundings, it was a silver Ford Focus with government license plates. It was stopped at the side of the dirt road. Wendy slowed the pickup, and Bear scanned the trees for some sign of the driver.

They were just a few feet away when the lady agent— Rita Paulsen, Bear reminded himself—stepped out of the trees. Wendy slowed further as Agent Paulsen flagged them down.

"It's one of the agents," Bear said, just in case Wendy went nuts and decided to run her down. It was the sort of reaction he wouldn't put past her brothers, though so far she'd appeared more reasonable than that.

"I know who it is," Wendy said grimly.

She stopped the truck.

Agent Paulsen drew her gun, her eyes seeming to take in Wendy, Bear, and Ren in a single sweeping glance. She wore no raingear, and was soaked to the skin.

Wendy stepped out of the pickup, her hands raised. "I brought the kids, Rita," she said. "You know me—when you and Gordon were together, we were sisters. You know I mean no harm. I'm just trying to fix this."

Agent Paulsen nodded, but she didn't put her gun down. There was something wild and sad in the woman's eyes. Ren squeezed Bear's hand. He glanced at her, his vision blurring at the edges again. He was freezing. Exhausted.

In the distance, he thought he saw a flash of red among the trees.

"They found Ariel," Wendy said, still talking in low, soothing tones to Rita. "It's almost over. I'm going to bring the kids back, and I'll get Ariel. Whatever happened...it's almost over now."

Agent Paulsen shook her head. This close up, Bear thought it looked like she'd been crying—though it was hard to tell with all the rain. "I thought I was fixing things," Agent Paulsen said. "That it would be... We could just go back. I was supposed to fix everything."

"It will be all right," Wendy said, her voice soothing. "Do you know where to find the other agents? Where they have Ariel?"

For the first time, it seemed like the agent snapped back to the present. She paused. "They found her? Alive?"

"That's what I heard," Wendy said. "Can you find out where she is? Bring me to her—let me take her home, take care of her. Please." Wendy's voice broke, and for the first time Bear thought he could see the toll this was taking. The strain she'd been under all this time.

The words seemed to snap Agent Paulsen back to attention. "She's still alive," she said. Then, she nodded—half to herself, like she was answering a question she'd asked in her own head. "I'll find out where they are," she said. "I'll get her, and I'll bring her to you."

Wendy nodded gratefully, lowering her hands. Agent Paulsen nodded toward her car. "Come with me," she said. "Leave the truck, and we'll bring the kids in together. Everything will be all right." This last was said like she was trying to convince herself.

Shaking, weak, barely conscious, Bear caught another glimpse of red in the wilderness. Was it a warning? Was Mary trying to find them; trying to tell him something?

It hardly mattered—what choice did they have?

He and Ren slid from the cab of the pickup, and limped toward Agent Paulsen's car. He saw Wendy glance at them, read fear in her eyes, and tried to tell himself that this was all good. They'd been rescued. They were safe.

No matter how much he repeated it to himself, he couldn't make himself believe.

●

"Stay away from me," I said into the darkness. Phantom pressed closer to me, her growl constant now.

Mary seemed frozen, unable to move forward or back as the darkness crept closer.

"I don't know what you are," I said, forcing strength into my voice, "but I know what you've done. I've found the bodies, all the people you fed on. It's over now."

It moved closer, and closer still. Phantom took a step forward. The screams began again. Mary flickered before my eyes. The physical world around me seeped in like cracks in the surface of a dream, and I looked down in time to see another trap already set, jaws gaping, just inches from Phantom. I wrapped my hand around her collar, pulling her back. I drew strength from the dog, since I was fast running out of my own. For a moment, it seemed that the shadow stilled.

"I'm taking these bodies, and I'm bringing them home," I said. "The tunnel will be sealed. There's no fighting that now."

Mary flickered once more, like a filmstrip fading to black. Beyond, I stayed focused on the darkness—no shape and no substance, nothing to identify it as a physical entity, yet the cold that enveloped me, the terrible fear, was undeniable. Beneath my feet, the ground trembled.

A gaping maw at the center of the dark cloud seemed to transform into a grin. The screams became shrill, deafening. Phantom barked, body squared and unyielding as the shadow moved closer.

Ariel stirred at my feet. My head throbbed, my heart pounding a staccato rhythm in my chest. My eyes never leaving the form in front of me, I leaned down and took Ariel's arm. The tremble beneath our feet grew.

There was no way I could get Ariel loose from that trap on my own.

"Ariel," I said. "Please—you have to wake up."

Debris fell from above us. Phantom was advancing on the shadow, trying to push it back, but it wouldn't retreat.

The screams reached an ear-splitting crescendo. The shadow was nearly upon us.

•

Agent Paulsen drove them back to the old church where everyone had been meeting, but the place was practically deserted. Bear heard an ambulance in the distance as they pulled into the parking lot. Normally he wasn't a fan of doctors, but right now he hoped to hell they were coming for him.

As Agent Paulsen stopped the car, Cheryl Madden appeared at the front of the church with two dogs, both straining at their leashes. Bear fought to keep it together as Casper and Minion practically dragged the woman down the steps.

A couple of stray tears coursed down Ren's cheeks. Bear squeezed her hand. "We did it," he whispered, his own voice rough.

She looked at him for just a second, staring into his eyes in that way that always felt like she was seeing straight through to his soul. "We did," she agreed. She leaned forward, and touched her lips to his.

Despite the pain and the fear and the fact that he hadn't bathed in, like, days, Bear leaned into it.

The rear passenger side door opened then, and they parted—they kind of had to, since Casper and Minion both piled into the back seat with them.

"The EMTs are on their way," Cheryl said. She'd given up trying to hold the dogs back. "But they were pretty insistent about seeing you first."

Minion clambered in and climbed into Ren's lap, and looked like she was setting up camp. Casper came in with surprising care, his eyes mournful, pawing gingerly at Bear's leg.

"It's okay, Caz," Bear said, his chest tight. He scratched the dog beneath his docked ears. "You did a good job, buddy—you really did. Good boy."

Casper grinned at him, hesitant at first, still looking up at Bear like he was apologizing. Bear gathered the dog in his good arm, and held him closer.

They'd made it.

"Where's my mom?" he finally remembered to ask.

"She found Ariel," Cheryl said. "They're just trying to get her now."

"Trying?" Wendy echoed. It was the first time she'd said anything since they'd pulled up. She looked smaller, older, now that she was away from her family. "I thought they had her?"

"She's in a tunnel," Cheryl explained. The ambulance pulled in then, barely coming to a stop before the rear doors flung open and two EMTs hopped out. "They're working as fast as they can, but I guess she's trapped under there."

"But she's alive," Wendy persisted.

"She is," Cheryl reassured her. "Unconscious, and I think she's in pretty rough shape. But she's alive."

"Where are they?" Agent Paulsen asked, inserting herself into the conversation. "I promised I'd bring Wendy to her."

"Excuse me," a male EMT said as he took in the scene. He frowned at sight of the dogs. And the blood. Overall, he didn't look happy. "You'll need to call the dogs."

Cheryl pulled Casper and Minion away with a lot of

effort, leaving the way clear for the paramedics to work

"You should stay with them," Bear told Ren as they loaded him onto a stretcher. She shook her head. Her hair looked wild. She was dirty and smelly, and still crying a little. Bear was sure she'd never looked prettier.

"I stay with you," she said. "They can bring the dogs to the hospital when you are well."

The EMTs weren't wild about that idea, but Cheryl nodded behind their backs. Before he could find out anything more about his mother or Ariel, the paramedics started doing their thing—asking if he had any allergies, was he on any medications, any conditions they should know about. He shook his head. Hopefully, talking to dead people wasn't the kind of condition they meant.

They loaded him into the ambulance, and Bear closed his eyes when they plunged a needle into his good arm. Ren pushed her way into the back with him, and took his hand. He saw Mary Wieland swimming in front of him—still worried, still sad. But she managed a tiny smile for him as she waved goodbye. They were safe.

So why did he feel like things weren't finished yet?

29

JACK WAS ABOUT TO go back in with bolt cutters and medical supplies when Rita arrived on the scene—and she wasn't alone. Wendy Redfield followed behind with unexpected determination, her mouth set in a grim line.

Gordon was still in shackles by the cairn. He and Rita exchanged a brief, loaded glance that Jack didn't understand, before the man turned his attention to Wendy.

"She's alive," Gordon said. He sounded like he didn't believe it. He took a step forward, eyes fixed on his sister. Wendy stepped back.

"Stay away from me," she said. "However you've done this, I know the truth about you—I know what you've done."

"I didn't hurt June and Katie," he insisted. "And I sure as hell had nothing to do with Melanie and Ariel."

Rita looked away at the exchange. Jack's doubts resurfaced all over again. He pushed them aside; now wasn't the time.

"I need to get back in there," he said. "But what can I tell Jamie?"

"Bear and Ren are both safe," Rita confirmed.

"Okay—good," he said with a brusque nod, downplaying the surge of relief that ran through him at the words. "Then

I'm going in. Emergency services are on their way?"

"They had to take Bear and Ren," Rita said. "But another ambulance is on its way. We should be able to stabilize her and carry her down to HQ ourselves, and they'll take it from there."

"I guess that means I've got company on this one?" he asked.

"You really think I'd let you have all the fun?"

"Jack," Gordon said. Rita shot him a chilling glare, and the man looked away. Before he did, Jack could have sworn he read fear in the man's eyes.

"Yeah, Gordon?" he asked. He moved away from Rita and toward Gordon, turning his back in an attempt for at least a pretense of privacy. "What is it?"

Gordon's eyes slid from Jack to Rita, now on the outskirts watching them. For the first time, Jack noted how worn she looked. Rita was a good-looking woman, had always been the sort who caught the eye and held it, but right now she looked almost…haggard. Her eyes were glassy with fatigue, a near-madness lurking beneath.

"Be careful in there, all right?" Gordon said quietly.

"Is there something you want to tell me?" Jack asked.

Gordon shook his head. Rita strode toward them, and he looked away. "Just be careful," he repeated.

"Are we ready?" Rita asked. She glanced at Gordon, but he wouldn't meet her eye.

"I guess so," Jack said.

"I'm going too," Wendy said, seemingly out of the blue.

"I'm afraid not," McDonough said, stepping forward for the first time. "There's been some seismic activity happening down there—we need to get in and get out fast."

The older woman brushed past him without looking back, headed straight for the cairn. "Then we'd better move," she said. "Ariel knows me—after everything she's been through, she needs a familiar face."

McDonough started to protest, but Rita shook her head. "Forget it—I know this family. Once they set their minds on something, it's pointless trying to talk them out of it."

She shot a not-insignificant glare toward Gordon, and stalked past them. Jack gave up trying to navigate the tumultuous family politics, and got moving himself.

Jamie was waiting.

●

"You're all right, Ariel—everything is okay," I said, trying to keep the girl's eyes focused on me now that she was finally coming to. Of course, my message was seriously undercut by the sheer terror in my voice. Her eyes widened as she took in the tunnel, the darkness…the shadow that had thankfully stopped advancing, but that hung in the air just a few feet away, as though waiting for something.

"What's happening?" she asked. The pain caught up to her then, and she looked down at the source. At sight of the trap and her mangled leg within it, the color drained from her face. "Oh my God. What the hell is this? What's happening? Where's Melanie?"

I didn't answer right away, waiting to see if the memory returned on its own. When it didn't, I answered the only way I could think of without sending her into a complete tailspin: I deflected.

"I need you to stay focused on me," I said. Tears coursed

down her face, her breathing coming in harsh gasps. She was panicking, and at the moment I had no idea how to help her.

Phantom moved toward the girl with her head down, and settled beside her. I may not have known what to do, but Phantom had guessed perfectly. I watched the same change I've seen a thousand times, when dogs extend that calm, comforting energy to a human in need. Ariel leaned forward until her head was on Phantom's chest. She draped her right arm around the dog's neck.

"Just breathe," I said quietly. "We're going to get out of this."

There was another tremor beneath our feet, and debris crumbled around us. The shadow pulsed, waiting—for what, I didn't know. Was there something holding it back, or was it simply biding its time?

"How long have I been here?" Ariel asked. Her voice was steadier now, but she continued to hang on to Phantom.

"I don't know," I said. "You've been missing for a couple of days."

"But we're getting out?" she asked. "You're getting us out of here?"

I ignored her use of 'us,' and nodded. "We're getting you out," I said, even as more rocks and debris fell from above. Phantom shifted uneasily, casting a questioning glance at me. *And we're staying here why, exactly?* Excellent question.

"Do you mind if I ask, um… How, exactly, are you getting us out?" Ariel asked. "Because this doesn't really scream rescue scenario to me."

I smiled—genuinely this time, relieved at her show of spirit. "I'm working on that."

"Jamie!" I heard Jack call somewhere behind us, and very nearly passed out with relief. Phantom got up, but didn't leave Ariel's side.

"We're here!" I called back. The voices forever in the background in these tunnels and caves had faded to a dull roar. The shadow, however, seemed to grow, pulse, at the sound of Jack's voice. Ariel noticed the change as well, and her eyes widened.

"What the fuck is that?"

"I don't know," I said.

"Keep talking," Jack called. "How's Ariel?"

"My leg's stuck in a bear trap and the cave's about to eat us," she called back. "I've had better days."

"Do you have something to get her out?" I called.

Jack appeared at last, about twenty yards away. He had Rita with him—and, surprisingly, Wendy Redfield. The urge to pass out with relief returned, and I realized that the last few days had been some of the most exhausting in recent memory.

"Bear and Ren?" I asked, half afraid of the answer.

"They're fine," Jack said. "Wendy brought them in. They're on their way to the hospital now."

Another tremor shook the tunnel. Jack reached for the closest wall and held on, head lowered, as debris rained down on him.

"How about we get on with this," he said. The shadow on the other side of us had receded, all but vanishing at the presence of so many others. I felt myself begin to breathe again as Jack brandished a sizeable pair of bolt cutters and introduced himself to Ariel.

"Paramedics will be waiting for us when we get back," he

told her. "You think you can hang on?"

Despite her earlier bravado, Ariel's color was bad, her eyes glassy, and I didn't think she could stay conscious much longer. As for the fact that she seemed to have no memory of what had happened to her and Melanie, I chose to look at that as a gift rather than something to worry about. Phantom moved out of the way as Jack knelt beside the girl, but she didn't go far. Ariel kept her gaze locked on the dog, while I noticed that Rita's attention was fixed on the girl. Wendy stood just behind her, seemingly uncertain what to do now that she'd made it this far.

"Cut the chain," I said. "Leave the trap for now—it's better if they remove it at the hospital." Since Ariel was conscious and listening intently, I spared the reasons for *why* it was better: that she could bleed out here and now if we removed it.

Jack nodded. He had to do some maneuvering to find the right position to cut the trap, but eventually he had the bolt cutters in place. Ariel buried her face in Phantom's fur.

I was so focused on what was happening with Ariel, I'd failed to pay attention to Phantom—or anything else, for that matter. By the time I had tuned in, Phantom was on her feet, head up, eyes locked on Rita.

Jack cut the chain with a snap that seemed to echo through the cave. When it broke, I felt it as an almost physical shift in the air. The shadow down the path returned, and the tremor that shook the tunnel this time nearly took my legs out from under me.

"Shit," Ariel said. "What the hell is happening?"

The other dead returned—no longer screams, but individual voices whose words I could almost make out.

Mary Wieland appeared in front of the shadow, just out of its reach, barely visible. Just behind it, I saw a glow that I hadn't seen before.

"I want to get them out," Mary said. "The shadow man—he's losing his hold. We can make it, I know we can. Please. You have to help us." I shook my head, caught between her plea and the sight of Phantom, hackles raised, as the dog took a step toward Rita.

Meanwhile, oblivious to the metaphysical drama, Jack scooped Ariel up in his arms and nodded toward the head of the tunnel. "We need to move," he said. Rocks rained down as a roar that seemed to come from the belly of the earth shook the world around us.

"Rita?" I said. She stood in our path, immovable, her gaze still fixed on Ariel.

"Do you remember me?" she asked Ariel.

Ariel looked at her blankly, one arm around Jack's neck. A shiver ran through me. Phantom growled, advancing another step.

"I don't know you," Ariel said. I could see her body shaking from where I stood, and knew shock had taken hold. I couldn't imagine a way they could save that leg.

That was assuming we made it out of here, of course.

"Get out of the way, Rita," Jack ground out, forehead furrowed as he glanced behind him. The walls were about to come down, and if we didn't move soon we would be under them.

"Leave her alone," I heard a voice behind Rita. Wendy—I'd almost forgotten her, she'd practically disappeared with everything else going on around us. "You heard her: she doesn't know you. You had nothing to do with us."

At the words, Rita snapped out of whatever spell she'd been under. She frowned. I got the sense the statement hurt her, but thankfully she didn't waste time now processing her pain.

"Do you have Ariel?" Rita asked Jack.

He nodded. Ariel was small, but I guessed she still weighed a solid hundred pounds—not to mention the fifty-pound trap still attached to her leg. "If we get a move on, I do."

Meanwhile, behind Ariel and Jack, Mary remained rooted where she was—pleading for me to help her.

I was committed to helping the living first, though.

Jack took a step forward, toward Rita and Wendy. Phantom was still advancing on the women. "We can talk about this when we get out of here."

"I don't think so," Wendy said. It was only then that I noticed the look on Ariel's face at the sound of her aunt's voice. It was as though every horrifying memory she'd blocked over the past three days came flooding back at once. Terror shone in her eyes.

Rita turned, and I saw the glint of a knife in the darkness.

Everything happened in an instant after that. Wendy moved with impossible speed considering the woman I'd thought she was all this time, jabbing deep into Rita's kidneys before she pushed past the agent and headed for Ariel.

"It was you," I said to Wendy. Rita fell to her knees, her hand clasped to her side as blood flowed freely between her fingers. "You killed those women?"

"Whores," Wendy said. The word came out in a hiss. "I killed the whores who tried to take my family from me. The ones who tempted Gordon—the ones who tempted Barrett.

And when that scourge reached my own blood, there was nothing I could do."

She looked at Ariel with pure, venomous rage. "Do you know what it would have done to your father if he knew what you were doing? After all he sacrificed—"

"I wasn't doing anything," Ariel said. "I told you that. Barrett asked us to come over. Melanie thought we'd maybe get some dates out of it—good God, woman. You move us out to the middle of nowhere, and what do you think we're going to do? But I sure as shit wasn't a whore."

Wendy all but roared with rage. She rushed the girl, her knife at the ready. I held the gun Jack had given me, but I had no idea where to aim it. Besides which, a single gunshot was all it would take for this entire tunnel to collapse around us. Wendy rushed on and Jack feinted right, Ariel still in his arms. Phantom dove into the space he'd left behind. I watched in horror as the now-bloody knife hit Phantom's side with a wallop that took my breath away.

Time stopped for a millisecond. I waited for Phantom to fall, then breathed again when I realized it had been a bad strike—or a good one, in this case. Phantom twisted away at the last moment, struck by the flat of the blade, and the knife fell harmlessly to the ground.

Caught off balance, Wendy stumbled. I watched in horror as she tripped over another of the traps we'd passed—the one Phantom had nearly been caught in earlier. Behind us, the shadow grew, the screams behind it deafening as rocks fell and the tunnel began to cave in on itself.

"Go!" I shouted to Jack. He ran on ahead with Ariel. I grabbed Rita and draped her arm over my shoulder, with no idea how I would manage this with my knee in the state it was. Wendy lay with her leg in the trap, eyes wide with terror. The shadow closed in on her, wrapping itself around her as her screams melded with the others.

Rita and I both stood mute, staring, until a final massive tremor shook the world around us, and the tunnel caved in on Wendy. Mary Wieland flickered before my eyes, unimaginable pain on her face. And then, she vanished.

The screams, muffled now by tons of rock and dirt and debris, continued. The shadow grinned at me.

Rita, Phantom, and I ran before the earth could swallow us the way it had Wendy, Mary, and the other dead it clung to.

EPILOGUE

"SO YOU FINALLY MADE IT for the grand tour," I said as Jack got off the boat and set foot cautiously on our island.

"I've got a lot more free time these days."

Two weeks had passed since the events in Glastenbury. My knee was healing well, though it was still in a brace and required nightly icing and a steady regiment of ibuprofen to keep the swelling down. Phantom, never far from my side before, had become my shadow in the last couple of weeks. It turned out we were all a little more shaken than I'd expected after everything that had happened in the tunnels and dense forests of the Bennington Triangle.

I'd read brief accounts of the events in Vermont on the news, so I knew the highlights. Chief among them was the discovery after Wendy Redfield's death of a secret chest of antique purity rings in the back of her closet, along with the cross earrings and the rope used to tie her victims.

"So there's no doubt now that she was the one who killed all the victims—even the prostitutes around the country over a decade ago?" I asked.

"There's always some doubt," Jack said. "But you heard her, she confessed. And we've been talking to Dean… She did some traveling back in those days, and it looks like the timelines match up."

"You wouldn't think someone like that would be strong

enough for a crime like this. At least, not alone. Capturing, tying, and torturing two women…"

"Two drugged women," Jack reminded me. "And according to the little that Ariel remembers, Wendy had no problem managing her and Melanie."

I frowned at mention of Ariel. "How's she doing?"

"Better than can be expected considering everything she went through," he said. "You heard they couldn't save the leg?"

I nodded wordlessly, thinking of the young athlete who had dreamed of being a personal trainer.

"She's handling it all right," he continued. "She's pretty tough. Very interested in what you've got going on around here, too."

"I emailed her just after everything happened," I said. "Maybe I'll pay a visit with Phantom while she's still in the hospital."

Jack nodded his approval. It was a gorgeous fall day, bright sun reflected off the blue sea. The scent of pine and salt were in the air. I could think of little I wanted to talk about less than the depravity of Wendy Redfield, but I was happy to hear that Ariel would be all right.

"What about everyone else?" I asked. "With Angie Crenshaw's death…"

Jack's face darkened at the mention, and I realized I still didn't know what had gone on between them. Clearly, though, it was something. "Claude's up on charges, but my guess is he'll be institutionalized—there's no way he's competent to stand trial. And Dean's awaiting trial for the kidnapping, though there's a chance he could get off since he wasn't in his right mind, either."

"Where does that leave Ariel?" I asked.

"With the State right now," Jack said regretfully. "Once she gets out of the hospital… She doesn't have any family left but Barrett and Gordon."

"I don't know that she'd be better off with either of them," I said. "What about Gordon? He's been cleared… I don't suppose Rita's interested in taking him back."

"No, thank God," Jack said. "I don't know what Gordon will do. He talked about doing some consulting, maybe even getting a license as a PI. As long as he stays away from me, I don't care what he does."

I wondered about Rita and McDonough, though I didn't ask the question aloud. Despite my initial dislike of McDonough, I thought the man might actually be good for her. Not that I was in any position to weigh in on anyone's romantic decisions.

"I'm still not completely sure I understand Wendy's motivation," I said, after a few seconds' thought. "I understand that she wasn't a fan of ladies of the night, but everything she did was so…extreme."

"She was trying to keep the family together, I think," Jack said. "And with June and Katie, I think it was a combination: Punish them for the path they'd chosen, and then punish Gordon by setting him up when it was clear he was never coming back—especially after he came in with the Bureau and helped take their house away."

"But why go this long without killing only to start up again in Glastenbury?" I asked. "She'd made it almost a decade."

"That we know of," Jack said. I looked at him, newly interested. "Dean's wife died four years ago under mysterious circumstances. I think she felt like she was losing control again, with Barrett's business dealings and his plans for Ariel and Melanie." He paused. "You know she was actually poisoning Dean and Claude? Not enough to kill them, just enough to keep them sick. She tried to do the same with Barrett, but he went to the hospital and then moved out."

I thought of everything Bear had told me about the black threads he'd seen spiraling in the air around Dean. Was that what he had seen? A physical manifestation of the poisoned thoughts swarming in his head?

"It makes sense, I guess," I said. "If she wanted to keep everyone together and make others stay away, that's one way to do it."

I led Jack from the boat launch up the hill to the wildlife rehab center we'd just finished building. Phantom kept pace at my left side as usual, head up and ears pricked forward as though searching for some hidden danger I might miss.

"So, you want to see what you've been missing all this time?" I asked Jack.

He looked sheepish. "That's why I'm here." The way his eyes met mine made my cheeks burn and my heart beat just a little bit faster.

The rehab center itself isn't really that heart stopping, however. It's a six-room wooden cabin made of repurposed lumber, but it's flooded with light and runs almost exclusively on wind power—courtesy of turbines installed by a local alternative energy company that gave them to us at cost.

Jack was suitably impressed, or at least he made a good show of acting like it.

"Sorry for the smell," I said as we moved past the still-gleaming front room, where my vet—Therese—was bringing in a crate of orphaned red fox kits we'd rescued early that morning. "It's clean, but there's only so much you can do with twenty-five wild animals in a space like this."

"Twenty-nine now," Therese said, looking up briefly from her new charges. "But I take your point."

"I've smelled worse," Jack assured me as we moved on.

Phantom followed along beside me as I introduced Jack to the injured raptors, held in floor-to-ceiling cages in a room with the shades drawn. Three buzzards, a bald eagle, a great horned owl, two barn owls, and a peregrine falcon whose wing had nearly been sheared off in a head-on collision with an SUV.

"They'll stay here or go to another facility, where they can help with education—if they take to that, of course. Some birds don't. In that case, they'll have an easy early retirement in the sanctuary out here."

"So, a happy ending for all," he said.

"Not always," I said. "Far from it… But enough to make this worth it."

We moved outside to one of the larger enclosures, where a motley assortment of injured and orphaned fawns grazed in the sunshine.

"See those two over there?" I said, nodding toward two dappled, leggy fawns standing together at the fence. "Phantom found them just before we left for Glastenbury."

Jack grinned. "I remember. They both pulled through?"

"They did. They're getting big now—we'll release them in a sanctuary up north in another couple of weeks. We want them to be settled before the first snow flies."

Bear was at the other side of the enclosure, Ren and Casper beside him. His arm was still in a sling, and he hadn't quite gotten his color back, but he was making progress. That progress was definitely aided by Ren's presence—since everything that had happened in Glastenbury, the two were even tighter than they'd been before. I sensed a shift in the relationship, but of course Bear wasn't about to confide in his mom about such things.

I waved across the enclosure. Both Bear and Ren waved back, but neither made any move to join us. Ah, teenagers.

I gave Jack a tour of the rest of the island, and then he shadowed me for much of the day while I did the things I usually do: trained dogs, fielded calls, fed buzzards and bears and honeybees, and a dozen other things that keep me busy from dusk till dawn. All the while, I kept thinking about the one piece I'd told no one about Glastenbury: the image of Mary Wieland, the screams I had heard underground… The shadow that seemed to feed on them all. Had they actually been real? Or had it been a manifestation of my own exhaustion, fear, and pain?

Finally, as we were heading back to the boat, I spoke up.

"You know, I went back to Glastenbury a couple of days after we found Ariel," I said.

Jack looked surprised. It was evening by now, the sky a rich caramel, the sun just going down on the horizon. "I didn't realize," he said. "Did you find anything?"

"No. The tunnel's completely caved in." I'd seen no sign of Mary that day, but I had heard cries that seemed to rise from the bowels of the earth. It felt like an indictment, proof that I had helped to save the living, but I had failed the dead. I wanted to ask Bear about it—to at least learn from him what he experienced when he saw these things. How did he know they were real, and not just a figment of his own imagination?

"Did you ever find out anything about the remains we found there?" I asked.

"No," he said. "There are some urban legends about a mad trapper who used to live out there in the 1930s. It could have been him, if he actually existed. Whoever killed the victims we found in that tunnel is long dead now, though. He can't hurt anyone else."

Dead, yes, but I wasn't so sure about the other.

The boat was idling at the dock, Monty waiting patiently at the helm. Jack looked awkward for a moment. I reached down and patted Phantom's head, feeling just a little bit vindictive. I waited Jack out, letting him squirm.

"I wasn't sure whether you're still shorthanded out here," he finally said.

"We are," I said. "We'll manage." I wasn't sure how, of course, but we always did. Jack shifted. At this point, I knew I was being cruel—he'd already told me he was officially done with the FBI, and had no intention of ever returning. I remained mute. I'd asked him once—this time, he would have to make the first move.

"Right," he said. "I'm sure. But, if you wanted another hand…" He cleared his throat. "I mean, I'm out of work right now."

I looked at him, trying to hide my smile. "Yeah, you've mentioned that."

His eyes narrowed, a grin playing at his lips now. "Wow—never let it be said that Jamie Flint doesn't have a mean streak. What I'm trying to ask, in as clumsy a way as possible, is… Does the offer still stand for a job?"

"It's not all crime solving, you know," I said. "We spend

a lot of time just rescuing ducklings and building latrines."

"I think I can handle that," he said. His voice was quiet, his eyes intent on mine.

I studied him for a long moment, as the sun went down behind him. Waves lapped at the boat as two bald eagles circled overhead. I smiled, finally, without reserve.

"Yeah," I said. "I expect you can."

A WORD ABOUT GLASTENBURY
AND THE BENNINGTON TRIANGLE

As mentioned on the copyright page of this novel, *The Darkest Thread* is indeed a work of fiction. I took liberties with respect to the geography of the town, but Glastenbury is a real place, as is the notion of the Bennington Triangle—a phrase first coined by paranormal author Joseph Citro. In 1946, Bennington College student Paula Welden mysteriously vanished after last being seen headed toward Vermont's Long Trail, and the failure to find Ms. Welden ultimately spawned the creation of the Vermont State Police. Despite an exhaustive search, no trace of the college student was ever discovered. Four other disappearances in the area between the years 1945 to 1950 inspired further speculation, which was fueled by multiple reported UFO and Bigfoot sightings in the area.

What interests me most about this area, however, are the stone cairns that have been found in the thick woods around Glastenbury Mountain and that part of the Long Trail. No one has been able to definitively date these cairns, and there's still some debate as to exactly who built them in the first place. These are exactly the sorts of mysteries that spark my imagination and inspire me to spin my own tales, and I was delighted to find such rich fodder right here in New England.

If you're interested in learning more, I recommend these sources:

- Abramovich, Chad. "The Vanished Town of Glastenbury and the Bennington Triangle." April 17, 2015. https://urbanpostmortem.wordpress.com/2015/04/07/the-vanished-town-of-glastenbury-and-the-bennington-triangle/

- Citro, Joseph. *Green Mountain Ghosts, Ghouls & Unsolved Mysteries.* Mariner Books, 1994.

- Garland, Matt. "Bennington Triangle." Documentary. YouTube, February 2011.
  Part I: https://youtu.be/fdyysF0VC20
  Part II: https://youtu.be/rBPMp8H3x3w

- Lord, Benjamin. "Lost Histories: The Story of New England's Stone Chambers." December 23, 2013. http://northernwoodlands.org/articles/article/stone-chambers

- Resch, Tyler. *Glastenbury: The History of a Vermont Ghost Town.* The History Press, 2008.

Looking for more from Jen Blood?

Turn the page for a free excerpt from
the first novel in the critically acclaimed
Erin Solomon series,
ALL THE BLUE-EYED ANGELS.

AUGUST 22, 1990

ON MY TENTH BIRTHDAY, I AM BAPTIZED BY FIRE.

I race through a forest of smoke, ignoring the sting of blackberry brambles and pine branches on sensitive cheeks and bare arms. Up ahead, I catch a glimpse of my father's shirt, drenched and muddy, as he races through the woods. I follow blindly, too terrified to scream, too panicked to stop.

A figure in black chases us, gaining on me fast. At ten years old, raised in the church, I am certain that it is the devil himself. He wears a hooded cloak; I imagine him taking flight at my heels, reaching for me with gnarled fingers. I run faster, my breath high in my chest, trees speeding past. The air gets thicker and harder to breathe the closer we get to the fire, but I don't stop.

The Lord is my shepherd, I shall not want.

I can hear him behind me, three or four steps back at most, his breath coming hard and his hands getting closer.

I skid into the clearing certain that I'm safe now—I've reached the church. The church is always safe.

But today, nothing is safe. Flames climb the blackened walls of the chapel, firemen circling with hoses to keep the surrounding forest from burning. My father has arrived ahead of me—I find him kneeling in front of a pile of rubble just feet from the flames. His shoulders shake as he cries.

He maketh me to lie down in green pastures. He leadeth me

beside the still waters.

I go to him because I know no one else will, and wrap my arms around his neck. When I scan the tree line, the man I felt behind me just moments before is gone. Now, there is no one but the firemen, the local constable, and my mother with her doctor's bag and no survivors to heal.

I pray in my father's ear, whispering words of comfort the way he always has for me. There is a smell that sticks in my throat and turns my stomach, but only when my mother comes for me, trying to pull me away, do I realize what that smell is.

He restoreth my soul. He leadeth me on a path of righteousness for His name's sake.

A coal black, claw-like hand reaches from beneath the pile of burned debris where my father weeps. A few feet beyond, I see a flash of soot-stained white feathers, china-blue eyes, and a painted smile that seems suddenly cruel. I stay there, fixated on the doll, until my mother takes me in her arms and forces me away.

She sets me on the wet grass and places a mask over my face so that I can breathe. The oxygen tastes like cold water after a long drought. I sit still while the rain washes over me and my father cries and the church burns to the ground.

I'm just beginning to calm down when I feel a presence like warm breath at the back of my neck, and I turn once more toward the trees.

The cloaked man stands at the edge of the woods, his hood down around his shoulders. Rain plasters dark hair against his head. Water drips down high cheekbones and a thin, sharp nose.

Yea, though I walk through the valley of the shadow of death, I will fear no evil.

The words of my favorite Psalm stutter in my head—*Thy rod and thy staff, they comfort me.*

The man in black turns his head, his dark eyes fixing on mine.

My cup runneth over.

He puts a finger to his thin lips and whispers to me through the chaos.

"Sshhh."

More than twenty years will pass before I pray again.

ONE

I RETURNED TO MY HOMETOWN of Littlehope, Maine, on a wet afternoon when the town was locked in fog. A cold rain filled the potholes and pooled on the shoulder of coastal Route 1, ensuring that I hydroplaned most of the drive up from Boston. I hadn't set foot in Littlehope since my high school graduation, when I left the town behind in a beaten-to-hell Honda Civic with the vow that I would never return.

That was fifteen years ago.

Littlehope is a fishing village at the end of a peninsula on Penobscot Bay, about two hours from Portland. It's known for Bennett's Lobster Shanty, the Ladies Auxiliary Quilting League, and a small but determined band of drug runners who rule the harbor. Littlehope also happens to be ten miles as the crow flies from the island where thirty-four members of the Payson Church of Tomorrow burned to death and where, a decade later, my father hanged himself in their honor.

They say you can't go home again. In my case, it seems more apt to ask why the hell you'd ever want to.

I walked through the front door of the *Downeast Daily Tribune* just after eleven o'clock that Wednesday morning.

The *Trib* has delivered the news to three counties in the Midcoast for over fifty years, from an ugly concrete block of a building on Littlehope's main drag. Across the road, you'll find the Episcopal Church, the local medical clinic, and the only bar in town. My mother used to joke that the layout was intentional—locals could get plastered and beat the crap out of each other Saturday night, stumble next door to get patched up, and stop in to see the neighborhood preacher for redemption on Sunday morning.

The first job I ever had was as Girl Friday at the *Trib*, fetching coffee and making copies for the local newshounds, occasionally typing up copy when no one else was around or they were too lazy to do it themselves. Walking through the familiar halls that morning, I soaked in the smells of fresh ink and old newspapers, amazed at the things people are usually amazed at when they come home after a lifetime away: how small the building was, how outdated the décor, how it paled in comparison to my golden memories.

My comrade-in-arms, Einstein—part terrier, part Muppet, and so-named not for any propensity toward genius but rather for his unruly white curls—padded along beside me, ears and tail up, his nails clicking on the faded gray linoleum floor. Plaques and photos decorated the concrete walls, some dating back to my teenage days with the paper. I passed two closed doors before I reached the newsroom—the last door on the right, with yellowed Peanuts comics taped to the window and the sound of a BBC newscast coming from within. Einstein's tail started wagging, his body shimmying with the motion, the second he caught scent of the company we were about to keep.

"Settle, buddy," I said, my hand on the doorknob—though in fairness the words were probably more for me than him. The dog glanced up at me and whined.

I opened the door and had only a second to get my bearings before I was spotted; it's hard to be stealthy when a bullet of fur precedes you into the room. Daniel Diggins—aka Diggs to almost everyone on the planet—greeted my mutt with more enthusiasm than I knew I would get, crouching low to fondle dogged ears and dodge a few canine kisses while I took stock of the old homestead.

The computers had been updated since I'd been there last, but were still out of date. The desks were the same, though: six hulking metal things with jagged edges and scratched surfaces, buried under the detritus of the newspaper biz—piles of paperwork, oversized computer monitors, and half-eaten bags of junk food. A couple of overweight, graying reporter-types were on cell phones on one side of the room, while Diggs and another man stood at a desk that had once been mine. Behind them, a wall-mounted TV was tuned to MSNBC.

Before Diggs straightened to say hello, the other half of the duo locked eyes with me. Though we'd never met face to face, it was clear from the man's pointed glare who he was—and that, unlike me, he had not been looking forward to this meeting.

"Are you planning on saying hello to me at all, or is this visit gonna be all about the dog?" I asked Diggs, if only to break the sudden tension in the room.

"It's always all about the dog," Diggs said. "You should know that by now." He stood and enveloped me in a warm hug. I held on tight, lost in a smell of wool and comfort that would forever be associated with the best parts of my youth.

"How're you doing, kiddo?" he asked. The words were quiet, warm in my ear—a question between just the two of us before I got started. I stepped out of his embrace with what I hoped was a businesslike nod.

"Good. I'm good."

"Good," he said. "And the drive was…?"

"The drive was fine, Diggs."

He smiled—a slow grin that's been charming women around the globe for as long as I can remember. Though I hadn't visited Littlehope in over a decade, Diggs and I never lost touch. Our latest visit had been a few months before, but he looked no different than he always does: curly hair stylishly unkempt, his five o'clock shadow edging closer to a beard than I'd seen it in some time. He was toying with me now. Diggs likes that kind of thing.

When it became clear that I wasn't playing along, he nodded toward the other man at the desk.

"Noel," Diggs said. "This is Erin Solomon. Erin, Noel Hammond."

Hammond extended his hand to me like someone had a gun at his back, and we shook.

"Nice to finally meet you, Noel. Thanks for coming."

"Diggs didn't give me much choice."

So, Diggs had come through again—this time by delivering a much-needed source at my feet. "Yeah, well, he knew he'd have to put up with my bitching otherwise. It won't take long."

"This is about your book, then?" he asked.

I glanced at Diggs, making no effort to conceal my displeasure. "You heard about that?"

"The whole town's heard about that," Hammond said. "It was the lead story in the paper about a month back. The book deal, you inheriting Payson Isle… Everybody knows about it."

I raised an eyebrow at Diggs, who raised his hands in surrender. "It wasn't my call, Solomon—there was no way I could keep it quiet. I figured you'd rather I do the write-up than somebody else."

He was right about that, at least. Still, I wasn't thrilled to think the entire *Trib* readership was in on my business. I suppressed a sigh and told myself to get over it. I was sure it wouldn't be the last surprise I had in this investigation.

"So, where do you want to do this?" Hammond prompted me.

He was a lesson in how deceptive a phone voice can be. In the one telephone interview he'd granted me in the past three months, Hammond had been articulate and reserved during a conversation that had been anything but pleasant. Though I'd known he was a retired cop, I had still pictured an aging professor-type—someone the local fishermen would hate, and the women in the tiny library on the corner would fantasize about. I was wrong.

Though he had to be at least sixty-five, Noel Hammond was built more like a linebacker than a man bound for the geriatric set. Over six feet tall and easily two-hundred pounds, he looked like he could bench press a buffalo without breaking a sweat. His hands were callused, his grip stronger than I'd expected.

"Do you guys mind coming back to the dock to check things out with me?" I asked. "We can talk there."

"Actually, there's been a little change of plan," Diggs said. "I got a boat for you like you asked, but we took her out to the island and set the mooring already. Noel said we can take you out there together—make sure you get set up all right."

This had clearly been Diggs' idea, since Hammond looked like he'd rather hog-tie a rattlesnake than spend the afternoon hauling my ass around the harbor.

"That would be great," I said.

"Great," Hammond repeated, with a notable lack of enthusiasm. He was out the door before I could respond.

Five minutes later, Diggs and I were headed out when a grizzled fisherman in coveralls and an orange hunting cap stopped us in the hallway. I fought the urge to run in the other direction the moment I realized who it was.

"You got that paperwork I asked you for, Diggs?" he asked. He didn't give me so much as a sidelong glance.

"I was just on my way out, Joe—can I drop it off later?"

The man shook his head; he didn't look pleased. Joe Ashmont was the fire chief in Littlehope—or at least he had been, up until the Payson fire. A week after the church burned to the ground, Ashmont turned in his resignation. Though the reasons for that were never quite clear, he always seemed to hold my family personally responsible.

"I've gotta get that boat fixed or I'm screwed—the season's about to start, I can't have her leaking oil all over the bay. You said you'd help me," Ashmont pressed.

Diggs glanced at me in apology. "Yeah, all right. Just hang on a second and I'll grab it. You wanna wait in the office, Sol?"

I started to nod, but Ashmont interrupted. "She can wait here with me. I don't bite."

Ashmont was probably in his sixties, though he didn't look a day under seventy-five. Still, he was lean and mean and, despite his claim to the contrary, I suspected that biting was the very least I had to worry about from him. Since he'd had a front-row seat at the Payson fire, however, I knew I'd need to break the ice sooner or later if I wanted any information from him. I sent Diggs on his way.

Einstein growled low in his throat, and stood with his body blocking my legs—just in case I did something crazy and took a step toward the psychopath in the hallway. He didn't need to worry, though. I planned on staying put.

"It's good I run into you," Ashmont said the moment Diggs was out of sight. The way he said it gave me the uneasy feeling our meeting didn't have anything to do with luck.

"Oh?"

"Payson Isle belongs to you now, don't it? Word is Old Mal left it to you."

'Old Mal' was Malcolm Payson—brother of Isaac Payson, the preacher who had led the Payson Church until their untimely demise. Ashmont took a step toward me. I smelled whiskey and stale cigarettes on his breath.

"I guess it does."

" 'I guess it does,'" he repeated, his voice up a tone to mimic me. "It does or it don't, right? I got fishing rights off that back cove—been pulling traps there for the past twenty years. Your old man didn't bother me, said I was welcome to it. Once he strung himself up, nobody said a word about it since."

My chest tightened at his words. "I'll look into it," I said.

A slow smile touched his lips. "You do that," he said. "You got your daddy's red hair, but you look just like your mum—you know that?" His eyes slid up and down my body, lingering on my chest. "You're littler than her—not much to you, is there?" I'm lucky to hit five-five in heels, and at the moment I felt about three feet shorter. "You got that fire in your eyes, though. A lot of secrets locked up tight in that busy head."

He took another step toward me, then leaned in more quickly than I would have thought possible. Einstein leapt for him, but he cuffed the dog in the side of the head with a swift, meaty-looking fist. Stein yelped and a split second later Ashmont's hand was wrapped around my upper arm, his mouth at my ear.

"Somebody might crack that pretty skull and let all those secrets spill out, you don't watch yourself. Go home, *Miss* Solomon. You got no business here."

Einstein was headed in for another go and Diggs was rounding the corner when Ashmont released me, turning on his heel.

"Mind that dog," he said, calling back over his shoulder as he reached the door. "A dog like that bites me, nobody'd say boo if I shot him where he stood."

I stared after him, too stunned to respond. As soon as Ashmont was gone, I knelt to check on Einstein.

"What the hell was that?" Diggs asked as he hurried to my side. The dog was fine, just a little shaken up; I hadn't fared so well.

"Did you see that? He hit my damn dog. Who does that? The son of a bitch actually *hit* my dog."

"What'd you say to him?"

Like it was my fault. I turned on him. Diggs held up his hands before I could light into him.

"Not that that justifies anything," he added quickly. "It's just—you know Ashmont."

That was true—I did know Ashmont. And it wasn't like I was actually *surprised* at his behavior, given the number of drunken brawls he'd started and hateful epithets he'd spewed in my family's direction when I was a teen. That didn't make it any more acceptable, however. I took a manila envelope from Diggs' hands.

"This is his?"

Diggs nodded. He didn't say anything when I tore the envelope open, and he did a fine job of keeping his amusement to himself while I skimmed the pile of paperwork inside.

"His boat broke down," he said. "There are a couple of places that offer financial assistance to lobstermen, but he was having a hard time with the paperwork. I told him I'd give him a hand."

Since I couldn't think of a fitting insult for this fairly innocuous revelation, I settled for a pointed glare as I returned the documents to the envelope and handed them back to Diggs.

"Newspaper man by day, guardian angel by night. What would Littlehope do without you?"

"I'm sure they'd muddle through."

A horn honked in the parking lot.

"That'll be Noel," Diggs said. "Not here half an hour and you've already got two men who'd just as soon watch you drown than toss you a line. Could be a new record."

"Give me time—I'm sure I can do better."

From the look on Diggs' face, that was exactly what he was afraid of.

For regular updates, free short stories, contests,
and giveaways between book releases,
visit http://jenblood.com/,
and like us on Facebook at
http://facebook.com/jenbloodauthor/.

More Mysteries from Jen Blood

In Between Days
Diggs & Solomon Shorts
1990 - 2000

Midnight Lullaby
Prequel to
The Erin Solomon Mysteries

The
Payson Pentalogy
The Critically Acclaimed 5-Book Set
Readers Can't Put Down!

Book I: All the Blue-Eyed Angels
Book II: Sins of the Father
Book III: Southern Cross
Book IV: Before the After
Book V: The Book of J

ACKNOWLEDGMENTS

As with all of my books, I would like to thank my family first and foremost, for your love and support during those tumultuous days when I'm not getting other things done because I'm a crazy person living in a made-up world. Mom, Dad, Mike, Brandi, Maggie, and Maya: I couldn't ask for a more loving and supportive tribe, and I thank the stars every day for each of you. And thank you from the bottom of my very full heart to Ben, who's taken the brunt of the Crazy this time around and doesn't seem terribly alarmed yet.

My deepest gratitude, as well, to my eagle-eyed beta readers and proofreader: Jan, Marie, and my wonderful proofreader Michelle Schweitzer have all proven invaluable in this process. And to the others who have helped and weighed in along the way, particularly the readers who continue to support this mad journey of mine, I offer my undying gratitude. You truly make this whole thing possible!

I always love to hear from readers—email me at jen@jenblood.com or follow me on Facebook at www.facebook.com/jenbloodauthor or Twitter @jenblood, and don't forget to join the mailing list for your free copy of *In Between Days,* my book of shorts featuring Erin Solomon in the years 1990 to 2000.